Reunification:

A Monterey Mary Returns to Berlin

by

Thomas Heinrich Edward Hill

T.H.E.Hill

T.H.E. Hill

Reunification: A Monterey Mary Returns to Berlin

Subject headings:

Cold War — Fiction

Intelligence service | Espionage | Spies — Fiction

Berlin (Germany) — History (1970-2013) — Fiction

ISBN-10: 1490490264

ISBN-13: 978-1490490267

Published simultaneously in the United States of America and in Germany to commemorate the Fiftieth Anniversary of the first permanent buildings on Teufelsberg, the operational home of Field Station Berlin.

www.VoicesUnderBerlin.com/Reunification.html

info@VoicesUnderBerlin.com

Cover design by T.H.E. Hill.

1 2 3 4 5 6 7 8 9 0

Preface

```
5001345 5001661 0012016 8460913 4766636
3500301 7502732 3506796 4258867 8402807
5428736 7476406 1478839 7575409 7711501
3725568 4505166 6557432 6625537 8784614
8888164 2864466 8994610 5109913 7406896
7967213 8755676 6756002 7272904 5842203
0300513 7800395 7851707 9012415 9500302
9350102 9855508 9994213 8805969 8857002
6371342 6535101 6647269 5340613 8904845
5040267 1080412 1090110 5287369 5295698
5483564 6810194 0241407 1340613 8395407
4425001 8897313 7947013 0445263 5321613
1322505 8320114 6322905 0376542 8411874
6451301 8515498 8555511 7572370 1658098
1755064 1011002 1966864 9054202 9344666
9695563 9495210 9595013 9891369 9295597
6474808 8536435 5290366 7305202
```

The Army of Occupation Medal

Awarded for thirty or more consecutive days of duty as a member of the occupation forces after World War II. While in Austria and most of Germany the period of qualifying service for award of the medal ended in 1955, Berlin was legally an occupied territory until the Reunification of Germany in October 1990. This is one of the things that made Berlin a unique place to be stationed.

Dedicated to the Army's top-ten-percent, the Army Security Agency and its successor organizations; not only to those who served at Field Station Berlin, but also to those who served in places I am not allowed to name.

2013 marks the Fiftieth Anniversary of the first permanent buildings on Teufelsberg, the operational home of Field Station Berlin. This novel, together with the issue of a sheet of Cinderella stamps commemorates that event.

To learn more about this commemorative issue of Cinderella Stamps, please visit: http://voicesunderberlin.com/Stamps5.html

The Army Security Agency

Adapted from *Wikipedia: The Free Encyclopedia*

The United States Army Security Agency (USASA) was the Army's Signals Intelligence Branch from 1945 through 1976. ASA's Latin motto of *Semper Vigilis* (*Vigilant Always*) reflects Thomas Jefferson's declaration that "The price of freedom is eternal vigilance." The color teal in the ASA shield is the color used in military heraldry for units not assigned to branch, which reflects the independent nature of ASA, after it was detached from the Signal Corps at the end of WWII. In 1976, ASA was merged with the US Army Military Intelligence Branch to form the United States Army Intelligence and Security Command (INSCOM).

For most of ASA's existence, the Army counted on conscripts to fill its ranks. ASA ceased to exist shortly after the draft ended in 1973. During the period of the draft, ASA filled its enlisted ranks from the top ten percent of the Army aptitude scoring range. Almost none of them re-enlisted. This led to an extreme shortage of cadre to fill the Senior NCO positions in ASA, and ASA was forced to go outside the top-ten-percent to the "regular army" to find candidates for these vacancies. The result was that the cream of the crop who did the actual work of intelligence collection were being led by those from the bottom-ninety-percent. This resulted in a "class war" within ASA that pitted the Army's best and brightest against their less-well educated "leaders." As a result, in the late nineteen-sixties, ASA initiated more complaints per annum to the US Army Inspector General and to their US Congressmen than the sum of all other Army units combined. Being well educated, this elite top-ten-percent recognized when their rights were being trampled on, and took appropriate action. This was a chronic problem within ASA.

ASA is a clear example of the severe waste and abuse of some of the Army's best and brightest enlisted troops during the period when the Army used conscription in the twentieth century. It was a failure in effective human resources management. Without the draft, it would have also been an operational disaster.

The educational level of a "Monterey Mary" (an ASA linguist) in the late nineteen-fifties is typified in a memoir by a graduate of ALS class R-12-80, the school's 80th 12-month class in Russian: He had an M.A. in one of the humanities, and had been working on a Ph.D. As he neared the end of his draft deferment eligibility at age 26, he decided to avoid the draft and enlisted in ASA. Today, of course, if someone with a graduate degree and test scores in the top ten percent volunteered for the Army at a starting pay rate of $1000 a year, the recruiting NCO would probably faint from shock.

A modern SIGINT Officer would probably be quite delighted with an old ASA type SP-4 from ASA's mid-life point of 1960, with a college degree and an I.Q. of 120 to 130. One would hope that he would not be used to peel potatoes on KP, or paint rocks, or drive a truck to pick up supplies and mail, duties that many old ASA-ers recall with annoyance.

The *Wikipedia* article suggests that things have changed, but have they?

From a 2009 post to a thread on the Military.com Discussion Boards:

I've recently read two novels about the ASA experience. The first was James Crumley's *One to Count Cadence* about the early exploits of the ASA in Nam. The second was *Voices Under Berlin* by T.H.E. Hill (an obvious pseudonym). ... I thought it was hilarious how some of the SIGINT/linguist jokes and eccentricities have virtually remained unchanged in sixty years, be it linguist vs. analyst clashes, clueless LTs, oversensitive OPSEC folks who throw out the "need to know" card at every single turn, reclassed soldiers deriding "overeducated" DLIers for not being "real soldiers," etc. I can assure you the same situations are being played out in Iraq and Afghanistan as I type this. :-)

I encourage anyone currently in SIGINT to read up on this stuff. It will make you smile a bit knowing that people have been going through the same crap you did as a SIGINTer for the past 60 years!

Acknowledgments

I would like to express my thanks to all those listed below, who read the manuscript and offered a variety of comments and editing suggestions to help improve it.

Carol Kasper, who has been in book publishing for over 30 years. She visited family in the former Czechoslovakia while it was still "behind the Iron Curtain," and is a frequent business traveler in Germany, particularly Frankfurt, Munich, and Berlin.

James Dunning, a veteran of USAREUR 2nd Support Command, 1970's. All his experience with Berlin is post-Wall.

Lou Novacheck who loves to travel. He has been to 41 states, 2 provinces, 3 U.S. possessions, and 34 countries on five continents, plus above the Artic Circle. He's ex-military, ex-international sales, ex-self employed, and just about ex-pired.

And last, but certainly not least, **my wife**, whom I met while stationed in Berlin, without whose help and encouragement, not to mention editing skills, this project would never have become a book.

They have all, in their own way, contributed to making this a better work of literature, but since I did not always take their advice, any shortcomings that it may still have remain those of my own invention.

Contents

German/GI Glossary

Some pieces of GI (soldier) slang, and a number of German words that were part and parcel of the vocabulary of even non-German-speaking GI's assigned to Berlin have been used to help recreate the linguistic atmosphere of the time. They are glossed here for the convenience of readers who have never been stationed in Germany. The first time that a word in the glossary appears in the text, it is prefixed with an asterisk: *word.

A-val — A-validity, an Intelligence-Report confidence rating equating to 'the truth'

Andrews - Andrews Barracks, on Finckensteinallee in Berlin (Lichterfelde), where the personnel of Field Station Berlin were billeted, now the Bundesarchiv

ARFCOS — Armed Forces Courier Service

Article 15 — non-judicial punishment in the Army, a step below a court-martial

AWOL — Absent WithOut Leave, unauthorized absence

AZORIAN — the covername for a CIA project to recover the sunken Soviet submarine K-129 from the Pacific Ocean floor

BB — Berlin Brigade

Bautzen — an infamous East German prison used by the Stasi

Berliner — a jelly-filled doughnut, typical of Berlin; called *Krapfen* in the rest of Germany

Berliner Weiße — A very popular wheat beer served in Berlin with a shot of flavored syrup, raspberry being the most popular flavor

B-val — B-validity, an Intelligence-Report confidence rating equating to 'probably true'

Call-sign Rota — the sequence in which radio call signs change

Case officer — an intelligence officer who recruits agents and manages their activities

Chow — food, a meal

Chow Line — the serving line in the unit dining facility

Chow Hall — unit dining facility

CI — CounterIntelligence

Class-A uniform — A dress uniform with a jacket and tie, a suit

COMINT — COMmunications INTelligence

Comm Center — communications center, the place where messages are sent and received

CoS — Chief of Station

Currywurst — A Berlin delicacy: a bratwurst with curry-flavored ketchup, best with potato salad

CQ — Charge of Quarters, the NCO on duty in the orderly room after normal duty hours

C-val — C-validity, an Intelligence-Report confidence rating equating to 'possibly true'

Days — the shift from 08:00 to 16:00

Das Volk — see: *Wir sind das Volk*

Day-weenie – someone who only works Days, in the jargon of the modern business world: 'a suit'

DCI — Director Central Intelligence, the Head of CIA

Dead Drop — a prearranged secret "mail box" for the clandestine exchange of intelligence information that avoids the need for a case officer and an asset to be present in the same place at the same time

DLI — The Defense Language Institute, Monterey, California, the graduates of which are known as "Monterey Marys," is the school where the Army trains its linguists

'Dumb Bar' — The rank insignia for a lieutenant is a single bar: a gold bar for a Second Lieutenant, and a silver bar for a First Lieutenant

D-val — D-validity, an Intelligence-Report confidence rating equating to 'might not be true'

East Herms — GI slang for 'East Germans'

Eierschale — a Berlin nightclub on Breitenbachplatz, popular with GI's and famous for its jazz, the name means 'The Eggshell'

Fatigues — short for *fatigue uniform*: the uniform to be worn on a fatigue detail, i.e. one where you get dirty and tired

Free University — created in 1948 to offer an alternative to the Humboldt University in the Soviet sector of Berlin

FTA — Fuck the Army

GDR - German Democratic Republic, the official name of East Germany

Genosse — German for 'Comrade'

Good Housing Post — an assignment that has a long list of negative descriptors in its Post Report that ends with "but the housing is good"

Grunie - GI slang for the Grunewald (literally: Green Forest), the Berlin forest that surrounds Teufelsberg

Grunie Pig — wild boar, living in the Grunewald

Guidon — a military standard (staff with a flag attached) that represents the unit and its commanding officer

Herr — mister

HA II — Hauptabteilung II (Main Department for counterespionage) of the Stasi

Head Shed — GI slang for headquarters, i.e. the place where the commanding officer and his staff hang their hats

the Hill — GI slang for Teufelsberg, the hill upon which the Field Station Berlin operations facility was located

HVA — *Hauptverwaltung Aufklärung* (Main Directorate for Intelligence) of the Stasi

IG — Inspector General, the guy who comes around to make sure you are doing things by the book

JAG — Judge Advocate General Corps, where the Army keeps its lawyers

JHS — *Juristische Hochschule der MfS*, Potsdam-Eiche, the Legal College of the Stasi

KP — Kitchen Police, the enlisted men who work in the mess hall on a rotating basis, peeling potatoes, mopping floors, washing dishes, pots and pans, taking out the garbage, and anything else the real cooks don't want to do: a very undesirable duty in my personal experience

Kudamm < Kurfürstendamm — think Fifth Avenue in New York

Luftgaukommando III — Third Air-Defense Command

The Man with the Golden Helmet — until recently, counted among the most famous of Rembrandt's portraits, it is now considered the work of one of his students; housed in Berlin's *Gemäldegalerie.*

MfS —*Ministerium für Staatssicherheit* (Ministry for State Security), the official name of the Stasi, the East German Secret Police

MHCHAOS — the covername for the CIA surveillance of antiwar activists during the Vietnam War

Mids — the shift from 24:00 to 08:00

MKULTRA — the covername for a CIA project to develop mind controlling drugs, in response to the use of mind control techniques on U.S. prisoners of war in Korea: this is the program that produced LSD

Monterey Mary — a graduate of the Defense Language Institute, Monterey, California, in other words, a military linguist

Newk — GI slang for a person new to the unit

Nilheard — operator jargon for 'nothing heard': when, however, all the operators report *nilheard*, it means a 'strike'

NCO — Non-Commissioned Officer

NVA — *Nationale Volksarmee* (National People's Army), the official name of the East German Army

O.D. — olive drab, the standard color for army equipment and uniforms

Omi — a pet name for 'grandmother,' think 'grams'

Op — operation

OPSEC — operational security

Ossie — an East Berliner (German)

Ostalgia — is a portmanteau of the German words *Nostalgia* and *Ost* (*East*), meaning 'nostalgia for the way things were in East (Germany)'

the Pit — the front-end of the Field Station, where the receivers were located

PNG — a Latin abbreviation used in diplomacy, meaning *Persona Non Grata* (an unwelcome person): it is the most serious form of censure which one country can apply to foreign diplomats, who are otherwise protected from arrest and other normal kinds of prosecution by diplomatic immunity

Re-up — GI slang for re-enlist in the Army

RIF — Reduction in Force, Government slang for 'downsizing'

S-Bahn — urban rail

SED — *Sozialistische Einheitspartei Deutschlands* (The Socialist Unity Party of Germany), the ruling Party in the one-Party East German State

SIGINT — SIGnals INTelligence

The Sov's — GI slang for 'the Soviets'

SP-4 — Specialist fourth class: An army enlisted rank equal to E-4, one step above Private First Class, and half a step below Corporal; pronounced [spec-4], sometimes referred to as a 'speedy-4'

SP-5 – Specialist fifth class: An army enlisted rank equal to E-5, one step above corporal, and half a step below sergeant; pronounced [spec-5]

SP-6 — Specialist sixth class: An army enlisted rank equal to E-6, one step above buck sergeant, and half a step below staff sergeant; pronounced [spec-6]

Special Services Club — the place to go for good clean off-duty fun; I remember BINGO games with good prizes, the woodworking shop, and the photography lab with great fondness, not to mention the tour of East Berlin described in this novel

The Special Services — Soviet bloc jargon for the intelligence community; from the Russian Спецслужбы (Spetssluzhby)

Speedy-4 — SP-4

Stars and Stripes — name of the daily newspaper published for the American Forces in Germany

Stasi — slang for *Ministerium für Staatssicherheit* (Ministry for State Security), the East German Secret Police

STRAC — officially: STRategic Army Corps; STRAC units were supposed to be able to move anywhere within 72 hours or less; in GI slang it means 'by the book professionalism,' expanded in that context to: Skilled Tough Ready Around the Clock

Straße — street

Swings — the shift from 16:00 to 24:00

Tberg — GI slang for *Teufelsberg* (Literally: *Devil's Mountain*), the location of the Field Station Berlin operations facility

TDY — Temporary DutY

Three Hots and a Cot — three hot meals (a day) and a bed

TKLUSTRUM — the covername for the CIA project to ▓▓

Trick — the team that works a particular *shift*, as in work 24 hours a day in three shifts: Days, Swings, and Mids

UB — Polish abbreviation: *Urząd Bezpieczeństwa* (Department of Security), Polish Secret Police

U-Bahn — *Untergrundbahn* (Underground Train), subway

Volkspolizei — People's Police (East German police)

Vopo — *Volkspolizei*

Wessie — a West Berliner (German)

Wir sind das Volk! — "We are the People!" was the slogan chanted by the East Germans during the demonstrations leading up to the collapse of the German Democratic Republic (GDR) in 1989 to underscore the fact that a democratic republic should express the will of the people, not merely the will of the *Sozialistische Einheitspartei Deutschlands* (SED: Socialist Unity Party of Germany), in English more commonly referred to as the East German Communist Party

Teufelsberg

The Operational Home of Field Station Berlin
Seen from the Air on Approach into Tegel Airport
Left-foreground: The Olympic Stadium
Photo: Kevin's Daughter

Freedom is indivisible, and when one man is enslaved, all are not free. When all are free, then we can look forward to that day when this city will be joined as one and this country and this great Continent of Europe in a peaceful and hopeful globe. When that day finally comes, as it will, the people of West Berlin can take sober satisfaction in the fact that they were in the front lines for almost two decades. All free men, wherever they may live, are citizens of Berlin, and, therefore, as a free man, I take pride in the words *Ich bin ein Berliner.*

— John F. Kennedy, June 26, 1963

Welcome Back to Berlin

Why do face wounds bleed so much? I had to buy a new shirt. I never could get the blood out of the one I had on that night. And I hate European shirts. They never fit right.

It was a great way to start my return to Berlin. I knew that I was going to run into a few ghosts of Berlin past, but I had no idea that they'd be so displeased to see me, and so physical about it.

I walked up to her and said, "Ilse?" I couldn't think of anything else to say. "Long time no see" seemed too casual. "I know I hurt you" seemed too cavalier.

She stared in my direction with a blank look, the kind you give people when they expect you to recognize them but you don't. Thirty-five years can do more to change your face than a Station disguise kit.

"I beg your pardon," she said. "I don't recall meeting ..."

Before she could say the word "you," the memory hit her. I could see it in the change in her eyes. They went wide. Without even blinking, she hit me in the face with the plate of *currywurst she was holding in her right hand. The plate was Meissen, pre-war from the look of it. It's a shame about the Meissen plate, probably irreplaceable. I don't think she was conscious of the plate. She probably just wanted to slap me, and forgot she had the plate in her hand. I guess you could say she wasn't pleased to see me again after all those years.

My host came running over to see what all the commotion was about.

"Mother!" he said, trying to sound calm. "What's going on?"

The curry in the sauce stung my face. Currywurst was one of the Berlin specialties that I'd missed. I'd never found currywurst anywhere else in the world that tasted as good. My preference, however, was to shovel it into my mouth with a plastic fork from a paper plate. Having it plastered on the side of my face with a piece of shattering Meissen china was never going to make my top ten ways of eating it. To eat it, you need to get it in your mouth, and not on your face and shirt.

The sauce was the same color as the blood that was streaming down onto my shirt, so my host didn't notice right away. I, on the other hand, did notice that he'd called her 'mother.' That meant that the complexity of my problem with Ilse had just been squared. My host was the Director of the *Stasi Archives where I was going to do research while on fellowship to the American Academy in Berlin.

I had the feeling that once he learned why she hit me with a plate of currywurst, I'd be lucky to be shown a bag of shredded Stasi files *before* they went through that miracle computer system that the Fraunhofer Institute had cooked up for the Archives to reassemble them.

Ilse walked off, ignoring her son.

"I can't apologize enough for my mother, Doctor Troyan," he said in American accented English. "I can't imagine why she would do something like that. Let me help you clean up," he continued, putting a linen napkin in my hand.

It looked to be damask. They'd never get it clean enough to use again.

Oh, well. In for a penny, in for a pound, as they say. I put the napkin up to my face and wiped off the bloody currywurst sauce, revealing a three-inch cut on the left side of my face. It started to ooze red again as soon as I finished the first swipe to clean up.

"*Mein lieber Gott!*" said Professor Johnson, reverting to his mother's native German. By this time Ilse was almost at the front door. "*Mutti! Was hast du gemacht!?*" he yelled in her direction, but I doubt she heard him. She just kept right on going, through the door and out into the night.

"We'll have to get you to the hospital," he said hurriedly, recovering his efficient Germanic sense of prioritization, and combining it with direct action. He grabbed another napkin from the pretty brunet on his right who had come over to see what was going on, and was staring speechlessly in my direction with her mouth wide open. Her napkin had a lipstick smudge on it. That was OK. It looked like a good color match for my blood.

"Manfred!" he yelled.

A starched and pressed butler appeared by his side almost by magic. I hadn't seen him anywhere nearby.

"*Mein Auto, und schnell!*" he instructed the butler, who vanished just as quickly as he had appeared.

The next thing I knew we were headed for the same door through which Ilse had disappeared. A brand-new Mercedes pulled up silently as we walked out the door. The butler had the car door open before we crossed from the house to the drive.

I had a sense of *déjà vu*, but that was a back street in Damascus, and the white cloth on my face then was soaked with chloroform rather than blood. And it wasn't damask either. I survived that trip, but not by much. There seemed to be sufficient reason to suspect that I'd survive this one too.

"To the hospital! And put your foot down!" commanded Professor Johnson in German.

The tires screeched as we left, and they screeched as we stopped in front of the emergency room entrance. Professor Johnson had called ahead on his cell phone and there was a team with a gurney waiting for us at the door. I was flat on my back and careening through the hall to a triage room faster than you could say *Krankenbahre*, which is German for *gurney*. Strange the way you remember words that you haven't used for years. It was a word that Ilse had taught me, and now she was the reason I remembered it.

They wheeled me under a bright light that made me shut my eyes. A cool, calm, deliciously female voice said, *"Und was haben wir hier?"* Her voice was competition for Marlene Dietrich at her best. It had that wistful quality that makes a woman's voice worth listening to.

"The gentleman is an American," said Professor Johnson.

"That's no problem," said Marlene's voice, this time with a clearly American accent. "I did part of my residency in Chicago. Let's take a look at your face," she said. "If you'll just remove your hand, I can see what's wrong."

I picked up my hand, leaving the napkin in place.

A shapely hand in a surgical glove lifted the napkin, but had to tug a little, indicating that the blood had begun to dry. An encouraging sign.

"A gentleman of your age, dueling? You should be ashamed of yourself. This is Berlin, not Heidelberg."

I tried to smile, but it hurt.

"The patient appears lucid," she said to the nurse in green scrubs with a computer tablet who made a note of that.

Marlene's voice turned to me again and said, "Please lie still, and try not to smile or talk. It will only make the wound start bleeding again."

She dismissed Professor Johnson with a wave of her hand.

He hesitated.

"You're still here," she said.

The nurse showed him the door.

Fifteen minutes later I was sitting up with twelve stitches in my face. I was something to look at, with my bloodstained shirt and a huge bandage on my head. It made me look like the mummy at a Frankenstein audition.

"No talking, no smiling, and no solid food," said the doctor who looked as good as her voice sounded. "Moving those muscles will tear out my stitches and make it start bleeding again. If you do that, I'll use a square needle to put them back again, and no anesthetic."

I pulled out my iTouch and thumbed a brief note for her to read on-screen. "Thanks, doc. How long?"

"At least three weeks," she replied.

"And the bandages?" I thumbed.

"The whole time. They are not just there to hold the dressing in place, but also to keep you from moving your jaw, which is what I suspect induced the lady to hit you with a plate of currywurst in the first place."

"The lady?" I thumbed. "Why think that?"

"You're not going to try and tell me that the suit who brought you in here hit you, are you? He'd have given you a black eye."

"His mother," I thumbed.

"How civilized of him to bring you," she replied.

"Follow my finger with your eyes," she instructed.

I did as I was told.

"There is no apparent problem with your eye. The cut was very close to it," she said. "When the bandages come off, you can either have plastic surgery to remove the scar, or you can just tell people that you went to school in Heidelberg," she joked.

"Ha, ha," I thumbed.

She smiled. "I recommend flowers for the lady, whether it was your fault or not, but especially if it was your fault."

"Mea culpa," I thumbed.

"In that case, my prescription is for roses, blood-red roses. A dozen, twice a day, until the inflammation subsides."

"Candy?" I thumbed.

"I think not. Perhaps an order of currywurst would be better," she said with a wink.

"U think?" I thumbed.

"Certainly. That will remind her of what she did to your face. Stand up," she instructed.

I pressed my hands on the examining table and pushed off into a more or less acceptable dismount.

"You seem none the worse for wear," she said. "You can go."

The left side of my face was numb from all the anesthetic she had pumped into it so that she could sew it up. She said that the pain would catch up with me later, and it did, with a vengeance.

"Take two aspirin, and drink through a straw," she'd said.

I had the sneaking suspicion that she was on Ilse's side. She knew it was going to hurt, and that the aspirin wouldn't help much. It didn't.

I walked out into the hall. Professor Johnson was at the end of it, sitting on an uncomfortable-looking couch.

"My mother won't pick up her phone," said Professor Johnson with more than a slight note of hostility in his voice. It seemed directed at me. "Why did she hit you?"

The answer to that wouldn't fit on the screen of my iTouch, or in a paper-back novel for that matter. I was glad that the doctor had told me to keep my mouth shut. It gave me an excuse not to say anything now.

"Can't talk - doc's orders - pull out stitches," I thumbed.

That didn't improve his mood, and he hit a speed-dial combination on his cell. I listened to the phone ringing for a minute until it switched him to Ilse's voice mail. The sound of her voice brought back memories. He didn't leave a message.

The ride back to the American Academy in Berlin on the Wannsee in the building that used to be the American Officers' Club took about 15 minutes. Neither one of us talked, but we were both doing a lot of thinking.

Welcome back to Berlin.

The Archives

Ghosts wander through the inner recesses of my mind all the time when I'm too tired to keep the doors closed that I put up to keep them out of the way. This was one of those times. I lay in bed, staring at the cracks in the ceiling that I couldn't see in the dark, wondering what had made me want to come back to Berlin on this fool's errand. I hadn't been looking for Ilse. I'd forgotten that she existed; well, sort of.

There are times in your life that you are really proud of, that you actively remember, like the time Samantha was born, or the time I kept the ambassador from being blown up. But there are also times that I'd really like to forget, like leaving Ilse, or having that affair with Irina because she reminded me of Ilse. Recollections like that make you want to pretend that it really wasn't you, but somebody else. Somebody you'd known, but had lost contact with. Somebody who didn't exist anymore, who was dead and buried in a shallow grave in a nameless wasteland you'd traversed on your way to an operation in Afghan that had gone terribly wrong. But the pretense was like a cover with no backstop, and you knew it the minute the thought started to take shape in the dark corners of your mind; unless, of course, you were still in that murky middle-ground between sleep and awakening. You could get away with it there, but not when you were wide awake or in one of those dreams that you woke up from in a cold sweat.

In the cold light of day, when the stuff that keeps my ears apart was doing its job, I could keep those memories locked away, like the other parts of my life that I really have forgotten, until some insignificant thing or event unlocks the door to the memory; something like a word, or a smell, or the taste of currywurst, something that was now inextricably woven—or should I now say 'sewn'—into the memory of Ilse. I had twelve stitches keeping my left check together that would leave a scar to remind me of her forever.

She wasn't the reason I applied for the fellowship. I don't recall being conscious of her at all during the time I was making the decision. I was full of grandiose thoughts like Kennedy's *"Ich bin ein Berliner"*—I feel like one too—and Reagan's "Tear Down this Wall" speech, in which he said *"Ich hab noch einen Koffer in Berlin."* That is a classic line from a nineteen-fifties German song that Marlene Dietrich made famous. "I still have a suitcase in Berlin" is to Berlin what Tony Bennett's "I Left my Heart in San Francisco" is to San Francisco.

Most people didn't get Reagan's allusion, because they didn't know the song, but it spoke to me. I can still hear Marlene singing it in my head, and I used to know all the words. What I'd forgotten was that the suitcase in Berlin was the place that she kept her memories, and she had to go back to Berlin from time to time to be able to look at them. If I'd been able to open up the suitcase in D.C. while I was writing the fellowship proposal, I might have had second thoughts. But I couldn't get it open in D.C.. I had to come back to Berlin to work the lock so that Ilse could jump out of the suitcase and hit me with a Meissen plate full of currywurst on my first night in town.

A look in the mirror the next morning convinced me that last night had not been a bad dream. My face was going to be the topic of conversation for the next three weeks at least, and probably longer. And not being able to talk was going to be a big handicap. A *case officer who can't talk is a pitiful creature indeed.

I made up a couple of screens of text that I could call up at a single tap. They began with "I walked into a glass door," and ended with "I can't talk or it will pull out the stitches."

When I showed the first one to Mary-Kate, the attractively put together Irish redhead of my vintage at the reception desk, she laughed.

"We've already heard the real story of your 'accident,' Doctor Troyan. You're the talk of the Academy. I can't wait to hear your side of it," she said with the gentle lilt of an Irish voice that matched her red hair. She was disappointed to learn that I couldn't talk, and tried to make me promise to tell her 'my side of it' as soon as I could.

"I never talk about a lady behind her back," I thumbed.

"How gallant. Gentlemen usually don't get hit in the face with a plate of currywurst," she said, "but you appear to be one."

Her pale gray-blue eyes broke into a subtle hint of a smile, and I pressed my advantage by asking her to help me fill Doctor Dietrich's prescription for roses twice a day. That enlarged the hint of a smile to a full-fledged one.

"If you'd be so kind as to get me a cup of coffee, Doctor Troyan?" she said.

"Cream? Sugar?" I thumbed.

"Black, one sugar," she replied with a twinkle in her eye. "Just around the corner," she continued, pointing the way.

When I got back she was just hanging up the phone. "Thank you," she said, taking the cup of coffee I'd brought her.

"If you go out the gate and turn right onto Am Sandwerder street, the Wannsee *S-Bahn station is about nine minute's walk away. There's a café with a great soup special every day, and a *florist*," she said as she gave me a hand-written note with Ilse's postal address and cell phone number.

"Elisabeth, Professor Johnson's secretary, was very obliging," she continued with a wink. "I've never met her, but we talk on the phone a lot. Practically every day at the beginning of the semester like this. She was thrilled to be able to help patch up your quarrel with the professor's mother."

"Thank U VERY much," I thumbed, and showed her the screen of my iTouch.

"Not at all," she replied. "It's clear that you'll be the sensation of the semester, and I don't want to miss any of the details. Please be sure to let me know what happens."

"Of course," I thumbed. I had learned early in my career that people like Mary-Kate and Elisabeth were good to have on your side.

„Only my second day in town, and already I'm the 'sensation of the semester'," I thought. „This is going to be a fun fellowship."

The florist was a lady of my vintage when I was younger. She had jet-black hair, and sparkling brown eyes that smiled, even when her mouth didn't. She was wearing a floral print smock that undulated with purple orchids. Her name was Trudi.

I showed her the canned iTouch text that said I couldn't talk, because it would pull out the stitches, and she smiled sympathetically.

I sent tulips to Mary-Kate at the same time I ordered two dozen roses a day for Ilse. I left six notes to go out with Ilse's flowers, and said I'd be back to write more. Trudi was obviously pleased with a big spender like me.

"But why the currywurst to go with the second delivery of flowers?" she asked.

I thumbed, "lady hit me face w/ currywurst." Her laugh turned to raised eyebrows when I continued, "plate cut face > bandages."

After the florist, I went to the café with the soup menu that Mary-Kate had recommended. It was practically next door to the florist. Mary-Kate was right. The soup was tasty. And the sturdy, but attractively put together lady behind the bar did her best to keep out the chewy bits so I wouldn't have to move my jaw. She said that if I was planning on coming back tomorrow, that she'd bring in her blender from home and 'pre chew' it for me.

"Wonderful idea," I thumbed. "Delicious! But 4 supper? I be in town all day."

"No problem," she said. "We have soup in the evening too."

I went back to Trudi's and bought a bouquet for Elisabeth, before I got on the S-Bahn heading for Magdalenenstraße on the U-5 *U-Bahn line, which was the closest stop to the Archives.

It was a strange sensation getting on the S-Bahn. When I'd been in Berlin the first time in the mid-nineteen-seventies, I was in the Army, and riding the S-Bahn was *verboten.* It was creepy. The hairs on the back of my neck were standing up, and I kept having this feeling that a bunch of *Vopo's or worse, *CI guys, were going to crawl out of the woodwork and drag me off in handcuffs. I tried to shake off that feeling every time it raised its head, because it kept turning into a flashback to Beirut, and that wasn't a pleasant memory at all.

The young guard at the gatehouse to the Archives was the model of Stasi efficiency and paranoia, even though he was probably still in diapers when the Wall fell. I showed him my passport, but he wasn't having any because my face was wrapped in bandages, and he couldn't match the photo in the passport to the face attached to bearer.

---

* Prohibited.

"You could be anybody behind those bandages," he said in German tinted with an accent that marked him as an *Ossie, an East German. "And I can't let just anybody in."

I whipped out my iTouch and thumbed, "Call Elisabeth Professor Johnsons secretary."

His face brightened at the thought. That signaled that she was probably not just an efficient gossip.

"There's a gentleman here," he said into the phone with a voice decked out in his best bureaucratic bib-and-tucker pronunciation, "who claims to be Doktor Troyan, but his face is all bandaged up and I can't make a positive identification from his passport picture."

He listened for a moment, hung up the phone, and said, "We'll do your photo ID after the bandages come off, Doktor Troyan. Fräulein Freitag will be right out to collect you." He handed me a generic 'Visitor' badge to hang around my neck. "Please have a seat. Would you care for a cup of coffee?"

I shook my head and pointed to my bandages.

"Oh, yes," he said. "I wasn't sure if you could, but thought I would offer you one in any event."

I thumbed out *Danke sehr*,[*] and showed him the screen.

The real reason that I refused wouldn't fit on the screen of my iTouch, and he'd never believe it anyway. Besides, it would take too long to type out with just two thumbs.

Despite all my years of government service—in uniform and out—I still didn't like the taste of coffee, which seems to be the lubricating oil that makes the government work. I don't know how people can stomach it. They wouldn't believe me on *Tberg the first time I showed up for work.

"Everybody makes coffee based on the roster over there on the wall," said the *Pit Boss, "It's your turn now."

"I don't think you really want me to do that," I replied. "I don't drink coffee, and don't know how to make it."

"Everybody drinks coffee," said the Pit Boss, "and there's nothing to making it. Get your can over there and make the coffee!"

---

[*] Thank you very much

I could see that there was no point in arguing, so I did as I was told.

Fifteen minutes later, after he'd tasted a cup from the batch I'd brewed, the Pit Boss came over to get me, and said: "Go pour it out."

I never made coffee on Tberg again.

When the next new guy showed up, the Pit Boss gave him the same introduction to operations that I'd gotten, but with one small difference.

"Everybody—except Mike—makes coffee based on the roster over there on the wall," said the Pit Boss. "It's your turn now."

"How come Mike gets to skate?" asked the *newk.

"The use of *poisonous* weapons of war is prohibited by the Geneva Convention," replied the Pit Boss.

I had barely started to warm the cold vinyl of the gray, government-issue chair in the guard shack, when Fräulein Freitag bounced into view. The gleam on the guard's face when I mentioned her name was certainly justified. Her silky auburn hair wasn't the only thing doing the bouncing.

She swung open the door, extended her hand, as she said: "Doktor Troyan, I'm pleased to meet you. Mary-Kate told me all about your unfortunate accident."

„My, how word gets around," I thought.

I turned her hand palm down, and made a slight bow as I brought it up for a kiss.

"Ach, Doktor Troyan!" she said, adding "How gallant!" with an emphasis and a shift in the direction of her voice that made it clear the remark was not addressed to me, but to the guard whose nametag said "Asch."

I whipped out my bouquet and presented it to her, gesturing 'from me to you.'

"But, Doktor Troyan," she began.

I held up my hand in a 'stop' sign before she could say anymore, and pulled out my iTouch.

"For ur help with the addr of Prof Js mother," I thumbed.

"Oh, how kind," she replied. "Mary-Kate said that you were a real gentleman." The second remark was again clearly intended for the erstwhile 'Gunner Asch.'

I nodded graciously.

"If you'll just follow me, Doktor Troyan," she said, opening the door.

Once we were outside, on our way to the main building, she continued, "Professor Johnson is unfortunately unable to look after you personally today, and has asked me to show you around."

"Perhps change aftr mother gets flowers," I thumbed.

"Perhaps."

She showed me into what was obviously the reading room. There were six readers sitting at large tables with low reading lamps. The chairs were the same bureaucratic gray as in the guard shack. There were ten other empty tables. The readers appeared absorbed in what they were doing. None of them looked up when we came in.

She marched me over to the only desk in the room. An obvious authority symbol left over from the previous owners that had been appreciatively commandeered by its present occupant, Herr Professor Luschke, who insisted on being addressed by his title. The reading room was his domain.

"Not THE Prof Helmut Luschke, author of *Record Keeping Systems of the *MfS*," I thumbed disingenuously, following the suggestion that Elisabeth made on the way in. The doctor's bureaucratic frown changed to the insinuation of a smile. I was doubly glad that I had bought those flowers for Elisabeth.

"How can I be of service, Herr Doktor?" asked Luschke, pleased to be recognized by another academic.

"Plz look abstract grant proposal," I thumbed, and handed him a copy of my 'elevator speech' for the proposal that got me this fellowship.

"*Dissuasion Techniques Used by the Ministry of State Security to Induce Dissidents to Halt Behaviors Detrimental to the State*," said the title. Professor Luschke smiled approvingly when he read it.

"Yes," he said. "I think that I can suggest a few avenues of approach to this problem," and started making notes on a pad with his left hand.

While he was writing, I thumbed out a note and showed it to him. "If not 2 much trub perhps look own file first?"

"You were in Berlin before?" he inquired.

I nodded, and thumbed: "1974-1977."

"Just fill out this form, and we'll see if you are listed," he said pulling a form out of the upper right desk drawer. "As a student?" he inquired.

"No, army," I thumbed.

He looked like he had a bad taste in his mouth, but he gave me the form anyway. After all, I had known about his book.

I filled out the form and handed it to him.

"If you come back tomorrow, we should have several things for you to read, Herr Doktor," said Luschke. "There are over 180 kilometers of files and there are only so many searchers in the stacks. They will need a little time to locate your material. Your personal file could be particularly difficult. Foreign names are often spelled incorrectly in the card catalog."

I thumbed "Thank you and until tmrw Herr Professor." Elisabeth then took me on the five-cent tour, showing me where to find all the really important things, like the toilets and the snack bar, before she deposited me back at the guard shack with her 'Gunner Asch.'

In and out in less than twenty minutes.

U-Bahn Station Surveillance Camera

The *Kudamm

„What the hell," I thought to myself. „Just like the Army: 'Hurry up and wait'."

I set off back toward the U-Bahn. „Might as well check out the Kudamm now rather than later," I said to myself, trying to justify my decision not to go back to the Academy this early in the day. The Kudamm had been the center of civilization when I lived here last. It might still be some fun.

A sign at the entrance to the Magdalenenstraße U-Bahn station that you could only see on the way in caught my eye.

That's the same reason the Stasi gave for keeping an eye on most of the population. I felt like the eye in the sign was focused right on me. I tried to look inconspicuous, for all the good that would do. Trying to look inconspicuous just made you more obvious to a trained observer.

If I had been doing the public relations for the Stasi Museum, I would have made sure that you could see this sign when leaving the U-Bahn, and there would have been another small sign underneath that said:

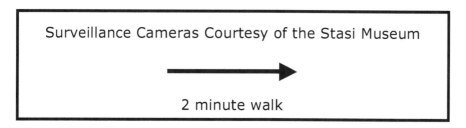

Surveillance Cameras Courtesy of the Stasi Museum

2 minute walk

It was 35 minutes from the Archives to Bahnhof Zoo. The ghosts of the Stasi, Vopo's, and the CI were still with me on this trip, but there were fewer of them. Maybe some of them stayed to visit friends in the Archives, or maybe camera surveillance meant that they didn't need as many of them to keep tabs on me.

The "Hollow Tooth" of the Kaiser Wilhelm Memorial Church was right where I'd left it: right next to the modern church that the Berliners called the "Lipstick and Compact." That gave me a sense of homecoming. I must have passed it a thousand times when I was stationed in Berlin. I turned right down Joachimstalerstraße, and headed toward the Kudamm and Kranzler's. Ilse had liked to go there, but it was expensive, so we didn't go that often. When we did go, however, it was a class date.

"Two cokes and one piece of cake. Chocolate."

"With two forks?" asked the smiling waitress.

We smiled and said "yes" in unison.

The waitress knew that there wouldn't be a big tip, but apparently she had a soft spot for young people in love and never complained.

The reality of the present beat the ghosts of Berlin past soundly around the head and shoulders. The place to take a special date for a coke and people watching at street level was gone. The street was filled with store window fronts, dominated by signs for the *Schuhhof.* "Welcome to the *Neues Kranzler Eck* Shopping Center," said a sign on the door where the café used to be. All that was left of Kranzler's was the sign and the red and white awning around a rotunda on the second floor.

I crossed the Kudamm, and turned left toward the Kaiser Wilhelm Memorial Church and the Europa Center. You could see them better from this side of the street, and it was nice to have something recognizable in view to counteract the disappointment of Kranzler's.

When I got to the place where the Kudamm turns into Tauentzien-straße, I noticed a bookstore on my right. I didn't remember it being there, but it didn't seem out of place either. The window display was artfully arranged with careful precision. I slowed to browse the books on display, checking the reflections in the glass for surveillance out of habit, when all of a sudden Professor Luschke's book caught my eye. I remembered the suggestion of a smile on his face when I knew the title of his book, and imagined his reaction if I'd ask him to sign a copy for me.

I continued slowly toward the door, recalling a hot summer day in Warsaw when a three-man surveillance team had followed me into a bookstore. They were in a panic because they thought that I was clearing a *dead drop and they'd miss it. They closed in so that they could see what I was doing with the books I was holding. A pungent odor preceded them, reminding me that deodorant was in short supply in Warsaw that summer. There was a dead drop in that store, but I wasn't clearing it. I'd only been looking for a kid's book with lots of drawings in it for Samantha to establish a pattern and a reason for being there. I found a good one full of illustrations and short on text. She literally 'read' it to pieces.

I took one last look at the reflection in the window to convince myself that I was still clear of surveillance—'black' as we call it in the trade. There was nobody behind me that I'd seen before, so I went in. I sauntered around a sale table stacked high with "bestsellers," none of which called out for my attention. Konsalik was obviously still popular even though he'd been dead for over ten years. He'd never been my style.

Just as I was finishing my first circuit of the sale table, a well-dressed, very presentable lady of indeterminate age maneuvered herself in front of me. She had blond hair, which was all the rage in my day, but seemed to have fallen out of fashion in the new Berlin. She, and Ilse were the only blondes I'd seen.

"May I help you?" inquired the comely saleslady, with an accent that said she had grown up here on the west side of the Wall.

I whipped out my iTouch and thumbed, "*Record Keeping Systems of the MfS,* by Prof. Luschke?"

"Yes, of course," she replied as if she ran into people every day who had bandaged faces, couldn't talk, and wanted books about the Stasi. She was a class act.

"Please follow me," she said, as she walked over to the window display where I'd seen Luschke's book. This was clearly the only copy in the store. She pulled it out of the window, and handed it to me. It was a hardbound, academic volume. I knew it wasn't going to be cheap, but I thumbed, "Thank you. I'll take it."

I left the store with my purchase in a bright blue plastic bag, and continued my way down Tauentzienstraße in search of the Ka-De-We, the Harrods of Berlin. Ilse and I had spent a good bit of time window shopping there. It was fun to pretend to be posh, even though the salespeople would ignore us because of the way we were dressed. Halfway to the Ka-De-We, a splash of yellow caught my eye. I don't remember what was there, but it wasn't McDonald's.

I remember when the first American fast food place opened in 1975. It was Burger King, and we'd send the duty vehicle with four guys on a "Burger King" run on *Swings, so we wouldn't have to eat in the mess hall.

"Hi, this is the American radar station on Teufelsberg. I'd like to place a take-out order for 127 Whopper Meals; 57 of those with onion rings. The car will be leaving to pick it up as soon as I hang up. We'll be there in 15 minutes."

I always wondered if they were glad for our business, or if we were just a huge pain in the ass. Some people ordered hamburgers every Swing. I couldn't afford to. Most of my money went to taking Ilse places. Things were different now; money-wise I mean. With my retirement and this fellowship I could afford to do both, but the memory of how the dull pain in my cheek got there reminded me that this wasn't a viable option.

A low rumble in my tummy suggested that a little something to eat wouldn't be out of place right now, but the dull pain in my face cautioned that chewing was not allowed, so a little voice inside my head put these two facts together and said, „McDonald's has milkshakes."

I continued purposefully down the street toward the golden arches. A McDonald's is a McDonald's, but there are little regional differences. You can order beer in one in Germany.

The ghosts of my Berlin who had been dogging my steps all day stopped at the door, unable to cross the yellow threshold into the present. They were replaced, however, by the memory of a little girl with bright shiny blue eyes tugging on my hand and asking if she could have a kid's meal with a chocolate shake instead of a coke. I said "yes." I always did.

I ordered a large chocolate shake, and sat in a back corner out of habit so I could keep an eye on the door. I had fun watching the people come and go. A kid with a green mohawk. A girl in Goth black with a piercing in her left eyebrow. A man in a gray pinstriped suit with a pink carnation in his lapel. A lady in a red coat with two kids. The boy in blue wanted ketchup for his french fries. The girl in pink wanted mayonnaise. A typically schizophrenic German-American family I guessed. It's funny how alone you can be in a crowd.

I finished my milkshake, but decided to skip the Ka-De-We. One of the highlights of visiting there had been the sixth floor, the *Fress-Etage*—the "chow-down floor"—a gourmet's delight, that wasn't as classy as the food halls in Harrods, but it did have more opportunities to graze as you walked through. I wanted to wait until I could chew again.

I left the ghost-free zone of McDonald's and turned left, back toward the Europa Center. I cut across the street and grabbed the first entrance to the Center. I got stuck in the foyer, however, transfixed by the stony gaze of two huge eyes staring at me from a double segment of the Wall. In my day, you had to go out of your way to find the Wall. It wasn't as pervasive as everybody who lived outside Berlin seemed to think. The one time I had visitors from the States, they wanted to see The Wall, and I had to look on a map to find where it was.

Now the ghost of the Wall seemed to have gone out of its way looking for me. I blinked first and dived inside the Center with trepidation. The water clock, however, was still there. Ilse and I had come back time and again to catch it when it changed hours. That was a real show. It was twelve minutes before the hour. I walked around killing time till the clock 'poured' two, but it wasn't as much fun alone as it had been with Ilse. I took the exit for Budapester Straße, but I didn't recall there being a Kentucky Fried Chicken in that spot before.

I crossed the street to what had been a line of chic shops full of rich people who stayed at the Hilton back in the nineteen-seventies. Ilse and I had gone there window shopping more than once. What else could you do on a *speedy-4's pay? The last time we'd been there together, we'd been looking at rings.

Things had changed, and the memories of my Berlin spun in their graves. Budapester Straße was another one of those places that you used to know, but that you'd rather have remembered as it was. There was a store that sold remaindered books from bins on wooden pallets, a cheap-luggage shop with lots of customers who didn't seem to be buying suitcases, and an even cheaper oriental import store; not the pricey jewelers and courtiers that I had remembered. And the Hilton was gone too.

"It's in Mitte now, across from Gendarmenmarkt," said the guy in the bookstore, whose German accent said that he didn't come from around here.

The ghosts of Berlin past swirled around me, and I felt a chill; or was that jetlag? I decided I'd head back to the café at S-Bahn Wannsee for some soup, and maybe a brandy. I'd seen a bottle behind the counter.

Double Wall Segment at the Europa Center

Good Morning

"Good morning, Doctor Troyan," said Mary-Kate with a smile on her ruby-red lips and in her pale gray-blue eyes as I approached her desk. "Thank you very much for the flowers. Elisabeth says that you gave her some too."

I nodded "yes."

"Has Professor Johnson's mother responded to your flowers yet?"

I shook my head "no."

"Then you must have done something really terrible to her, if two dozen roses won't make amends."

I nodded "yes." My neck muscles were getting a real workout this morning.

"But you seem like such a gentleman?" she continued.

"I was younger then," I thumbed, "and foolish."

"Ah, the follies of youth," she said with a sigh. "Who doesn't have a few of their own?"

"Can't talk on phone wud U call her ask to lunch?" I thumbed on my iTouch.

"You really want to apologize?" she asked with a hint of doubt.

I nodded "yes."

She picked up the phone and dialed without asking me for the number. I could hear the phone ringing, then Ilse answered with a non-committal "Hallo."

"Frau Johnson," said Mary-Kate, "This is the American Academy in Berlin. Doctor Troyan …"

The line went dead.

"She doesn't seem to want to talk to you Doctor Troyan."

"Thank U," I thumbed. "U can call me Mike."

"I think that I will wait until I learn what you did to Frau Johnson, Doctor Troyan," was her cold reply.

I headed up Am Sandwerder to S-Bahn Wannsee and the café with the soup. The lady who ran the place had brought in her blender. The soup for the day was vegetable-beef. It was delicious. The straw made a slurping noise when I got to the bottom of the bowl. An older gentleman alone at the next table with a *Berliner Weiße looked at me disapprovingly for disturbing the peace and quiet of his tête-à-tête with his beer.

I got up and took the empty bowl back to the counter.

"My thanks, dear lady," I thumbed.

"Call me 'Helga,' please, she said with a smile, lifting her hands to sweep back her chestnut-brown hair. This is a gesture that always fascinates me. It's a seemingly natural thing that women do unconsciously all the time. I've seen six-year-olds doing it as well. Samantha did it. Her mother did it. But Helga did it with a kind of slow-motion ease that spoke of practiced poise. I stared in awe.

"With pleasure," I thumbed in German. "My name's 'Mike.' I'll be back this evening for a re-fill. Tschüss!*"

The next stop was the florist.

"Good morning, Herr Doktor," said Trudi, who was wearing a different floral print smock from the one I'd seen the day before. Today's was a multi-colored profusion of tulips. "More flowers?" she asked.

"Yes," I thumbed. "4 Mary-Kate @ Academy roses."

"Herr Doktor, Casanova so many flowers did not buy," she said with an ostentatious wink.

---

* Berliner slang for "bye-bye"

I selected a 'Thank you' card from the rack on the counter, and wrote a note for Mary-Kate.

"The least you can do for the 'sensation of the semester' is to call him 'Mike.' The older me is really a nice guy."

I gave it to Trudi who I was sure would read it before attaching it to the bouquet of roses she had just wrapped up. I suspected that this information might make its way to Helga, so I thumbed, "Another dozen and a single rose to go."

"No card?"

I shook my head "no."

She looked puzzled, but I decided that an air of mystery would stand me in good stead with her, so I didn't say anything.

On my way to the S-Bahn, I dropped back into the café, and gave Helga the dozen roses. Her green eyes sparkled.

"Mike," she said, "you shouldn't have."

"They're no match for your beauty, but they will have to do until something better comes along," I thumbed.

I left, basking in the rays of a very pleased smile.

I settled down in the S-Bahn with the ghosts of my Berlin past for the fifty-minute ride to the Archives, and opened Professor Luschke's book to a random page.

Typical dossiers consist of five to thirty pages. The top page is invariably a justification for the investigation of the subject. The second is the adjudication of the investigation. Brevity, not lucidity, is the key characteristic of these pages. They are primarily formulaic. The top two pages are followed by multiple, often repetitive, voluminous reports on the subject's private life contributed by various informants, who are identified by a covername rather than by true name. While these reports appear to be just so much boring, personal trivia, they were extremely useful to the Stasi for creating a personality profile of the subject so that those who exhibited "politically negative conduct," or those who presented an "operational interest" could be induced to cooperate. The repetition was a result of the use of multiple sources, which was essential for cross-checking the information, and making sure that the informant reports were factual.

That had a familiar ring to it. I'd done a bit of that kind of reporting myself.

The ghosts who had me under surveillance seemed to have lost contact with the subject—me—in the crush of humanity at Alexanderplatz where I changed to the U-5 U-Bahn line. Places with lots of people milling about were always good for giving your surveillance the slip. I used to teach that in the counter-surveillance course at the Farm.

I was still black when I got to Magdalenenstraße.

"Good morning, Doktor Troyan," said Elisabeth's Gunner Asch.

I put my single rose on his counter, and thumbed, "G.M. rose 4 U 2 give 2 Elisabeth be 'gallant'."

"But Fräulein Freitag is not speaking to me," he replied.

"She was talking U not me yesterday when she said 'gallant'," I thumbed, glad for auto-complete with a sentence that long.

He looked unconvinced as he gave me my badge, but said "Thank you," nonetheless. It showed that he at least had a good upbringing.

I found my way to the reading room, and tiptoed over to the symbol of Professor Luschke's authority, his desk.

"Good morning, Doktor Troyan," he said in a mock whisper, even though we were the only two in the room. What is it about library reading rooms that makes you feel like you have to be quiet?

"It appears that you do not have a file," he said.

I'd suspected that something like that might happen. I frowned in mock disappointment, but it hurt, so I quickly relaxed my face. Professor Luschke seemed not to notice, but I'd bet dollars to doughnuts that he had.

"You are only listed in the *HA II Counterespionage index of Western embassy staff," he added.

His book had said that the spelling of your name in the main index did not always coincide with the way that it was spelled on your passport. German phonetic spellings were used when your name was first encountered in an audio operation—a bug or a phone tap—or had been heard by an informant with no access to documentation.

"Variant spellings?" I thumbed.

"Possibly," he said. "Frau Asch wanted to hear you pronounce your name so she could look for that. You can do that when she brings out your HA II cards. I'll just give her a call," he said, reaching for the phone.

I hesitated while it sunk in that Gunner Asch's mother was one of the guardians of the Stasi files. The hesitation dragged on as I applied that tidbit of information to the giant jigsaw puzzle of life in the Archives. A little nepotism can go a long way, if you know how to use it. I forced my wandering consciousness back to the process at hand.

If Luschke had noticed the hesitation, his Sphinx-like deadpan hid the fact. He had the practiced facial control of a professional, which made me wonder about his past. I'd have to make inquiries.

I waved my hand to catch his attention, and when I saw his eyes following the motion of my fingers, I pointed to my bandages.

"Oh, I'd quite forgotten," he said.

My galloping paranoia pointed out that this was an old interrogator's trick to try and catch you out in a faked injury. I tried to calm it with the thought that he was an absent-minded professor, but my paranoia wasn't taking any, especially in what used to be Stasi Central. I quickly changed the subject before this got out of hand.

"While I here wud U sign copy Ur book 4 me?" I thumbed.

He did a good job of suppressing his surprise, but there were telltales in the eyes, and the right corner of his mouth, exactly where it should have been for someone left-handed. He was good, but I was better.

"But certainly, Herr Doktor," he said with restrained enthusiasm as I fished his book out of my briefcase. He put the book down on his desk, positioned it carefully, and opened it to the title page, where he wrote:

Archiv der Zentralstelle der BStU

to Dr. Troyan

Helmut Luschke

The graphologist at Headquarters would probably have said that the right-angled, 90-degree slant of the subject's letters indicates an analytic and unemotional person who would tend to be sincere and reliable, because he or she always recognizes their obligations. The uniformly straight lines suggest that the subject has willpower and determination, though he or she might exhibit a tendency to rigidity. The small size of the subject's letters indicates an intellectual and scholarly person with a keen sense of observation, who will tend to be meticulous and methodical.

Stasi files had graphologists' notes in them. It said so in Luschke's book. I wondered if he suspected what I was doing to him by asking for an autograph.

"Thank U very much," I thumbed.

"You're welcome," he replied. "If you just take a seat, Frau Asch will be right out."

I sat down at a table facing Professor Luschke's desk to wait for the appearance of Frau Asch with visions of Connie from *Smiley's People* dancing in my head. The mispronounced whisper of my name in my left ear made me jump. I hadn't heard her coming. I knew people who worked in Surreptitious Entry who couldn't be that quiet.

"Ur brother on the gate?" danced my thumbs.

"My son," she replied.

"He cudn't be your son. You'd have to have been about 6 when U had him."

"Fräulein Freitag said that I'd have to look out for you," she replied. "Don't waste your time," she continued. "I'm immune. I grew up with case officers. My father worked here."

That made things a lot clearer. She was in the family business.

"What makes you think I case officer?" I typed.

"These cards record the identities of confirmed intelligence officers," she said, placing three on the table in front of me. "The information on these came from cooperating counter-intelligence services."

"I wonder where they cud have gotten idea," I countered. The funny thing about women is that they can make you feel guilty even when you're not. My counter to this power of theirs is refusing to admit to any guilt at all, even for things of which I am guilty. Sometimes it works. Sometimes it doesn't. This was one of the times that it didn't.

```
        T R O Y A N                    |        H-DE
Name                                   | Erf. in Inf-Speicher/Erf.-Nr.
                                       | A3750
Geburtsname                            | Ablage
weitere Namen                          | DOKNR/PI
        Michael  Alexander             |
Vorname                                | Diensteinheit/Mitarbeiter
        22.08.1953                     | HA II-10
geb. am              in                | Erfaßt am
        Sta.: USA                      |
Wohnanschrift                          | F402 am
Mitarbeiter des Verteidigungsminis-    |
teriums der USA.                       | an
Gehilfe des Luftwaffenattachés         | Schlagwort/Kurzfassung — SV/
                                       | Maßnahmen/Entscheidungen
                                       | (auch Rückseite benutzen)
der Botschaft der USA in Warschau      | SO VRP 11.9.84
401   °                                | ODD 4/174/84
```

"Perhaps because the position you filled was always filled by CIA officers," she observed calmly. She did a woman's enigmatic smile, the kind that speaks volumes.

She had a head on her shoulders like Connie, but she didn't look anything like her. She had to be over 40 to have a son at the gate, but she didn't look it. A skirt that suggested it had a designer label on the inside, an understatedly elegant blouse brushed by shoulder-length blond hair, and fiery blue eyes all suggested Veronica Lake rather than Beryl Reid playing Connie Sachs. On any other woman of her age, her dress and bearing would have been called too young, but she carried it off with ease.

When I missed my cue to reply, she continued the conversation on her own.

"The abbreviations are generally troublesome, even for people with German as good as yours," she said. "I've brought you a glossary," she added, placing a small stack of papers with three staples down the left side on the table next to the cards. Locally produced working aids like that were generally much better than the ones printed by Headquarters on an off-set press.

"Thank you," I thumbed, for lack of anything more intelligent to say.

"To continue to search for your files, I need to know how to pronounce your name," she said.

I thumbed energetically on my iTouch, and turned it around for her to read. "Sounds like 'Treu - Jan' w/ accent on 'Jan'."

"An interesting name," she answered. "What's its origin?"

"Russian," my thumbs typed.

"Really?" she said.

"Used to be Troyanovskij," said my prancing thumbs.

"You speak Russian, then, Doktor Troyan?" she asked, to practice pronouncing my name.

I nodded.

"You should tell Doktor Luschke. He might have a few other things you could look at in that event," she said. "I'll leave you to your cards, then. They are copies. You can take them with you." She turned gracefully, and left as silently as she had come.

The first card in the stack was from my assignment in Poland. The information was nothing more than my passport data along with my official job title. It was the card file it was in that was important. "Confirmed intelligence officers," she had said. The source notation in the lower right corner said that it came from the Polish *UB. So much for the cover that Headquarters believed was as tight as a drum. The second card was from Prague, and the third from Damascus. There was nothing from my tours in Vienna and Munich. Guess the Austrians and the Germans weren't "cooperating services."

It was hardly an earth-shattering revelation. The amount of surveillance I'd had in all those places made it clear to anybody with horse sense that they'd figured out who I was.

I put the cards in my briefcase. They'd make good show and tell for an evening of war stories and drinks sometime.

As I turned in my badge, Gunner Asch beamed at me pleasantly.

"Thank you, Herr Doktor," he said. "I'm taking her to dinner tonight."

I didn't have to ask whom he was taking to dinner. It was Elisabeth Freitag. I'd made a friend in low places. They were always handier than people thought.

Snapshots of a Younger Me

The next morning Gunner Asch greeted me full of smiles and *thank-you*'s for the 'Herr Doktor.' There were some other people in the guard shack, so I didn't hang around for a full report on his date with Elisabeth.

"U R ++ welcome," I thumbed, but before I headed for the reading room, I pulled another rose out of my briefcase for him to give to Elisabeth.

Luschke was polite, but reserved when I approached his desk. His bow tie was crooked, but I wasn't going to tell him.

"Herr Doktor," he said, "The MfS manual that I ordered from the stacks for your research has arrived."

He got up, went to the bookshelf that formed the wall behind his desk, selected a thickish hardbound volume from the second shelf from the top. He turned around and presented the book across his desk to me title up so that I could read it: *Methods of Reconciling the Interests of Society with the Interests of the Individual*. The title page showed that it had been published by the *JHS in 1968.

"Unfortunately it can't leave the Archives," he said. "You'll have to read it here, but I'll keep it in the reading room until you are done with it."

I nodded comprehension and sat down at an empty table. It didn't take a lot of effort to find one. I was the only reader this early in the morning. I picked a table that let me sit facing him, and opened my briefcase to form a shield so that he couldn't see what I was doing. I got out my pen scanner and started scanning the book into memory. It's amazing what you can buy on the open market these days that started as a great piece of tradecraft.

It was almost all text, with just the *de rigueur* portraits of the Party leadership, but I didn't care about those, so I set the scanner for 200dpi. That meant I could get 150 pages into memory before it filled up, or my fingers got tired, whichever came first. I'd run the images through the OCR on my laptop when I got back to the Academy. Soft copies of a text were so much easier to mine for information.

Frau Asch was suddenly standing next to me. Her stealth approach caught me in mid-scan, but she didn't say anything about the scanner. I didn't have any illusions that she hadn't noticed. Case officers' daughters usually know exactly how the game is played.

"I would like to consult you, Doktor Troyan, about a series of photographs I have been trying to identify," she said. "A younger you is clearly one of the people in this shot," she continued, placing four black and white 8X10 glossies on the table in front of me. "I was hoping that you could tell me who the others are."

The photos showed four American soldiers in uniform sitting at a table piled high with food. One of them was me. They were a little underexposed, but otherwise a good likeness. The kind of thing you get from concealed cameras inside without a flash; not great art, but a mug shot for a file.

Placing the event was easy. It was the only time I had been to East Berlin when I was in the Army. It was on one of those *Special Services tours in an O.D. green army bus. I had forgotten the date, but it didn't really matter. The backs of the photos had a date stamp.

The reason that I could be so sure of the *where* is that all of us in the photos were in class-A dress uniforms. It was a requirement for the tour, and one of the few times I had worn mine while in Berlin. At work, we wore *fatigues, and off-duty, I was always in civvies.

One of the ground rules for the tour was that we couldn't wear nametags on our uniforms, hence the lack of ID in the file. We'd been told that the reason for the "no nametag" rule was to confuse the Stasi. It seemed to have worked, otherwise I'd have had a file, which would most likely have raised my stock a few points in Luschke's eyes. I hadn't seen or heard from the other three guys in years.

"Hmmm," I thumbed. "That's Jerry Whatshizname, George Somebody-or-other, and Professor Johnson's father."

That generated a genuine look of surprise on Frau Asch's face.

"Our Professor Johnson?"

"Yes," waltzed my fingers. "Small world, isn't it?"

"Small indeed," she said, as she quickly put her case officer's daughter face back in place. "The file is labeled 'Operation MAHLZEIT,' and there are no names to go with the photos. You are simply identified as 'Army Security Agency soldiers'."

So much for confusing the Stasi. Clearly, no nametags and unassigned brass gave us away from the get-go.

"Is there anything else in the file?" I thumbed hopefully.

"There is an audio recording with transcript, and a foot surveillance report."

I mimed: "Could I see it?" and she just as silently put an accordion folder down in front of me.

"If you remember the surnames of the other two gentlemen ..." she said.

"Of course," I thumbed.

"Just leave the file here when you've finished with it."

"And note re names," responded my thumbs.

The tour was a big deal for us: a trip to the lion's den of the Commie threat, and a chance to see how the target lived. The price we paid was a list of restrictions as long as your arm. In addition to the uniform, we were only supposed to exchange our west marks for east marks at the official rate of one to one, at the official window at the border, where we crossed. The minimum exchange was twenty marks, about five bucks at the time. It was a one-way exchange. You couldn't change your unused east marks back to west marks when you left. Everybody looked at this as a cover charge for the tour.

Some people—myself and the rest of the guys in the photo included—seemed to have more east marks than the exchange receipts in their pockets said that they should have had. I had bought my "extra" east marks at Bahnhof Zoo, where there was a thriving black market that offered you eight to one. We had all dutifully stood in line with the rest of the bus for the obligatory exchange of twenty marks, and then went off to spend our ill-gotten gains in the Workers' Paradise.

The flag store was a popular stop. At the unofficial rate of eight to one, flags were cheap, and could be sold or bartered back on our side of the Wall. I got an East German and a Soviet flag, both of which I eventually sold. I think I got twenty bucks each. Not a bad profit margin.

After that, I headed for the Russian book store, where I bought a bunch of books that were listed on the foot surveillance report: Хоббит (*The Hobbit*), *Schwierigkeiten der russischen Sprache* (*Difficulties of the Russian Language*), Русское словесное ударение (*The Accented Syllable in Russian*), Подпоручик Киже (*Lieutenant Kizhe*) by Tynyanov, and another six books in a similar mix of grammar and literature.

I still had most of them on the shelf at head-level in the bookcase back home that was right behind my desk. No need for the foot surveillance behind me that day to guess what I did. Mighty efficient of them to get the book titles. I'd worked with teams that would not have thought of it.

When it got to be lunchtime, our tour-bus load of GI's invaded some poor restaurant, where the tour organizer had reserved tables. The four of us figured that with a week's advance notice we were coming, the Stasi would have the place wired for sound. The transcript in the folder proved we were right. It was labeled "Table 23."

The guess was that the bug was in the vase with a single wilting flower in the middle of the table. Actually, it was probably under the table-top, but we didn't know that. I only learned that a lot later, and the other guys most likely never did.

Jerry pointed at the vase, and said, "Eins, zwei, drei, wie hören sie mich?" I didn't need to remember. It was the first line of the transcript.

We all broke up laughing at his "audio check" for the Stasi microphone in the vase. The second line in the transcript was a transcriber comment that said, "Unrestrained laughter. (How very droll.)" The guys working the tape didn't seem to have much of a sense of humor, or maybe they got this kind of stuff all the time.

I chimed in with, "Раз, два, три. Как слышно?", just in case this was a joint Stasi-KGB *op. That was in the transcript too, but in Latin letters, not Cyrillic.

"Give 'em a break," said George. "They're English Marys, so that's what they want to hear. One, two. Radio check, over."

Practical to a fault, Fast Eddie said, "Where's the waiter with the menu? I'm hungry."

The waiter showed up, as if on cue. "What'll it be, guys?" he said with a clear American accent.

"See? Didn't I tell you?" said George.

Snapshots of a Younger Me
Illustration by Herb Gardner from *Enemy Agents and You*,
DA Pamphlet 355-15, 3 October 1960.

We ordered like four Diamond Jims, 'cause we all still had wads of east marks in our pockets, and couldn't think of anything better to do with them. You couldn't change 'em back to west marks on your way out.

The waiter had trouble finding room on the table to put all the plates, but he finally made it, and vanished, before George noticed that there was no ketchup for his french fries. That was when the photo was taken. There was no bottle of ketchup in the picture.

George looked around for the waiter, but he was nowhere to be seen.

Jerry noticed that George wasn't eating, and stopped shoveling his schnitzel into his mouth. "Hey, George, this is great. You're not thinking about sending it back to the chef, are you?"

"No," said George. "There's no ketchup, and I gotta have ketchup for my fries."

"We'll just tell the guys in the back room," said Fast Eddie into the vase. "Hey, guys, tell the waiter to bring some ketchup for my buddy George."

Sure enough, half a minute later, here comes our waiter with a bottle of ketchup.

"Sorry I forgot the ketchup," he said placing the bottle exactly where it was supposed to be: in front of George. "Will there be anything else, guys?"

We left him a big tip, all our leftover east marks, and there were plenty of them.

"Thanks for the ketchup," said Fast Eddie to the vase. "Tell the waiter we said to split the tip with you."

The comment about the tip didn't make it onto the official transcript of our "entertaining" table conversation.

The next four lines, however, did.

"The air drop is planned for the eighth at 23:00," said Jerry.

"They'll all be dressed as street sweepers," said George.

"They'll have the dead drops filled before anyone knows they're here," said Fast Eddie.

"And the uprising can begin on time," I added.

It's a wonder we got out of there and back across the border. It must have been that they just wrote us off as unreliable sources when we started doing 'radio checks.'

I scanned myself a copy of the photo and transcript, and went back to the book. I made it to page 129, which coincided with the end of a chapter, before I decided to call it a day. I grabbed a 3X5 card from my briefcase, and left Frau Asch a note with Jerry's and George's surnames. I figured I didn't have to write down Fast Eddie's name. I imagined that the discovery of a file on Professor Johnson's father was already being broadcast over the local grapevine, and that the folder would be on his son's desk ten minutes after I left; maybe less.

I took the book back up to Luschke and headed for the guard shack. Fräulein Freitag and Gunner Asch were the only two there. She was holding her rose, and talking animatedly. Women think that talking is an infallible index of feelings, but I don't trust words, they're too easily said. She broke off in mid-sentence as I opened the door.

"How interesting that you knew Professor Johnson's father," she said, turning to me. "And to think that we've had a file with him in it all this time, and nobody knew."

"Why someone not recognize him fm photo?" I thumbed.

"No one here had ever seen him," she replied. "He died before the Wall fell. A traffic accident, I think."

That explained a lot: Frau Asch's surprise, why Ilse was at the reception alone.

"I didn't know," said my thumbs.

When the S-Bahn deposited me back at Wannsee, I went straight to my favorite Berlin florist. Trudi's smock of the day was overgrown with ivy.

"Lilies," I thumbed. "A dozen. 4 Frau Johnson."

"Someone has died?" she asked.

"An old friend."

I grabbed a black-rimmed card from the rack on the counter, and wrote: "I only just learned about Eddie. My condolences."

U-Bahn 'Stasi Headquarters'

My File

I picked a table facing Luschke, put my open briefcase on it to claim my spot, and went over *the* desk to retrieve *Methods of Reconciling the Interests of Society with the Interests of the Individual.*

He said "Good morning, Herr Doktor," in that stage whisper of his. "It appears that you *do* have a file, Herr Doktor," he continued, turning up the volume in recognition of the expanse of his desk that separated us. "Frau Asch found you among the 'reconstructs,' Herr Doktor, based on that phonetic spelling you gave her."

Three *Herr-Doktor*'s. It was clear that I had taken a step up in his estimation. You weren't really somebody unless you had a file. It meant that you were important enough for the Stasi to have taken notice of you. And if it was a reconstruct, it meant that you were important enough for them to have tried to destroy your file. I had arrived. I was officially somebody with a capital 'S' for 'subject,' at least in this little corner of the world.

"I will call and tell Frau Asch to bring it out, now that you're here, Herr Doktor," said Luschke.

As the writing on the wall got clearer that the days of East Germany were numbered, Stasi officers did what any sane intelligence officer would do in similar circumstances. They implemented the Standing Operating Procedure for such an occurrence, and began shredding documents. The result was about 16,257 bags of shredded documents that are now stored in the Archives. That's about 45 million pages of jigsaw puzzles mixed together in batches of 3,000 puzzles, for a total of 600 million individual pieces.

In the good old days, we considered shredding a secure, ecologically friendly method of destroying classified documents. I'd personally seen more than one classified-document burn get out of hand and set fire to something that wasn't supposed to be burned, so I understood why this was the preferred modern solution. They'd burnt down the classified destruction shed on the roof of the embassy in Warsaw, and almost taken the whole building with it. I ran up three flights of stairs with a fire extinguisher under each arm. You should never take the elevator during a fire.

Before the Fraunhofer Institute applied computer technology to the problem of shredded files, estimates for reconstructing a bag of shredded documents were in the hundreds of years. I had my doubts about shredding the first time I saw it, and expressed them to my boss.

"If you can put just one document out of this bag back together, I'll get you promoted two grades and throw in a cash award," he said.

I tried for about half an hour and gave up.

"On top of this," my boss said, "before we throw it away, we run the bags through a disintegrator that turns the cross-cut confetti into something that looks like gray flour. If you mix that with water, if turns into a sort of papier-mâché, the kind of stuff that they make egg cartons out of."

Luschke's book said that the Stasi had been planning to truck the bags to a quarry near Magdeburg for a giant classified burn, with real fire, but they simply ran out of trucks and time. Before they could complete all the steps in the emergency destruction procedure with typical Prussian single-mindedness, they were overrun by *Das Volk, the same people who brought you the Fall of the Berlin Wall.

There was so much material to shred that even the industrial strength machines the Stasi had bought began to overheat, but the Stasi officers were dedicated to the cause, and knew that the show must go on, so they started ripping up documents by hand. The Archives had already had some success at putting bags of hand-torn documents put back together. Reassembling hand-torn documents was painstaking and laborious, but it was nothing that a patient twelve-year-old jigsaw buff couldn't do. This approach, however, had only reconstructed about 300 bags of documents.

Estimates were that it would take a team of thirty puzzle enthusiasts at least 600 years to finish the job by hand, which is hardly a viable time frame for Stasi victims who need these documents to press compensation claims, or to seek rehabilitation. Some of these bags might even contain evidence that could be used in outstanding murder cases.

The application of computers to the task changed the whole equation. At US$8.53 million it would be cheap at twice the price. The German Income Tax Authority was putting up a quarter of the money for the project. They had visions of recouping their investment in short order by reassembling the shredded financial records of a number of firms whose existing bookkeeping didn't seem quite kosher.

"The bastard! If he wasn't already dead, I'd kill him," exclaimed a well-dressed, not unattractive mature woman at one of the other tables. Anger makes some people peal off words with the staccato beat of a metronome. She wasn't one of them. The syllables left her mouth like bullets coming out of the barrel of an Uzi. Nice weapon in a tight spot. You can empty a twenty-five round magazine in 6.7 seconds.

Everybody looked up. It wasn't the kind of thing you'd expect to hear from a mid-sixties lady in a dark blue dress with a bright string of pearls around her well-preserved, slender neck.

Saying 'everybody' makes it sound like there was a crowd in the reading room. There wasn't. Luschke, Frau Asch, and I were the only others.

"She just found out that her husband was the Stasi informant reporting on her," whispered Frau Asch, bending down to put my file on the table in front of me. "It wasn't in her main file. I only just found it in one of the new reconstructs. She has a standing request for any new information, so I called her as soon as I found it. I didn't expect an explosion like that though. It's very much unlike her."

In another incarnation, higher on the path to nirvana, the lady in blue might have smiled, but I could see the vein pulsing in her neck all the way over here, and the knuckles of her hands clinching the crumpled file folder had gone white. Her eyes had glazed over, and she was staring absently at the folder, without seeing it.

"Bomb 4 me = hers?" I thumbed for Frau Asch, pointing at my folder.

"It has the covername for the Stasi informant who was reporting on you," she said. "But there's no equation for it … as yet."

„So much for any thought of sleep tonight," said a little voice in the back of my mind that immediately ran off to start thinking up possible suspects to be my Stasi informant.

One look at the lady in blue, and I could tell that the siren call of revenge was ringing seductively in her ears.

"I'm going to go piss on your grave," she said icily with the staccato beat of a metronome that meant her anger had been replaced with determined resolution. Her voice was edged with the threatening whisper of a buzz saw. This was the woman who generated fury for Hell to distribute to other women who had been scorned.

A vision of her pissing on her husband's grave flashed on the screen of the theater of my mind. The scene was somewhere in the Friedrichsfelde Central Cemetery. That's where all the notable old Socialists, like Rosa Luxemburg and Karl Liebknecht are buried. The grave was covered with red carnations, like it would be on the second Sunday in January every year, in a display of *Ostalgia, when the old guard remember the martyrs of the revolution of 1919, and lament the passing of the People's Republic of Germany.

I know that revenge is a dish best served cold, but it's hard to enjoy serving it, if the recipient is cold too. Then I thought, maybe it's hot where he is, but that thought passed as quickly as it had formed when I recalled that Communists don't believe in Hell. I guess pissing on his grave was the best she could get under the circumstances. It was a Berlin problem— unsolvable—but resolved with typically unique Berlin practicality. Like they kept saying when I was here in the Army, everything about Berlin is unique.

The ludicrous idea of asking her to comment about her husband for my book sprang into being, but sanity regained control of my head before this rogue thought reached my tongue. Her face was now a sea of calm. She stood up, left the file folder wide open on the table, and walked purposefully out the door. I imagined she was on her way to Friedrichsfelde. That's only one stop on the U-5, but I couldn't see her on the U-Bahn. She probably had a chauffer waiting with a Mercedes.

"Who was that?" I thumbed to Frau Asch.

"You know very well that I can't tell you that," she said.

"Pretty please," I thumbed.

"No," she replied with a smile that belied the curtness of her answer. "Will you be alright by yourself until Herr Professor Luschke gets back? I've got a few things to retrieve for him from the stacks, and he'll want them on his desk when he returns."

I looked up at Luschke's desk. It was vacant. Frau Asch didn't miss a trick.

"Yes," I thumbed in answer, pasting on a poker face, which was made easier by the bandages.

She smiled again, and headed for the door to the stacks, with the self-assured step of a woman who knew that she was firmly in control of the situation.

I counted to fifteen after she disappeared from sight before I got up. I then walked unobtrusively over to the table with the file that the mystery woman had been reading. I thought that I heard something behind me, and looked back over my shoulder at the doorway through which Frau Asch had disappeared. I couldn't see a thing in the darkness beyond the curtain, but I could sense that she was there. I casually looked down into the folder. Two quick passes with my pen scanner, and I had a copy. I nonchalantly closed the folder and strolled back to my table.

Her name was Romaine Schreiber. She and her husband had been the dynamic duo of the dissident set, so I wasn't surprised that they had been keeping tabs on her. The surprise was that they had co-opted him to spy on her. If they could do that, then I had to concede that they just might have been able to get Ilse to spy on me. I reluctantly left her name at the top of my list of suspects, while I sat there staring at the back of my eyelids, trying to force my paranoia to cough up some more names to add to the list. I didn't want it to be Ilse, because that would mean that those poltroons in security had been right, and I didn't want them to be right. They couldn't be right. No, they were definitely wrong. It had to be somebody on *the Hill.

I had seen the reports. There had been enough 'moles' at the Field Station over the years. Four for sure: James Hall, an Army sergeant, Jeff Carney, an Air Force sergeant, Geoffrey Prime, RAF Sergeant, and another source called OPTIK, whom they had never identified. It didn't have to be Ilse. I opened my folder.

The reports I'd read had included the Stasi covernames for Hall, Carney, and Prime, too. They were PAUL, KID, and ROWLANDS. I peeked inside my folder. Add one more. My 'mole' was covernamed MUSIK.

41

Diensteinheit HA II		Datum	16.4.75
		Sichtvermerk	

Treffbericht

Kategorie/Deckname VIM "Musik"

Datum/Zeit	Treffort	Mitarbeiter	Teilnahme durch Vorgesetzten
18.00-20.30 Uhr	IMK "Schumann"	Kaufmann	Hartmann
Nächster Treff	am	Zeit	Treffort
wird telefonisch vereinbart		Anfang Sept.	IMK "Schumann"
Ausweichtreff	am	Zeit	Treffort

1	2	3	4	5	6	7	8	9	10	11	12	13	14	15	16	17	18	19	20	21	22	23	24	25	26	27	28	29	30	31
															1x															

Treffvorbereitung:
(z.B. Treff geplant/kurzfristig festgelegt, Kurzfassung des geplanten Treffablaufes, Schwerpunkte der Auftragserteilung, Instruierung, Erziehung und Befähigung)

Der Treff mit dem VIM MUSIK war kurzfristig geplant.

Like any good covername, it didn't give you an idea of the identity of the source. Back to square one. I ran my pen scanner over the reconstruct so I could study it when I felt like it, without coming back here.

It wasn't like there was a lot to scan. There was only half a page of a standard Stasi form entitled "Report of Meeting" that had been taped together from about sixty pieces. It had my name in the narrative, misspelled the way I had "pronounced" it for Frau Asch.

The body of the report said:

Debriefed MUSIK at safe house SCHUMANN as a part of operation SANDBURG.

MUSIK reports that subject TREUJAN is a Russian transcriber at Field Station Berlin in the section covernamed TREADMILL. According to MUSIK, subject's generally slovenly appearance in uniform is reluctantly tolerated because of his skill as a transcriber. Case officer comment: The neighbors would be very pleased with access to the type of information he undoubtedly has access to.

MUSIK observes that subject speaks passable German, and takes Russian classes at the Free University. <u>Case officer comment:</u> Request subject's university records from KUBUS.

MUSIK remarks that while subject is voluble in his excoriation of the army, subject exhibits anti-socialist tendencies. <u>Case officer comment:</u> A political approach would probably be unsuccessful.

MUSIK advises that subject's lifestyle matches his income. <u>Case officer comment:</u> Money is ruled out as an approach.

MUSIK describes subject's alcohol consumption as …

It ended in mid-sentence, but I didn't need the whole thing to tell me what this was. It didn't look a lot different from the information we generated for a case work-up. The style was exactly what Luschke said in his book: formulaic, but the case officer running MUSIK did have his plus points. He had found six different synonyms for the verb 'reports.' That meant he was an old-timer. It takes a while to build up that kind of vocabulary.

He also had great operational security. He didn't use any pronouns, which as any grammarian will tell you are marked for gender. One 'he' or 'she' can eliminate a whole bunch of potential suspects. Why'd this guy have to be so good? Why couldn't he have left one sloppy little 'he' in the report so that I could have eliminated Ilse?

I stood up.

"Have a great day, Doktor Troyan," said Frau Asch, just coming back in through the door with a stack of file folders in her arm.

I mimed a kiss of the hand at her, and closed my file.

I didn't want to think about who could have been providing the Stasi with that kind of information on me, because the answer to that question could be very uncomfortable. Finding the answer to that question, however, was the only thing I could think about. It was an intrusive thought that kept echoing in my head. I knew it wouldn't go away until I figured out the identity of MUSIK.

And it wasn't as if MUSIK had just faded into the woodwork when the Wall fell. I hadn't seen anything on MUSIK before, and if we had busted him or her, I would have seen something. I knew that the Stasi had passed on their best sources to the Russians as East Germany collapsed around their ears. MUSIK's case officer looked to be as good as I was, and if MUSIK had been my source, I would have made the handover to the Russians personally. Now the question was not just who was doing a targeting work-up on me, but what did MUSIK give the Russians access to? And since nobody ever really retires from this business; what did he or she have access to now?

Frau Schreiber's outburst insinuated that Ilse should be the first and only name on my list. Ilse knew all those things about me. I couldn't believe Ilse would do that to me, but then Frau Schreiber obviously didn't believe that her husband could do that to her; until today.

Busting an unknown source on the Hill would be worth a promotion. Wait! I'm retired and can't be promoted any more. ... Maybe they'd make an exception for uncovering an unknown penetration that was still active. It wasn't out of the question.

I headed for the U-Bahn, aiming for a lunch of 'pre-chewed' soup at the café near the Wannsee S-Bahn station.

S-Bahnhof Wannsee

Après Vu — Déjà Vu — Jamais Vu

There's not a lot to see out the windows of an U-Bahn train. Dark is dark, no matter how you look at it. My mind wandered off into some even darker corners of my subconscious that I hadn't visited in over thirty years, where it dredged up a few possibles for the title of MUSIK, by imagining who could I have recruited at the Field Station, if I had been the Stasi case officer targeting Tberg?

First on my list was Wild Bill Hiccup. I don't think I ever knew his real name. Everybody called him that. And even though I got this story first-hand, it was told over a beer or eight. When Wild Bill left, it became one of those 'legends' that floated around the bars just outside the gate at *Andrews. Wild Bill could have known the things that were in my file. Anybody could have. It's not like you had a lot of privacy living in the barracks. What made Wild Bill's name bubble up to my consciousness was his threat to spy for the Russians.

The way Wild Bill told it with a beer in his hand, was that when he got down to six months before his enlistment was up, the First Sergeant called him in for the standard re-enlistment talk.

"There's a six thousand dollar bonus," said the First Sergeant. "And I can guarantee that you'll get promoted to *SP-6. That's almost a hundred dollars more a month."

Wild Bill's answer for why he didn't want to *re-up was a showstopper. There was no possible logical response to it, and it put an end to the re-up talk then and there. It was crazy, but we were all a little crazy then, and truth be told, some of us still are. It was so crazy that at the time, nobody listening to Wild Bill tell the story even considered for a minute that it was true. We all thought it was just a piece of *FTA bravado, told for the enjoyment of those who would listen. The tale was the thing. It didn't have to be true. Nevertheless, it could have been true. Sometimes the best way to cover up something is to tell a truth that nobody will accept.

"Let me see if I've got this right, Sodge," said Wild Bill to his attentive audience, pronouncing 'sergeant' in a way that would have got him six months of cleaning latrines, if he had really said it that way to the First Sergeant, who was Army green through and through. "I can re-up for *six* thousand dollars, a promotion, *three hots and a cot. If I stay in for sixteen more years, and make it to twenty, I'll get half-pay for the rest of my life. That right?"

"Yes, that's right," came the reply in an imitation of the First Sergeant's southern accent. "I thought it was a good deal. That's why I stayed in. And I think it'd be good for you too."

"The economics just aren't there," said Wild Bill in his own voice. "I mean I could get a much better deal spending the time from now to the end of my enlistment on courier duty between the various sites. While I'm driving from one site to the next with all this classified stuff, I just make a short stop, take a photo of everything in each pouch, bundle it up neat and pretty with a ribbon on it, then sell the package to the Russians for a cool million. They'd say cheap at twice the price."

"What!" cried Bill, switching to his imitation of the First Sergeant's voice. "You'd get ten and ten."

"Yeah, but the ten years and ten thousand bucks is only if they catch me," countered Wild Bill. "After I collect the million dollars, I immediately squirrel it away it in a secret Swiss bank account. Then I will go to CI and turn myself in, cop a plea, and it's only five and five."

"Yeah, sure. You pay the five grand out of your Swiss bank account," replied Bill's mock First Sergeant's voice, "but there's still the five years at Leavenworth, and that ain't no picnic."

"It's all a matter of perspective," says Wild Bill, warming to the reaction of his audience. "I go to Leavenworth, but it's only for five years instead of the sixteen I'd have to do to retire. I get the same three hots and a cot. And the BS there can't be any worse than it is here. On top of that, I could get an early release for good behavior. When I get out, I'll be 27 max, and I'll have $995,000 plus five years of compounded interest sitting in the bank. Sounds like a better deal than the Army's got, Sodge."

We all figured that it was just another war story. If he'd really have said all that to the First Sergeant, they'd have pulled his clearance and sent him to some infantry outfit for the last six months of his enlistment. With my paranoia set on 'high,' it was easy to believe that his story had some correlation with the truth, which as any case officer knows is stranger than fiction. I penciled him in on my list — lightly.

Time flies in the *après vu* of another time-space continuum. When I rejoined the present, I was at Alexanderplatz. Time to change for the S-Bahn back to the Wannsee and soup. I got off, and started that way, but my feet seemed to have a mind of their own, and I ended up on the U-2 to Wittenbergplatz, which landed me in the *déjà vu* of the trip I must have made a thousand times. Into town to see Ilse. Back to classes at the Free University, or to the PX across from Berlin Brigade Headquarters.

It had been thirty-five years since the last time I had made this trip, but I remembered each stop as if I had been there yesterday. A little girl with her mother at Hohenzollernplatz, on their way back from a visit to grandma. I remembered the lady bug on her dress. A guy at Heidelberger Platz, cursing because he had just dropped his currywurst on the floor. Been there, done that. And there I was with Ilse at Thielplatz, so wrapped up in each other that we forgot to get on the train. I'd seen them all before. This was my Berlin.

I got off automatically at Oskar-Helene-Heim, and it felt like my Berlin all the way to the top of the stairs, right up until I turned left for the PX and the Snack Bar, and walked into the *jamais vu* of a temporal causality loop. It was as if this was the first time I'd ever been here, even though that was rationally impossible.

Truman Plaza, where the PX, Snack Bar, and Commissary had once formed the center of the American shopping experience in Berlin was a rash of construction activity with a big sign that announced that this was the future home of "The Dahlem Urban Village."

Across the street where the alleged leaders of Berlin Brigade had been ensconced in imposing grandeur, there was an even bigger sign that proclaimed you could soon be the proud owner of "Three Rooms, Kitchen, and Airlift." In the context of three rooms and a kitchen, 'Airlift' seemed like the odd-man out, or maybe my German was rustier than I thought, and this was a new kind of elevator.

It took a moment for the pun in the advertising copy of the sign to trigger a state of comprehension. The smile generated by the pun contained in "Airlift" was immediately replaced by a frown, which was quickly wiped clean, because it hurt. Another of my Berlin memories was being exorcized, modernized, and monetized.

The Headquarters Compound for Berlin Brigade where General Clay had planned the Airlift was being converted into luxury apartments. One could be yours for a mere €4,500 per square meter. The smallest apartments were 40 square meters, or €180,000. The largest could have been yours for the paltry sum of €700,000, but it was already taken. It was good to see that somebody had money. I didn't, not that kind anyway.

I guess I should have been thankful for small favors. The Berlin Brigade buildings were on the historical register, which meant that the exteriors had to be preserved. Truman Plaza, on the other hand, was not, and it was toast. They were thankfully not changing the name of the street that the compound fronted on. It was still Clayallee ... for the time being. The name of the apartment complexes, on the other hand, weren't even in German. The one in *BB Headquarters was going to be called *The Metropolitan Gardens*. The English names seemed to lend the place a sense of continuity with the American community that used to be there, but they didn't.

These names in and of themselves would be enough to rid the place of any ghosts that were hanging about, either as paranormal ectoplasm, or as transient memories in the corners of the minds of the thousands of people who had worked there. Maybe this would lay the ghost of the *Feldwebel*[*] whom numerous sane—and hopefully sober—duty officers and NCOs had reputedly seen late at night wandering the halls of Berlin Brigade in search of his head. Nobody in his right mind would make an entry about that in the duty log, so his presence was undocumented, but widely known. The new owners would find out soon enough if they had hung around after dark for any amount of time, so I didn't think I would bother them about him.

---

[*] Sergeant

Logically, however, it was the same process that had made the Third Reich's *Luftgaukommando III* into the U.S. Army's *Berlin Brigade*. When we took over the place on the Fourth of July 1945, the dead bodies of the ghosts inhabiting the place were still strewn about the street outside and scattered throughout the rooms inside. This time the victors had had the decency to observe a respectable period of mourning. The buildings had stood empty since we pulled out in 1994. The number of people harboring the ghosts of Berlin Brigade past amongst their aging memories was getting smaller all the time. That was a worrying thought for me, but not for the investors.

In Berlin, the past is in the ruins, and there has been no shortage of people ready to supply Berlin with them. The Thirty Years War laid waste to the city in the seventeenth century, and World War II blithely did it all over again in the twentieth. The Kaiser Wilhelm Memorial Church was left as a ruin to remind people of what happens when you get belligerent with the neighbors.

At the end of World War II, there were no streets in Berlin. They were all covered with rubble, so crews of women—there being a definite shortage of German men at the time—removed it one brick at a time by hand, and the rubble got dumped in mounds on the outskirts of town. The mounds grew into hills. I spent almost all my Army tour in Berlin in the nineteen-seventies working on one of those rubble hills. Teufelsberg was the highest point in the city, which had a certain utility for SIGINT collection.

In the West, those mounds kept growing for over twenty-five years. The clean-up took longer in the East. In fact, it didn't really get finished until after the Wall fell forty-four years after the war, and the West came in with lots of money to pretty things up.

In typical Berlin fashion, when the Wall was opened, the Berliners gave history short shrift, and quickly tore the Wall down. They then neatly wrapped up the pieces small and large in an attractive consumer package, complete with certificate of authenticity, to sell to tourists. Why should I have expected the Berliners' sense of history to be any kinder to Truman Plaza? They were just doing the same thing they did to the Wall and the Palace of the Republic where the East German Parliament met.

The Parliament building represented the historical irony of Berlin at its best. The Palace of the Republic had been built on the ruins of the old Hohenzollern Palace that had been so conveniently leveled by the war. Now the Germans were going to replicate the Hohenzollern Palace atop the ruins of the Palace of the Republic. That's Berlin's idea of preserving the past. The new Truman Plaza cum "Dahlem Urban Village" would have a supermarket, a snack bar, and a bunch of small shops just like the old one did. That was a good piece of Berlin irony too.

I walked down to the end of the block. The sidewalk was full of people speaking German as they went about their business. All of them were unaware that they were walking down a street full of English-speaking ghosts who shimmered before me on their way to a PX that didn't exist anymore. The sensation was as surreal as an episode of *The Twilight Zone* or *The X-files*. The message was clear: you can't go home again. Your old home has been taken over by strangers.

I gave up trying to revisit my Berlin, and went back to the café at S-Bahn Wannsee for soup through a straw, washed down by a triple brandy. I was in a new Berlin, but I seemed to belong here. The lady serving the soup knew my name. Nobody living near Oskar-Helene-Heim did.

U-Bahnhof Oskar-Helene-Heim

Cultural Hegemony

When I woke up the next morning, the sun was shining, so I was sure that I was in a new Berlin. It was always raining in the Berlin I remembered from the days that I wore Army green.

"No messages for you today, Doctor Troyan," said Mary-Kate with an Irish lilt in her voice that brought back pleasant memories of a long *TDY in Ireland.

"You shud always wear green, Mary-Kate," I thumbed, "especially when you're going to lunch with me."

"Get away with you, Doctor Troyan," she replied. "I've not agreed to have lunch with you."

"You can't blame me for trying to have lunch with the loveliest Irish colleen east of the Elbe," I thumbed.

That produced a frown and a raised arm pointing toward the door. The frown, however, was restricted to her facial muscles. Her eyes were smiling. I figured I might get that lunch date yet. A non-chewable breakfast was the next order of the day, and I headed for Helga's.

"Mike, you're spoiling me with all these flowers," said Helga as she ran my soup through the blender to 'chew' up the big pieces.

"It's no more than you deserve," I thumbed. "And you can cook too."

That produced a big, gushing smile that said maybe I did belong here.

The next stop was Trudi's flower shop. The smock of the day was hibiscus, the really big ones. There couldn't have been more than half a dozen on the whole smock, but it was full of them.

"Do you have shamrocks?" I thumbed.

"No, but I can get some," said Trudi.

"Great. A pot to Mary-Kate @ the Academy," I thumbed.

"And your usual roses?"

I just nodded, because my thumbs were getting tired.

While she was getting my roses together, I filled out a card for Mary-Kate that said: "♪ When Irish eyes are smiling, they just steal your heart away ♫. Lunch?"

Trudi pretended not to read the card, but she didn't fool me for even a moment.

"I'll have the shamrocks tomorrow, Herr Doktor," she said, as she handed me my roses.

I nodded again, and left to drop off the first batch of roses at Helga's.

As I was going into the S-Bahn station, the headline on the front page of *Der Tagesspiegel*[*] caught my eye.

Greece Braces for General Strike Against Austerity

I bought a copy to read on the way to the Archives. It was a longish trip. It would give me something to do besides think about MUSIK and Ilse.

> ATHENS—Life in Greece will grind to a tumultuous halt Thursday when the country's biggest unions hold another general strike to oppose the new round of austerity measures planned by the government in order to meet requirements for the activation of the next tranche of its bailout loan.

---

[*] *The Daily Mirror*

The Greek situation had been dragging on forever. The article was full of the normal complaints, but then I saw something that was not normal. The author wandered off into a discussion of 'cultural hegemony' as an outgrowth of the bourgeois ideology of 'humanity.' This was nothing out of the ordinary for people whose idea of small talk is to discuss the philosophical differences between Gramsci and Althusser, but it felt very much out of place in an article in a Berlin daily, aimed at people who had no idea who Gramsci and Althusser were.

I'll bet I could ask the first ten people I met on the S-Bahn who Gramsci and Althusser were, and not a one of them would know.

"Doesn't Gramsci play for Bayern München, and Althusser for Hertha?"

I could probably ask the first ten people I met at Headquarters—past the gate, of course, and inside the secure area—and none of them would know either.

"Wasn't Althusser something with the *Rote Armee Fraktion*, and Gramsci one of the *Brigate Rosse*?"

But ask some of the guys I worked with on Tberg, and you could fill a dull Mid with a discussion of the differences between the two, which is why the mention of 'cultural hegemony' in the context of a strike took me back to my Army days in Berlin.

The Great S-Bahn Fiasco was precipitated by a drunken Russian Mary from Tberg who had slept past his stop on the S-Bahn and was rolled up by the Stasi when his train crossed the sector border into East Berlin. The result was that all the officers in the Field Station—none of whom any of the enlisted men would have recognized without a cheat-sheet—were unceremoniously packed off to destinations unknown and probably less than desirable. With my case-officer hat on, the new crew of officers seemed to have been handpicked by the Stasi to give a boost to their recruiting efforts at the Field Station.

The company bulletin board was suddenly full to overflowing with notices "FOR ALL PERSONNEL," stamped "EFFECTIVE IMMEDIATELY" in large red letters, courtesy of the new colonel. Despite the fact that most people at the Field Station couldn't have found the bulletin board unless you hit them over the head with it, word of these pronouncements from on high eventually wound their way through the grapevine to the site, which none of the new officers could have found with a map, a compass, and three tries to get it right.

The Great Mess Hall Strike, as it came to be known in the official records before they were summarily destroyed to protect certain reputations—was precipitated by the "EFFECTIVE IMMEDIATELY" notice that appeared the Tuesday before Thanksgiving.

FOR ALL PERSONNEL
EFFECTIVE IMMEDIATELY

The Thanksgiving Day noon meal has been designated a Dining-in.
The Field Station will be honored by the presence of the Berlin Brigade Commander.

Dining-in is a long-standing tradition that encourages pride of service, high morale, and loyalty.

Uniform for the Dining-in will be *Class-A. There will be an inspection prior to the head-count station, and those with uniform violations will not be admitted until they are corrected.

Colonel Erich F.E. Mielke
Commanding

"The new officers are just trying to brown-nose the BB Commander and establish their own brand of cultural hegemony," said Vinny, when this *A-val rumor reached him on *Mids.

"I've got better things to do with my break day than dress up for a dog and pony show. They can take their Dining-in and shove it." This evaluation of the situation was likewise expressed on *Days, Swings, and by the *Trick on Break.

The consensus was that a Dining-in with the Berlin Brigade Commander for Thanksgiving wasn't an honor, and that even if it was, it wouldn't be any fun in Class-A's. Not a soul said they weren't going, or suggested that others not go, but on Thursday, the only people at the Dining-in were the new officers, the NCOs who had been shipped in with them, plus the BB Commander and his staff.

The embarrassed silence with which the meal was being eaten was broken unexpectedly when the general saw a face at the door. It was the *CQ making his rounds of the barracks, checking to be sure that there were no fires, earthquakes, overflowing toilets, or pieces of trash on the floor. As required by another "EFFECTIVE IMMEDIATELY," he was wearing the prescribed uniform for those on CQ: fatigues.

"Soldier!" said the general amicably, motioning to the CQ, "Come in and join us, won't you?"

"I regret not, Sir" said the CQ, who was obviously someone with a head on his shoulders. "I am on duty and inappropriately attired for a Dining-in, Sir. Besides, Sir, my runner and I already had hamburgers from the snack bar, Sir."

That didn't particularly improve the general's mood, which raised the colonel's blood pressure, but there was nothing the colonel could do to the CQ—in front of the general. The CQ had been polite, and had stated the irrefutable facts clearly and succinctly.

The headcounts for the Swing and Mid meals tightened the colonel's jaw even more. They were both well attended, and there were even a number of people who paid to come with their dependents.

The new colonel was certain that the humiliation of the Dining-in was a subversive plot to make him look bad in front of the BB Commander.

"He doesn't need any help in that department," said Vinny, when this *C-val rumor reached him on days.

The new colonel's overreaction to the "boycott" of the Thanksgiving Dining-in went into overdrive.

"I'm going to find the 'ring leaders' behind it and make them pay!" said the colonel to the Sergeant Major, a little more loudly, perhaps, than he should have, because the clerk in his outer office, who was one of the roots of the enlisted grapevine, could hear him too. "Come payday, I'm going to hold an all-hands evolution for the noon meal, and anyone who fails to show up for *chow will be court-martialed for mutiny."

This declaration was toned down a bit the following Monday in the new "EFFECTIVE IMMEDIATELY" notice on the bulletin board that nobody read.

FOR ALL PERSONNEL
EFFECTIVE IMMEDIATELY

All personnel not on duty, including those on Mids, Swings, Break, and on separate rations, will report to the Mess Hall for the noon meal on payday.

Uniform will be Class-A. There will be an inspection prior to the head-count station, and those with uniform violations will not be admitted until they are corrected.

Those who do not check in with the headcount for the noon meal will not be paid, and considered *AWOL.

Colonel Erich F.E. Mielke

Commanding

"Sounds like the colonel's not happy," said Vinny, when this new A-val rumor reached him on Days. "Good thing I'm working payday. If I wasn't, I'd just walk through the *chow line, dump the food in the trash can, and collect my pay."

This assessment of the situation quickly made the rounds on Swings, Mids, and the Trick on Break.

Unbeknownst to any of the players in this battle of wills, the menu for payday called for liver and onions. If it had been steak and baked potatoes, things might have gone differently. The steaks were really good, and there were always plenty of takers for them.

When the chow line opened that day, a major, who someone thought was the Field Station Adjutant, and a master sergeant driving a clipboard with coffee-cup accessory, whom nobody recognized, were standing in front of the headcount.

"You need a haircut. Go get one now," said the major, whose nametag read 'Wolf.' The master sergeant wrote the man's name down on his clipboard with the annotation "haircut".

"Your brass is smudged. Go polish it," said the major. "Hagerty, brass," penned the master sergeant.

"Your five-o'clock shadow is showing. Go stand closer to the razor," said the major. "Nelson, shave," put down the master sergeant.

"You pass," said the major. "Douglas, OK," noted the master sergeant.

Douglas showed his meal pass to the headcount. The headcount made a check mark next to his number on the list. Douglas grabbed a metal tray, and walked through the chow line. If it had been steak and potatoes, he'd have sat down and eaten, but he couldn't stomach liver and onions, and never ate in the mess hall when they served them. He walked straight to the garbage can, dumped the contents of his tray into it, put the tray in the window for dirty dishes to be washed, and walked out past the major and master sergeant, who didn't realize what was happening, because they were too busy sending people back to their rooms for haircuts and shoe shines. By the time they caught on, Kozlovski, Hagerty and Nelson were back in line. This time they passed.

"You better eat everything you take," said the major, as they showed the headcount their meal passes.

Both Hagerty and Nelson got to the end of the serving line with empty trays, which they promptly put in the window for dirty dishes to be washed. Kozlovski had taken a serving of apple crumble.

"But I like apple crumble," he said when we questioned him about it.

The headcount that day was one of the highest ever for a noon meal, but only twenty-eight portions of liver and onions were served, and all of them went straight in the garbage.

The colonel and the Adjutant were now both furious, and more determined than ever to find a scapegoat they could make an example of so the troops would respect their authority.

The next morning the colonel called a meeting of all his officers, NCOs, and NSA civilians who were treated as officers for protocol purposes.

"Gentlemen," said the colonel to his assembled staff, "I think there's a conspiracy afoot among the enlisted men to undermine good order and discipline, and we have to take firm steps to suppress it."

The civilians, all of whom had been enlisted men before they went to work for NSA, started laughing.

"Since you 'gentlemen' can't seem to take this seriously, I will ask you to leave us," said the colonel, and the NSA civilians left, taking our source of information about what happened next with them.

The thrust of the decision that concluded the meeting was clear from the rising depth of the O.D. green army bull shit, unit of issue: 5 pound bag. There were inspections, alerts, guard duty, endless formations for no apparent reason other than to show us who was in charge.

When they couldn't find enough infractions to suit them on the third inspection that week, the major came up with an imaginative idea.

"What kind of underwear do you have on under those trousers, soldier?"

"Beg pardon, Sir. I don't understand."

"What type of shorts are you wearing under your trousers? Boxer shorts? Y-fronts?"

"Y-fronts, Sir."

"Regulations prescribe boxer shorts," said Major Wolf, turning to the master sergeant behind him driving a clipboard. "He's out of uniform. One demerit."

It may have been a good idea, but it only worked on that one inspection. By the next inspection, everybody knew the correct answer to his question.

So many complaints about unjustified mass punishment were submitted to the *IG, that he called the colonel to see what was going on. Rumor had it that the IG would be holding office hours in the barracks to meet with everyone who had such a complaint. This rumor produced such a large turnout that the crowd stretched all the way down the hall to the rotunda.

The rumor was clearly bogus, because a platoon of armed MPs came out of the mess hall, followed by the colonel and the Adjutant.

"You are to disperse immediately," said the colonel through a megaphone, citing the articles of mutiny.

All the while a photographer was taking pictures of those present. Unfortunately, all his film was fogged when he went to process it. For the rest of his tour, his money was no good in a bar with ASA folks present. All his drinks were on us.

The crowd dispersed silently, and that silence spread to Tberg, which caused an expression of concern from the general who ran NSA to land on the colonel's desk with an almost audible thud.

WHATEVER YOU ARE DOING TO CREATE A *NILHEARD, STOP IT IMMEDIATELY!

The official word was that the new colonel and major had reconsidered their position after consultation with the IG, but we had friends in the *comm center who knew otherwise.

Things quickly returned to abnormal for an army unit, but normal for an ASA unit.

The next paragraph in the *Tagesspiegel* article said:

> An era comes to an end when the people who advanced an idea are replaced by people who only see it as an illusion, and can't understand how anyone could have believed in the unchallengeable power of an idea to shape a millennium, oblivious to the shadow of catastrophe that it casts before them. From their perspective, the double vortex of crisis should have been clear to anyone who could read the signs.

> But events tend to move faster than elites can react, especially when the events are as confusing as the unforeseen collapse of the basic Weltanschauung that led to the fall of the Wall. That's the long view—and if the rubble under Teufelsberg could speak, it would probably agree.

That sure sounded like Vinny on his soapbox on a Mid. The article was signed Vincent Cortese, but I couldn't remember Vinny's last name for the life of me. I did remember that he'd taken a European out, and that his German was real good.

I put Vinny down on my list of suspects. I could have recruited him with a political pitch. It would have been a cinch after the Great Mess Hall Strike.

So much for not thinking about MUSIK or Ilse on the S-Bahn.

I silently swapped Gunner Asch a rose for my badge, and went in to get down to work. I was disappointed that his mother wasn't there to greet me with another reconstruct, but at least I had another candidate for the title of MUSIK. One thing leads to another. I'd get it figured out in the end.

Rathaus Schöneberg
Where Kennedy gave his "*Ich bin ein Berliner*" speech
Home of the Liberty Bell (*Freiheitsglocke*)

Ban the Bond

The Academy didn't want us just milling around Berlin without soaking up some Berlin-American culture, so today's obligatorily optional tour was to Rathaus Schöneberg.

"But you'll be back in plenty of time to go to your liquid lunch at Helga's," said Mary-Kate with a broad smile when I checked in with her to try and wriggle out of going.

That was the straw that broke the back of my resistance to this outing. I've always been susceptible to the Irish charm of a well-contoured colleen whose red hair was real, and not out of a bottle. A couple of *b'gosh-and-begorrah*'s would have helped, but she didn't need them. The smile did the trick. I got on the bus.

"I was here when General Clay first rang the Freedom Bell in 1950, but I was only five years old at the time," said the tour-guide who looked to be about my age when I was older. "And later I was here to hear Kennedy deliver his famous '*Ich bin ein Berliner*' speech in 1963."

He had lots of little tidbits of information that I'd never known about the Freedom Bell, even though the Army had tried to pack us full of that kind of information.

"The design of the Freedom Bell is based on the Liberty Bell in Philadelphia," he said, as we walked toward the entrance. "After a tour of twenty-six major cities in the States, it was put on a boat and shipped to Bremerhaven, where it was transferred to an American military train for the trip across the Soviet Zone to Berlin. There was some concern that the Russians would be difficult about it, and perhaps even 'blockade' it, but it got through just fine, if you don't count the anti-American 'Ban the Bond' graffiti that got scribbled on it as it made its way across East Germany."

I knew that what I heard couldn't be right. He must have said "Ban the Bomb," because "Ban the Bond" was a slogan from the nineteen-seventies, and not from the nineteen-fifties, and the Soviets wouldn't have known about it, unless MUSIK told them, but I hadn't seen any reconstructs about it … yet.

"Ban the Bond" was a reaction to the great Savings Bond Campaign that the colonel instituted while I was at the Field Station. Word had come down from on high that Commanding Officers who had one-hundred-percent Savings Bond participation within their commands would be ranked higher for promotion than their peers. As if that was not enough, they would be awarded a "Hundred Percent Bond" streamer for the unit *guidon. Since the Field Station had never been in combat, it did not have any battle streamers, and streamer-envy worked its evil magic on the colonel.

Word trickled down from the colonel to the major to the captains to the lieutenants who had been designated "Bond Drive Officers" under the great catch-all in everybody's job description that said: "Other Duties as Assigned." By the time the word got down to those of us at the working level, there had been a slight semantic shift. At this lowest level of the low, the word was that while participation in the Savings Bond Campaign was strictly voluntary, those who did not "volunteer" to participate might find promotions, passes, and leaves to be few and far between. That did wonders for morale. Most of us were not making enough money to be able to afford a bond and continue to do laundry, get haircuts, and go down town on the same paycheck.

People who took out bonds either quit doing laundry, which drew the ire of their coworkers, or quit getting their hair cut, which drew the ire of the First Sergeant, or both, but nobody quit going down town. Bonds were cashed the day they came in. You could always tell when that was. Suddenly lots of people who hadn't had them before had clean clothes and a haircut.

Shortly after the second installment of bonds was cashed, a rumor was noted making the rounds at the working level. It said the Bond Campaign was an intentional part of the Field Station's security program to keep us out of town and out of touch with all those locals of the female gender who were officially viewed as a big threat to security.

With the hindsight of the Ops Course, I can see that the "assumption" behind this line of thinking was all wrong. While a honey trap is one of the classic tools of KGB and Stasi tradecraft, there was actually a bigger threat in alienating the work force. "An ax to grind with the system" was one of the top hot buttons to push when you made a recruitment pitch.

Compared to the colonel, Ilse was no threat to the security of the mission. The odds were against it. The colonel, however, had just given one-hundred percent of the enlisted men in his unit an incentive to screw the mission to get even with him. I made more than my fair share of recruitments based on just that premise.

It wasn't long before the "Ban the Bond" graffiti started showing up. It didn't attract too much attention as long as it was in chalk on the sidewalk between the operations building and the mess hall on Swings or Mids, or in pencil on the wall of the latrine. It was just more work for the people pulled out of operations to clean the area. When, however, it showed up in felt-tipped marker on the "Great Savings Bond Drive" campaign-status thermometer sign in the hall outside the colonel's office, the *Scheiße*, as they said up in BRANDFLAKE, hit the fan.

The duty cleaners were told to drop everything else, grab some brushes, and paint it over. That instruction, however, was not coordinated with the colonel, who had called his buddy over in the MPs to ask for a crime-scene technician to check the sign for fingerprints. By the time the MP who knew how to dust things for fingerprints arrived, there wasn't a fingerprint anywhere to be found on the sign, not even the prints of the duty cleaners. They were efficient, if nothing else. You tell a guy with a 120 IQ to clean and repaint the sign, and you can be sure he'll get it done, especially if he hears the colonel yelling into the phone at the top of his voice that he wants a crime scene tech to go over the sign for fingerprints. The colonel had one of those parade-ground voices that could be heard at the far end of a regimental formation.

What none of the powers-that-be noticed about the newly repainted sign was that the duty cleaners had made a slight adjustment in the height of the red column inside the thermometer that showed what percentage of the unit had a Savings Bond allotment. That came from painting over the "Ban the Bond" graffiti, which was in the red part of the thermometer. The cleaners didn't have any red paint, but they had plenty of white, and orders are orders, so they just whited out the slogan. The new sign, therefore, showed a precipitous drop of almost twenty percent in bond participation. This incorrect reflection of the number of people with a savings bond allotment did more than the graffiti slogan "Ban the Bond" ever could have done if it had not been painted over.

The slogan was just part of the disgruntled background noise that would be a topic of conversation for a week. It was not a rallying cry that would get any of those "big-mouthed" chair-borne rangers with bond allotments to rush to the barricades. At best, they would only say: "That's the way to show 'em," and even that would not be said too loudly.

Emboldened, however, by what they saw as a sudden rash of people with brass balls enough to cancel their bond allotments, they decided to put their money where their mouths were, and prove that they had a pair too. They promptly went to the orderly room to cancel their allotments. So before the powers-that-be discovered the error on the repainted campaign-status sign, the status of the campaign had adjusted itself to match the sign.

To make matters worse, the powers-that-be didn't notice the discrepancy between the real figures and the figures on the sign until they had ordered the sign repainted to reflect the twenty percent drop in allotments, which meant that the sign showed a forty percent drop before the *head shed caught on, but by then it was too late.

The colonel's last-ditch stand was to send Lieutenant Dunbar to give a bond pep talk to each Trick as it got off duty. That was a big mistake for two reasons. At the end of a shift, the only thing that anybody was thinking about was the food in the *chow hall, and how cold it was getting, because they never told the mess cooks that we'd be late due to the meeting.

The other mistake was the messenger. Lieutenant Dunbar wore bloused, spit-shined boots, aviator mirror sunglasses, and carried a sawed off pool cue as a swagger stick. He was about as subtle as a whack upside the head with a two by four, and was an honor graduate of the course on how to lose friends and alienate people. No matter what he said, you immediately wanted to do exactly the opposite. We called him Lieutenant 'Dumb Bar.'

He was the one who had the brilliant idea of putting a lock on the elevator in the ops building on Tberg so that the enlisted men would have to take the stairs, as a way to keep us in shape. It only took two weeks for everybody to get a key. Even the people who used to take the stairs, took the elevator after that.

When he finished his spiel for the Trick coming off Mids, he asked if there were any questions, and was as amazed as the rest of us that Fast Eddie had the temerity to actually ask a question.

"How does getting one-hundred-percent participation in a Savings Bond Campaign make someone a better commander, worthy of being ranked higher for promotion than his peers?"

"Because it shows that he can command the loyalty of his troops," replied Lieutenant Dunbar.

Once that pronouncement made the rounds, participation dropped to two percent. It couldn't get any lower than that, because that was the number of people for whom the colonel personally wrote a performance appraisal.

It was the end of our six-on-two-off cycle, and Fast Eddie had a leave approved, though I have no idea how he did it. He didn't have a bond allotment. His plan had been to grab some chow, get some sleep, and take the Duty Train at 20:31 out to Garmisch for the next cycle. I didn't notice that he had changed his mind, until Lieutenant Dunbar and the Company Commander came into the mess hall looking for him. He wasn't there.

Turns out that he'd gone straight to his room, grabbed his suitcase, signed out on leave, and disappeared. They went looking for him on the Duty Train. He had a reservation, but he wasn't there.

When he got back eight days later, there was a note on his door.

"Do not report to work. See the First Sergeant immediately!"

He'd been planning a European out, and normally you work right up to the last day when you do that. Eddie had two months to go, but he was put to work mowing grass for a few days while the paperwork was done for an expeditious discharge. They were sure he was the one behind the "Ban the Bond" Campaign. He might have been. He was a man of principles.

I wondered if I could have turned those principles into a recruitment. I put his name on the list, ... and then crossed if off again. The principles would win out.

"General Lucius D. Clay inaugurated the Bell on October 24, 1950 before a crowd of more than 400,000 Berliners, some 100,000 of them having risked crossing the border from East Berlin," continued our guide when my thoughts caught back up to him. "The then Governing Mayor of West Berlin, Ernst Reuter, declared that Germany 'will never rest or relax until freedom will shine over the countries of Eastern Europe that are at present forced to live in slavery'."

We'd made it to that day, alright, but it didn't look like the Germans were going to take a break or relax. Over twenty years after the Wall fell, and they were still industriously cleaning up the East so that the *Ossies* could get with the program.

The cheerless articles I'd read in the newspapers made me have my doubts about the *Ossies* getting with the program any time soon. It usually takes about three generations to get over the 'not invented here' syndrome, and we were only at the start of post-Wall generation II. I figured it was about as likely as getting the Army to implement that suggestion award I had once foolishly submitted.

The convoluted problem for which I saw an easy solution had nothing to do with operations. It was a real-army problem. The real-army played bugle calls to help regulate the course of the day. They started with *Reveille* at 06:00, progressed to *Assembly*, *Chow Call*, *Retreat* and finished with *Taps*. None of those coincided with our 24-hour work schedule, but they were obviously important to the real-army, because the real-army made a big deal out of it and they posted a call for suggestions, offering a cash award to the person who found a solution. I read about it in a copy of *Stars and Stripes* that I had found on the Trick bus when I was headed back in from a Mid.

The source of the problem was that the army did not have a real bugler. All they had was a phonograph record of the bugle calls. Dropping the needle on the correct track of the record fell to the real-army CQ, who—typically for all hierarchical organizations—had his runner do it. Sometimes the needle would slew across the well-worn record, producing a sound somewhat akin to a *grunie pig singing opera. Other times, the needle would end up in the wrong track, and an inappropriate bugle call would get played, causing untold confusion in the ranks, especially when *Chow Call* was played instead of *Assembly*. Like I said, those bugle calls actually did mean something to the people in the real-army.

I suggested that they requisition a reel-to-reel tape recorder, transfer all the bugle calls to tape in the correct order for the day, and then all they would need to do is start and stop the recorder. No need to reposition the needle for each call. The tape would remember for them. Don't forget to rewind at the end of the day.

You would think that anybody, even the permanent PFC who had to put the needle down in the wrong place, could see the utility of such a brilliant suggestion. I was merrily imagining how I was going to spend this windfall. A week went by, then two, and finally the envelope arrived from the real-army. I ripped it open, expecting to find my check inside, but there was just a sheet of army letterhead that said:

```
We thank you for your participation in the
suggestion awards program to find a solution to the
problem of daily bugle calls. You suggestion,
however, could not be implemented for two reasons:
1) We could not locate the recommended device in
army supply channels,
2) No one in this command has the requisite
technical training required to operate the
recommended device.
We look forward to your next suggestion.
```

They never got another suggestion from me. We had racks and racks of tape recorders on the Hill, so they must have been in army supply channels. Besides that, a tape recorder was what we called a "banana machine," because you could teach a monkey to run one if you had enough bananas, and the mess hall seemed to have plenty of those. You could get one at every meal.

"The Bell is rung daily at noon, and at midnight on Christmas Eve and on New Year's Eve," continued our guide. "It is also rung on several special occasions, like the East German Uprising of June 17, 1953, the Hungarian Uprising of 1956, and the Reunification of Germany of 1990."

I wondered if they'd ring the Bell if I got Mary-Kate to go out to lunch with me. Probably not. Even though it would be a big 'international' deal for me, it wouldn't be have the same kind of international impact that those two revolutions and the Reunification of Germany had.

Bell or no Bell, I'd ask her to lunch again when we got back.

TRASHINT

Illustration by Herb Gardner from *Enemy Agents and You*,
DA Pamphlet 355-15, 3 October 1960.

The Man Who Wasn't There

The message that Mary-Kate handed me was short and to the point.

"I have something for you. Frau Asch."

"Thanks," I thumbed. "Lunch?" I added, noticing that my roses were in a vase on her desk.

"Why are you asking me to lunch when you can neither chew, nor talk?" said Mary-Kate.

"Soup at the café that you recommended, and you can do all the talking. Tell me about yourself."

"I'd rather learn more about you first, Doctor Troyan."

"Bandages off tomorrow. I can talk then. How about it?" I pushed my luck.

"You don't give up, do you?" she said with the hint of a smile.

"No," I thumbed, encouraged by the suggestion of a smile. "Think of someplace nice to go where there is food you can chew."

"Ask me again when the bandages are off and you can say the words. I can't tell if I should trust them when they are written on a screen."

"I shall return," I thumbed. It had a familiar ring to it. I wondered if she got the allusion. It probably wasn't all that well known in Ireland.

I dropped by my favorite Berlin florist's to refresh Marty-Kate's vase, and to grab some roses for Helga and one for Gunner Asch. Trudi was wearing yet another flowered smock this morning. It had carnations all over it. I hadn't seen the same one twice.

"Why not see you in same smock twice?" I thumbed.

"I subscribe to a 'smock of the day' service for florists," she replied. "Before I take your order, Mike, some advice for an old Casanova from his florist."

I tilted my head, and gave her the best quizzical look I could manage with a bandaged face full of stitches.

"Helga's husband's been in, asking who's been buying all those roses for her," she explained. "Even when you *were* as young as you think you are, he could tie you in a knot and beat you to a pulp."

That didn't sound promising. I'd been there, done that, and had the scars to prove it.

"You didn't give me away?" I thumbed.

"No, but I can't have him scaring off all my customers," she said. "He's been stopping everybody who comes out of here with roses. It's not good for business. Turn around and pretend you're looking at the window display. That's him over there, holding up the tree."

Holding up the tree was right. He could do it, even though it was a big village-smithy type chestnut tree, because the muscles of his brawny arms, as Longfellow said, were strong as iron bands. When you see someone like him, even if you aren't very scared to begin with, if you have a bit of imagination—which few people have—you can frighten yourself sufficiently to decide that discretion is the better part of valor. I was getting my bandages off tomorrow, and didn't want them held over 'due to popular demand.'

"No roses," I thumbed. "What flower says 'I'm sorry'?"

"Purple hyacinths," said Trudi.

"A dozen to Frau Johnson. ... 'Give me a chance. I'm really a nice guy'?"

"Gladiolas," replied Trudi.

"A dozen to Mary-Kate. ... 'Good-bye'?"

"Sweet pea," she said.

"A bunch to Helga. ... 'Love'?"

"Orchids."

"One to go," I said.

Trudi whipped a box out from under the counter. It had cards with pictures of flowers on them, and the meaning of each one. She had this down to a science. That's why I love dealing with professionals. I put a message on the back of each card, except for the orchid. That was for Gunner Asch to give to Fräulein Freitag.

I kissed Trudi's hand, gathered up my orchid, and 'bravely' left the shop to run the gauntlet of Helga's husband. He didn't need any help. He could be a gauntlet perfectly well all by himself.

I got a kick out of seeing his thunderous face glare in my direction as I left, but I didn't have any roses, so his face went back to neutral, and I kept on walking towards the S-Bahn. I'd have to find another place to eat. Good thing the bandages were coming off tomorrow. The message of the bunch of sweet pea would call off Helga's husband, and Trudi's business could get back to normal.

I swapped Gunner Asch the orchid for my badge, and headed for the reading room. I hadn't even pulled out the chair to sit down, when Frau Asch appeared through the draped door to the stacks. I swore that if her son wasn't tipping her off to my arrival somehow, she was psychic.

I clicked my heels and made a slight bow as she arrived. She demonstrated that she really was immune to the likes of me, and got right down to business, deftly avoiding my attempt to kiss her hand.

"MUSIK was also reporting on Fergie Howard," she said. "An *SP-5 legacy German speaker. That's all we have for now," she added, placing a quarter-page reconstruct on the table in front of me.

If I hadn't had my mouth all bandaged up, I'd have laughed. As it was, the smile I cracked felt like it tore a stitch or two.

"That's not quite the normal reaction," she said. "Could you perhaps enlighten me?"

"Fergie Howard doesn't exist," I thumbed. "He's the man who wasn't there."

"I can assure you, Herr Doktor, that he does exist," she replied sternly. "This is not a covername, or an alias, and his file would not be in the burn bag where I found him, if he did not exist. The Stasi did not catalogue nonexistent people."

"Files are not reality," said my thumbs rushing to keep up with the speed of my train of thought. "Files are someone's perception of reality.

Fergie Howard was someone that we made up. It's a very long story. Can I tell you when I get my mouth back tomorrow?"

"Tomorrow," she said, "or I'll tell Professor Luschke about the pen scanner in your briefcase."

"You're only a case officer's daughter?" danced my thumbs.

She donned a pleasant, but enigmatic smile. Women smile better than men. Their smiles always look pleasant, no matter how unpleasant they really are.

"The strange thing about your files, Doktor Troyan," she said, "is that neither the first one, nor this one are complete, while the pieces for all the other reconstructs I've seen were in the same bag and could be completed."

"My case officer must have worked TRASHINT," I thumbed.

"TRASHINT?"

"Intelligence derived from the recovery of trash," dashed my thumbs. "It is very frustrating if the material is spread across several bags, so if you ever worked TRASHINT, you know to split things up among several bags."

"I see," she said. "Tomorrow, and if you're not here …!"

She turned to float silently away, leaving me alone with thoughts of SP-5 Fergie Howard.

Fergie Howard was a person we invented at the school at Goodbuddy, but his name wasn't Fergie Howard when he was born. It kept changing. Tony made him up as a way to game the system that was used to assign duties to those of us who were in casual status waiting for classes to start. He went to the thrift store, and bought a bunch of fatigue shirts with different names and ranks on them. He would wear one of these shirts to the morning formation where they handed out all the dirty jobs that made casual hell. The sergeant in charge of the casuals would begin by calling the roll based on the barracks roster. When his name was called, Tony would always answer, "Here, sergeant!" in a loud, clear voice.

When it came time to assign warm bodies to whatever shitty jobs he had on his list for the day, the sergeant would walk the formation, picking "volunteers" at random, and writing down the names on their shirts so he could keep track of who was doing what.

"I need three volunteers who studied political science in college," said the sergeant.

Two hands went up. It was their first day on casual status.

"Kozlowski and Andrews," said the sergeant. "And now, one more. You with the wrinkled shirt. Schildkraut," spat out the sergeant. "Go clean the latrine, and make it *shine*."

Schildkraut was the name on Tony's shirt of the day.

Tony's trick worked, because the names the sergeant wrote down were the ones on the shirts from the thrift store and not Tony's own name. The sergeant couldn't tell one warm body from another, because the casuals under his "command" changed on a daily basis, and he never had time to match names on shirts with faces.

When Tony got assigned to some detail he didn't want to pull, like clean the latrines, he would go back into the barracks, change to a shirt with his real name on it, and head for the PX or library till lunch, dropping the "used" shirt off in the thrift store on the way. When he got assigned some cushy job, like headcount at meals, he would keep the shirt with the fake name on and show up for duty. This kept the disappearance of a casual from becoming a daily occurrence, so the sergeant didn't catch on to what was happening.

When the name-of-the-day shirt didn't show up for duty, the sergeant would get hot under the collar, and head for the PX and library, looking for his missing goldbrick.

"Troyan, you seen that deadbeat Goldfarb?" said the sergeant, when he looked in to see how I was getting on with cleaning the latrine.

"No, sergeant," I said, even though I knew that Tony had been wearing Goldfarb's shirt that morning.

Since Tony had his own shirt on by then, the sergeant never found him. And all the rest of us played along. We thought it was a great joke. Whenever the sergeant asked for name-of-the-day at the morning formation the next day, the standard reply was "he got shipped out this morning." And, sure enough, name-of-the-day would not be on his barracks roster, which was retyped on a daily basis, because people really were coming and going every day.

Howard was the name on the last name-of-the-day shirt that Tony had. He had kind of forgotten about his scam once we started class and got off casual. He only wore his "Howard" shirt to class when he was too lazy to take his uniforms to the laundry. He was wearing it the day that they called him over to the orderly room to answer some stupid question about his orders.

He walked into the office and said, "They told me that you wanted to see me about my orders to Berlin."

The clerk looked up at Tony's nametag. He looked down at his list.

"You ain't on my list. That must be what they wanted. I'll fix it," and put "Howard" down on the orders for Berlin with the rest of the class. This shirt had SP-5 stripes on it, and he was put in charge of the group.

Fergie Howard got advance pay and a travel advance, which was split equally among everybody in the class. When we got to Berlin, we couldn't let Fergie be AWOL. There would have been an investigation. Fergie shared a room with Tony, who kept up his locker for inspections. Whenever someone asked where Fergie was, he was on leave, on duty, on TDY, on sick call, or on pass.

When payday came, there was even money for Fergie. He couldn't come claim it himself—he was on TDY—so the pay officer said he should have a direct deposit, and gave Tony the forms to give to him the next time he showed up in their room. We opened a bank account for him, filled in the paperwork in his name, and split the money. He was a SP-5, and got pro-pay because he was a linguist. That made everybody's life a little easier, until Tony up and made Fergie a deserter. We weren't exactly pleased about that, but Tony was the one who had his neck out the furthest, so there wasn't a lot we could say about it after the fact.

I checked the date on the Report of Meeting for MUSIK. It was five weeks before Fergie disappeared. With my case-officer hat on, it was easy to see what happened. The Stasi worked up an approach to Tony, and Tony gave Fergie the push to turn it off. Nobody could prove that Fergie never existed, and without that proof, everything was copasetic. We had orders, pay stubs, duty rosters, and a dozen people who would swear he was real.

Rumor in the bars just outside the front gate at Andrews was that Fergie had run off to Sweden to avoid a levy to Field Station Shemya. It made sense, if you didn't know the real story, and no one who did know was about to talk.

I crossed Tony off my list of suspects to be MUSIK, but that still left Ilse on it.

Now what was I going to tell Frau Asch next tomorrow? If all else failed, I could tell the truth. But only as a last resort. She was, after all, a case officer's daughter. She would expect me to lie.

Rumors Persist

Mary-Kate, the quietly efficient, some might say 'bossy,' Irish "colleen" behind the reception desk was wearing green today. It looked good on her. It brought out her red hair.

"The first time I've seen you without your bandages, Doctor Troyan," she said. "Your scar is less prominent than I had expected."

"Mike, please," I replied, thankful for all the experience I had picked up applying makeup from the Station disguise kit. "And now that I can talk, how about that lunch date?"

I could tell she was suspicious about me, but I'd gotten used to that. It's an occupational hazard that crops up as soon as people guess what you do for a living, and she had access to my Academy file, so she wasn't guessing.

"Rumors persist, Doctor Troyan," she said, ignoring my gambit, "that you made an untoward proposition to Professor Johnson's mother. Perhaps you would like to clarify matters?"

"Rumors are part and parcel of a place like this, Mary-Kate." I replied, glad to be able to speak with my mouth, instead of my thumbs. "Rumors have been a part of every place I've ever worked."

"It's the grapevine's job to crank out 'news' about the Fellows, Doctor Troyan," she countered. "But it is my job to separate the 'rumors' from the 'news,' and I go to a great deal of trouble to do so. The least you could do is to make a sensible reply. Otherwise, I will have to validate the 'news' about you."

That wasn't exactly an original approach for coercing someone into providing a direct answer to a question, but it was effective. Now that I was between a rock and a hard place, how did I want to answer it? With the truth? Some creative non-fiction? A flat-out lie? I'd had this conversation with myself a hundred times before, so I just did the executive summary, before coming to what would be a foregone conclusion.

What's the truth? Whatever you can make someone believe. The truth can be a lie repeated a thousand times, or it can be an objective reflection of reality. More times than not, the lie works as well as the reality.

At work, we always tried to stick as close to the truth as we could, because when you're asked the same thing for the thirtieth time in your twenty-eighth hour without sleep, it's easier to keep your story straight. But when all else fails, tell them what they want to hear, no matter how far-fetched it is.

Deep down inside of me, the small voice of my conscience said, „I'll know if it's a lie the minute you open your mouth, and I won't let you forget it either."

The cold analytical side of my logical mind sneered at this crude attempt to dissuade a man of my principles from using an economy of the truth, but the words that came out of my mouth surprised me.

"Ilse—Professor Johnson's mother—was my girlfriend when I was stationed in Berlin in the mid-seventies, and we had gotten to the point of talking about making our relationship permanent, but close and continuing relationships with German women were prohibited by the unit I was assigned to, but this only mattered to the powers-that-be, and if they didn't know anything about those relationships, everything was alright, up until somebody turned us in, at which time I got called into Security, where they told me that I could either keep Ilse and be reassigned to an infantry unit to go slogging around in the mud at Grafenwöhr, or I could drop Ilse, and stay in Berlin, so being young and scared, I made the wrong choice, and let her go without even saying 'good-bye,' which is why she hit me with the Meissen plate," I said, running out of breath as I neared the end.

An old case officer I once worked with had told me that if you want to make your audience believe you're telling the truth, tell them with the shortest possible sentences. So much for his good advice. The nimiety of the sentence I'd just created wouldn't make anybody believe what I had to say.

If I'd written my answer down and rehearsed it like I normally did for an approach, the sentences would have been lean and mean.

"And you expect me to believe that?"

"Not necessarily, but it is the truth."

"That's a terribly weak reason to believe it," she said as a smile flittered across her face before vanishing behind a polite mask. "I can't get away for lunch, Mike, but you can take me to dinner at the *Dicke Wirtin*.[*]"

I kissed her hand. "Your servant, my lady."

„That came off better than you expected, now didn't it?" said my conscience.

„I'm surprised that it came off at all," I replied to my conscience under my breath, as I headed for the door on the way to the Archives.

Gunner Asch was talking to Elisabeth when I came through the guard shack, so I didn't give him her rose in exchange for my badge. I'd catch him on the way out. I picked up my current book from Luschke, and settled down comfortably for some serious scanning behind the screen of my open briefcase. It was a Russian training manual on how to intimidate people. I was picking up some useful pointers.

Frau Asch's silent feet let her sneak up on me again. She didn't say anything about the rose in my briefcase, but I didn't have any illusions that she hadn't noticed it. I wondered how long it would take her to put my rose, her son, and Elisabeth together. Maybe she already had. She was not just a pretty face.

"Another MUSIK reconstruct has come out of the system, Herr Doktor," she said, as she placed the blue-buff folder on top of my book. "I wonder if you could identify any of the people it mentions?"

```
MUSIK reports that there is a rumor to the effect
that the wife of a C-Trick BRANDFLAKE transcriber
is sleeping with a D-Trick 'Low Life' Russian op
who works in the pit. This state of affairs is made
possible by the fact that the wife is a traffic
analyst on D-Trick, therefore her work schedule is
```

---

[*] The Fat Landlady.

not synchronized with her husband's. <u>Case officer</u> <u>comment:</u> A blackmail approach is recom...

MUSIK's report was the standard fare of targeting work-ups. The Stasi did it. The *Sov's taught the Stasi how to do it, not to mention the Poles, the Czechs, and everyone else in the East Bloc. I liked to think that we did it better, but the Stasi were working up Tberg, so I had to give credit where credit was due. The people who go on and on about the FBI, CIA and NSA invading their privacy would go off the deep end, if they had lived in Stasiland. In the States, it's paranoia. I never worked an American target. In East Germany, it was the real thing: they were out to get you.

Not having any privacy was one of the things about living in the microcosm of a small embassy in the East that some people couldn't get used to. My ex was one of them. The briefers who gave you and your spouse the warm-up for your assignment called it the "Goldfish-Bowl Effect."

They called it that because you had about as much privacy as a goldfish living in a small bowl on a sideboard in the living room. There were bugs in your phone, in the walls, and probably cameras too. Even without those, if you had a fight with your wife at breakfast, everybody in the embassy knew about it by lunchtime, and the friendly Western embassies knew about it by dinnertime. If you wanted to have a "private" fight with your wife, you had to take a walk in the park. It's hard to bug a park; doable, but hard.

Not everybody can live under those conditions, and there were a few people who left short of tour because of it. That kind of life is a symbiotic relationship of reflexive exhibitionism and voyeurism. You put on a show for the host service and the embassy, and they watch.

While I was in Warsaw, a new political officer came in who was married to a Dutch lady. They spoke Dutch at home. About a week after they moved into their quarters, a note magically appeared in my car when it was parked on a side street near a national day celebration we were attending. I treated it like a walk-in contact and wrapped it in a handkerchief until I could get it to the office to dust it for fingerprints. There were none.

The note said: "Please tell Mr. Handley and his wife to speak English at home. We don't have an extra

Dutch linguist to cover them with. A *PNG at this time would be very inconvenient for us both."

They weren't giving anything away by telling us that they listened in on what was said in the Handleys' house, and the threat was real enough. I reported it through my channels, and went to see the ambassador, who reported it through his.

The consensus from Washington was that the Handleys should speak English at home, as there was nobody available to replace them if it came to a PNG, but Washington wanted a tit-for-tat.

"OFFICER HANDLEY AND SPOUSE CAN BE INSTRUCTED TO SPEAK ENGLISH AT HOME, PROVIDED THAT HOST IS PREPARED TO DROP ITS OBJECTIONS TO THE BI-MONTHLY SUPPORT FLIGHT," said the cable.

The ambassador and I called Handley in and told him about the note and the threat to PNG him if he and his wife didn't stop speaking Dutch at home.

"We can speak Polish at home, if it makes it any easier for them," he said. "Both our degrees are in Slavic Linguistics and Literature. That's what made this assignment so desirable for us."

They could have done it too. Both of them spoke excellent Polish.

"No," I said. "I don't think we need to bend over backwards to make it easy for the host service."

"Now that's out of the way," said the ambassador, who was practical to a fault, "how do we let the host service know what we want in return?"

"I have an idea that just might do the trick," I replied.

Handley went home that evening, and he and his wife went out for a walk in the park. When they got back home, they started speaking Dutch like they always did. Somewhere between the soup and the main course, he switched into English and said: "Darling, there's this really tiresome problem that we're having with the foreign ministry about the bi-monthly support flight for the embassy, and if we don't get it fixed soon, there won't be anymore of that American peanut butter that you like in the Commissary, and we might have to switch entirely to Dutch ...... peanut butter."

"That would be really inconvenient," she said, and the conversation resumed in Dutch.

The next morning about eleven, a note arrived from the Foreign Ministry that said: "If the ambassador finds it convenient, we would be prepared to sign the new protocol about the embassy's bi-monthly support flight, based on your proposed draft c.8, on Friday at 14:00 in the Ministry."

That was the draft that gave us what we wanted. That Friday at dinner, Handley and his wife spoke English at the table and throughout the evening. For the rest of their tour, as a matter of fact. The first support flight landed the next Tuesday.

The Goldfish-Bowl Effect, however, was not limited to embassies in less than friendly countries, and people working at Tberg. The inhabitants of East Germany were goldfish too. The kilometers of files in the Archives attested to just how little privacy they had in their lives. If you had a fight with your wife at breakfast, the Stasi knew about it by lunchtime, and the KGB by dinner, which was three hours earlier than in Germany, because of the time difference.

"I'm sorry," I said to Frau Asch, "I sort of remember the story but not the names, because I didn't know the people involved. I was on B-Trick, and there wasn't a lot of cross-Trick partying. That's what made it so hard on husbands and wives on different Tricks."

"Thank you, Herr Doktor," said Frau Asch, as she picked up her folder and walked silently away, almost as if her feet weren't touching the ground. I wished I could do that. There are more than a few times I can think of when it would have come in handy.

From the point of view of a Stasi case officer targeting Tberg, putting husbands and wives on different Tricks was one of the better decisions that had come down from Field Station head shed. If I'd been the case officer for Tberg, I'd have been all over MUSIK's report, up to the point that the wife divorced her C-Trick hubby and married her D-Trick lover. That took away all the leverage for a blackmail approach.

From a counter-intelligence perspective, blackmail was all that ever counted with an affair. Petraeus would still have been the *DCI, if that FBI agent hadn't taken the rumor of the affair out of channels. Headquarters would have offered Petraeus the same choice they offered me: "You can resign right now, or you can tell your wife about your affair in the presence of an officer from Security."

I told Margaret. Margaret slapped me, and headed straight for a lawyer. I was reassigned to a desk in the basement to cool my heels while the divorce was processed, "so I could be available for the proceedings."

My guess is that Petraeus would have opted to tell his wife, too, if he had been given the choice. Easy enough to guess what his wife would have done. The only reason he resigned was that the affair went public. If it had stayed in-house, the way it should have, he could have stayed in place.

With my case-officer hat on, the way I saw the lady playing musical husbands is that the Stasi pitched her, using the affair as leverage. She got divorced and remarried to cool the approach. Before the head shed realized what happened, she managed to get pregnant, which earned her an immediate discharge, and kept the head shed from moving her onto C-Trick with her ex, and away from her current husband. A neat little package; or maybe I'm giving her and the Stasi too much credit.

Ilse had known about the lady playing musical husbands. Hell, everybody in the Field Station at the working level had known. That meant that the only people I could cross off my list were the members of the lovers' triangle, whose names I didn't know. The MUSIK reconstructs were going to have to come up with something better than this, if I was going to cross Ilse off my list.

The World Clock on Alexanderplatz

The *Dicke Wirtin*

The *Dicke Wirtin* has plenty of atmosphere. It's on Savignyplatz, which is officially in Charlottenburg, but in my day I'd have just thought of it as 'downtown.' I wondered how I had missed the *Dicke Wirtin* the first time I was in Berlin. It's only a short walk from the Kudamm, which means I'd been on Savignyplatz more than once or twice before. Probably not the age group I'd been looking for in a pub when I was in the Army. The crowd looked to be mostly locals of my vintage—if I were older, with a distinct absence of suits, and an overabundance of well-worn shirtsleeves and sweaters. I took this as a good sign.

I ordered currywurst. What else on my first time out for chewing food? This is Berlin, after all. Mary-Kate ordered a Wiener Schnitzel with warm potato salad.

"Why a Wiener Schnitzel in Berlin? I know this great place in Vienna. *Figlmüller's*, right near the cathedral. I should take you there some time."

"I think you're getting ahead of yourself, boyo," said Mary-Kate. "First explain to me why your daughter's mother is the *former* Mrs. Troyan, and why the older you is better and more reliable than the younger one."

Older women have a kind of inner wisdom that younger ones seem to lack. And they have a quality of mercy—the hallmark of a successful woman—that, as the Bard said, is not strained. Well, most of the time.

"One of the things that makes the older me better is that he has a degree in 'Life' from *The School of Hard Knocks*," I replied. "*Divorce 101* seems to be a required course for case officers, because so many of them have taken it. The prerequisite for me was an affair with an Austrian college student who reminded me of Ilse. Margaret didn't like being a case officer's wife anyway. She didn't like living overseas, or the hours I had to put in. She took this as her cue to exit stage left. Headquarters took her departure as their cue to put me in limbo behind a desk. I might have sat there until Judgment Day, but there was a sudden, unexpected vacancy at a Station with hazardous duty pay, and I leapt at the chance to get back to the field. There's nothing as exhilarating as being shot at without effect, and nothing that inclines you to re-examine your life more than being shot at with effect. Hospitals are good places for philosophizing."

"And I suppose that Professor Johnson's mother's application of a plate to your face was a 'refresher course'?"

"More like a graduate course on Hemingway's paradox of youth and old age," I replied. "He said 'the error of youth is to believe that intelligence is a substitute for experience, while the error of age is to believe experience is a substitute for intelligence.' Ilse is an error of my youth come back to haunt me. I like to think that I've overcome it, and that I now combine both experience and intelligence."

"We'll have to see about that," she said.

I pondered the significance of that "we." Maybe there was an 'us' in Mary-Kate and me after all.

The conversation stopped at this point, because the waiter showed up with a Wiener Schnitzel that hung off the edge of an incredibly large plate, just like at *Figlmüller's*.

"Where's the potato salad?" she asked.

"It's under the Schnitzel, Fräulein," said the brisk waiter who either needed glasses, or was fishing for a big tip. "Otherwise it won't fit on the plate, and it helps to keep the potato salad warm."

She lifted up a corner of her Schnitzel to check, and took a forkful to sample.

"Your stealth potato salad reminds me of a story from when I was here in the Army," I said, trying to move the topic of our conversation away from 'confession is good for the soul.'

She raised an eyebrow, which—since her mouth was full of potato salad—I took as a signal to continue with the story.

"There was a new German Mary monitoring the *SED line. It was his job to identify important conversations for immediate processing, but being new, he wasn't all that good at it yet. Well, he got this conversation between two ladies, one of them complaining about how hard it was to find decent potatoes, and about the ridiculously high prices that grocers were being allowed to charge."

"It's unconscionable, *Genosse," said the first lady.

"I quite agree, Genosse," said the second lady, at which point the newk made a note on the tape jacket:

"Indication of possible potato famine."

"Let me check," said the second lady. "I'll call you back."

The call-back came about an hour later, but the newk was so overwhelmed just trying to keep fresh tapes on the recorders that he couldn't put the two calls together in his head, which hurt from the heavy headphones he had to wear. A more experienced Mary wouldn't have had any trouble tying two calls together. They were only an hour apart.

"The only person who can release potatoes from your warehouse is TDY here in Berlin for a produce managers conference," said the second lady. "He's scheduled to return to your place tomorrow. The supply and price should return to normal when he does. My boss made a point of telling him to be sure that they do. Even if he's getting a cut from the grocers, he won't want to ignore my boss. The last guy who did was sent to the Soviet Union to study produce distribution in Siberia."

"That just goes to show you ...," I began, but she cut me off.

"... not to make snap judgments when you don't have all the facts," she said, taking my story for a reproach, when it was nothing more than a funny story about potatoes that seemed to be missing, like the ones on her plate.

The School of Hard Knocks had taught me that a woman's mistakes should never be corrected, so I didn't.

Telling the story, however, had made me conscious of one of the pieces of the MUSIK jigsaw puzzle that I hadn't seen before. I hadn't seen it, because it was invisible. I'd forgotten one of the tenets of deduction: the absence of information is information. The fact that there hadn't been any operational material in the MUSIK reporting suggested that it was somebody who was not in operations. That wasn't a comforting thought. Ilse didn't know anything operational, because I didn't talk to her about ops. That meant this missing puzzle piece could point to her.

On the other hand, the operational reporting could have been *COMINT Channels Only and had a higher priority for destruction, or was stored someplace else, or had been shipped off to Moscow. That meant that the lack of information was just circumstantial, rather than conclusive proof that Ilse was MUSIK.

Unlike most places "with atmosphere," the food was actually good. The currywurst was just like I remembered it, maybe better. The Schnitzel was more than Mary-Kate could eat, so I got to try a bite. Not bad at all. *Figlmüller's* was better.

The decor is what gave the place its atmosphere. It was a cross between an overfull antique shop that kept its stock on the walls, and post-Wall Berlin kitsch typified by a mannequin sporting a Soviet Air Force officer's uniform, guarding the corridor that goes back to the toilets. The mannequin looked a bit young to have a "Battle of Berlin" medal, but, sure enough, there was one on his chest. I'd seen plenty at the flea markets, which is where the uniform probably came from too. He seemed very out of place to me. You didn't see any Soviet officers in this part of town in my day.

"Why the Soviet Air Force officer, guarding the bathrooms?" I asked the brisk waiter when he brought the bill.

"Soviet?" said the waiter. "I thought he was Stasi. The Stasi claimed to know everything, including how often you went to the toilet. At least, that's what we tell all the tourists."

"I guess it passes the realishness test for that audience," I said.

The waiter looked confused, but smiled when he saw the tip I'd left.

"The realishness test?" asked Mary-Kate, as we headed toward the door. "Seems real enough to me."

"That's exactly what the realishness test is. Does it seem real to the person looking at it? You don't have to lead people too far down the garden path to get them to leap to conclusions. Half a truth in the desired direction, and their own assumptions will happily take them the rest of the way. The 'potato famine' interpretation of the SED conversation seemed realish to the new guy who wrote it down, but not to the analyst who'd been working the target for two years. The information about WMD in Iraq from CURVEBALL seemed realish to the politicians who were making the case for invasion, but not to the case officer who was handling CURVEBALL. The mannequin guarding the toilets seems real to you, because you don't know what a Stasi uniform looks like, but I do, so it doesn't pass the realishness test for me."

"So how do I tell if you're 'real' or just 'realish'?" asked Mary-Kate.

"You can't," I replied, turning up my smile to show no hard feelings. "I spent so many years living undercover that even I don't know where my cover ends and the real me begins. You'll need an expert on the subject. Ask my daughter when she gets here. If anybody knows the real me, she does."

"I saw Samantha's planned stopover in your Academy file. How can she afford the time off to visit you for a month?"

"She teaches Art History at a small, but prestigious college, and her sabbatical to tour all the European art museums just happened to coincide with my fellowship," I replied.

"You'll be showing her around?" asked Mary-Kate.

"Not the art museums. She knows more than I do in that area," I said. "And since so much has changed since I was here, there's very little of 'my Berlin' left to show her, even if she was interested, which I doubt."

"When people go back to a place they've been before, they generally spend a lot of time being astonished that it isn't at all like they remembered," said Mary-Kate. "They shouldn't be. Change is, after all, the only constant. You really should be surprised if it hasn't changed."

"That's very philosophical."

"And why shouldn't it be? Is there some law that says 'an Irish country colleen can't be philosophical'?" demanded Mary-Kate.

"Don't get your dander up," I said, trying to deescalate this impending disaster. "I'm just verbalizing a discovery. Knowledge doesn't exist until a phenomenon has been observed and verbalized. The acquisition of information is not merely mental gymnastics, but a philosophical necessity. Life is only possible if we know about things and how to cope with them. You see, I don't know if you're 'real' or just 'realish' either, so I'm collecting information."

"That's very philosophical," said Mary-Kate.

"I told you hospitals incline you to be philosophical, not to mention the fact that we're walking down Kantstraße. He's the man who said: 'There can be no doubt that all our knowledge begins with experience'."

"Now I've seen everything: a spy who can quote Kant," quipped Mary-Kate.

"You didn't think that we're all really like James Bond, did you?"

"The thought had crossed my mind," she replied, "and you didn't do anything to convince me otherwise with all that talk of being shot at without effect, and how exciting it was."

"No, I never was a 'double oh' series spy," I said. "I was a '451F' series. We're licensed to quote. Though, according to my daughter, there's little difference between the two. Death by quotes just takes longer."

"Licensed to quote, and the best you can do of an evening after taking a colleen to dinner is to quote Kant?" challenged Mary-Kate.

"Your image accompanies me even in places the most hostile to romance," I responded.

"What do you mean by that?" she snapped.

"James Joyce, *Araby*," I said. "I thought an Irish author could rescue an Irish colleen from the clutches of a German philosopher hostile to romance."

"The man's impossible," she said with a laugh. "He's kissed the Blarney Stone three times over."

"All the best case officers have," I replied. "Would you care for a nightcap, Mary-Kate?"

"I think the nightcap will have to wait until I can tell if it's the real you, or if it's your cover, Michaleen."

"Fair enough. Dinner again tomorrow night?" I asked, encouraged by the hint of favor in her calling me "Michaleen," which—for an Irish colleen—was a step, or two, above 'Mike.'

Phantom Streets

Today's research stop was the Hohenschönhausen Memorial, out east in the Lichtenberg district. I'd been putting this trip off, because I don't do ominous places like this well. It was the Stasi Detention Center for those under investigation. But it's not easy to write a book about the way that the Stasi dealt with dissidents if you haven't been to Hohenschönhausen, so I couldn't give it a miss, like I did Auschwitz, Buchenwald, and Dachau. Just the mention of those names makes my skin crawl.

The fifteen-foot walls, topped with barbed wire and proximity sensors didn't look welcoming at all. *The Lives of Others* was set at Hohenschön-hausen, but it wasn't actually filmed there. The director of the Memorial objected to the script, and wouldn't issue a filming permit, because the script makes Wiesler—the main Stasi character—into a hero.

"If you could make your Stasi captain more true to life ..." said the Memorial's Director. "There may have been a Schindler, but there was never a Wiesler."

I liked to think that I would have had the guts to be a Wiesler, but I never found myself in a position where I needed to make his choice.

Hohenschönhausen had been one of these phantom places that didn't exist, so when the Wall fell, and overt Stasi offices were being stormed by *Das Volk*, the prison had plenty of time to complete its emergency destruction plan. No records survived, and the only history of the facility is from eyewitness accounts, which pretty much puts the people who ran the place out of harm's way, because their lawyers have been able to claim that the witnesses are not credible.

"The problem with oral history," said the lead counsel for the defendants, "is that after a while, even the people with firsthand knowledge of events begin to believe the story the way it's told, rather than the way it actually happened."

"Locals had no idea what was going on here," said the guide with humorless dark eyes, who had been 'detained' here, as he so politely put it, in the late-nineteen-eighties. "The prison was hermetically sealed off from the outside world in a restricted military area. It was a blank spot on East Berlin maps. The vans that delivered prisoners were made to look like innocuous delivery trucks, bringing in baked goods and food stuffs so as not to arouse suspicion. Once you were inside these walls, you didn't exist."

Back in my day, we had phantom streets in West Berlin, too. They weren't as ominous as the officially sanctioned redaction of Hohenschön-hausen from the city's maps, or even official. They were part of a running joke that was played on newks time and time again. Knowing where they were and what they hid was one of the things that marked you as an old-timer.

"You've been here for a while, Mike," said a new Russian Mary from New Jersey who wanted to be called 'Pete.' "Where do you go for a good time?"

"You can't beat the *Kein Einfahrt Ecke* on Einbahnstraße," I told him. "Any taxi driver can take you there."

"I can't remember that. Write it down, yeah?"

The taxi drivers who dealt with GI's on a regular basis would just smile when they read the address, which said "*The No Entry Corner Bar* on One-Way Street." They would drive the unsuspecting newk around till the meter read five Marks, and then deposit him at some GI dive like the *Scum* or the *Baby Doll*, or if he were lucky, at the *Eierschale or the *Eden*.

"Boy, they really know how to party down at that place you sent me to, Mike," said Pete the next time I saw him. "Thanks for the tip."

"You're welcome," I said, with no idea in the world where he'd been. If he'd had that good a time, he probably didn't know himself. The next time he gave a taxi driver that address, he'd probably end up somewhere else, where the party might not be as much fun.

The German girls who partied at GI watering holes like those had equally enigmatic addresses.

"Sure, you can pick me up for dinner tomorrow night: seven thirty. I live at the corner of Sackgasse and Umleitung Allee. Third floor. Apartment 'D'."

If you were lucky, the taxi driver would be a real Mensch.

"She was giving you the brush off, buddy. That address means 'Dead-End Alley and Detour Avenue.' Let me take you to this classy place I know, where they really like Americans."

If you weren't lucky, you'd wake up in the French Sector with a bump on your head, and a long walk back to the barracks ahead of you, because you didn't have any money. Hardly in the same class as being whisked off the map to the phantom streets of Hohenschönhausen, but not on my top-ten list of things to do in Berlin.

"Many of those incarcerated here had been apprehended trying to escape to the West," said our guide, staring off into the middle distance, as he pointed to the door of a windowless isolation cell that would have made a broom closet feel big. "Since border crossers had the potential of being sold to the West for hard currency, which the regime badly needed, they were not subjected to physical torture, which could be easily demonstrated, but rather to psychological intimidation by threats against family and friends, and by the kind of repressive techniques that left no telltales, like sleep deprivation, and total isolation."

I tried not to think about being in that cell alone, with the door closed, but my imagination got the upper hand, and I broke out in a cold, claustrophobic sweat. I'm cursed with too much imagination.

That's the thing about imagination. It's a double-edged sword. On the one hand, it's the creepy sensation of what unpleasant things could happen, but on the other hand, like Einstein said, "Imagination is greater than knowledge," because it helps you think outside the box, which is a key to being a good case officer. You never know when some small, seemingly inconsequential piece of information will be the key to the problem you're working on. The way that the guy at the next table stirs an empty cup of coffee. The fact that his newspaper is upside down. A whiff of perfume you've smelled before. All those can tell you something, if you've got the imagination to look at them the right way. Off the record, I was a *very* good case officer.

"The light stayed on all the time, and you had no sense of time," droned the guide blankly.

I knew what he was talking about. You lost all sense of time working at the Field Station. On Days in the winter, it was dark when you got to work, and dark when you came out. There were no windows, and you only got to see real daylight when you went out to the mess hall for lunch. That was depressing enough, but at least there was something to do, and you could talk to other people.

This would have been a good place for our tour guide to break into a joke for some comic relief, but he never did. His expressionless face never even cracked a smile. If I'd been running the tour, I'd have regaled my audience with the one about how Mister Stasi himself, Erich Mielke, was the last prisoner detained here. His defense lawyer got him transferred to the Moabit Detention Center in West Berlin, because conditions at Hohenschönhausen were inhumane. Now that's irony with a capital 'I.' I would have laughed. It's a wonder the judge who issued that order could keep a straight face. Maybe he couldn't. I wasn't there, so I couldn't say.

"When I was detained," said our guide, mechanically buttoning and unbuttoning his coat, "the door bell rang, and it was a pleasant-looking gentleman who solicitously inquired of my health."

"'Herr Boltzmann,' said the gentleman. 'I trust you are feeling well this evening.' It was the kindest, friendliest voice I'd ever heard," continued our guide, gazing obliquely past me.

"Yes, I am, thank you."

"You're under arrest," said the gentleman, smiling good-naturedly."

Yeah, I know the type. One of those people you want to keep smiling at all costs, because the minute you do something they don't like—not doing what they say, for instance—the smile vanishes, and you tend to need bandages, stitches, and plaster casts. Doing what they say is an interesting textbook example of a successful coping mechanism for a psychological disorder known as fear.

"The interrogations went on for months," said our guide, looking at his shoes. "And they always asked the same question: 'Who were you working with?' They wouldn't believe I was acting on my own. I eventually made up names to give them to make them stop."

The Stasi didn't have a monopoly on pointless paranoia, nor did the Soviets who taught it to them.

A new company commander came in while I was in Berlin, and he was actually a human being. He was five-foot-nothing, and probably actually under the Army's minimum height standard, but what he lacked in height, he made up for in soul. His First Sergeant was on his retirement tour, and despite all his years in the Army, he was still a human being as well. They both put the mission first, and treated the guys in the company like people instead of like animals. Things were running smoothly, and after six months there hadn't been any *Article 15's, and they even had people re-upping.

Rumor had it that they were called into the colonel's office to explain what was going on.

"Why haven't there been any Article 15's in your unit, captain?"

"No one has done anything that would require an Article 15, Sir," replied Captain Goodwin.

The First Sergeant and the Sergeant Major were having the exact same conversation at the same time in another room. Double teaming at its best.

"If the enlisted men aren't doing anything to deserve an Article 15," said the Sergeant Major, "then they must be plotting against the officers and *NCOs."

The search for the ringleaders of "The Great Enlisted Men's Plot" began immediately after that. It's probably a good thing that they didn't have the resources of Hohenschönhausen at their disposal. They might have gotten somebody to confess. When they couldn't uncover a plot, Captain Goodwin was reassigned to a staff job where he would have no contact with enlisted men, and the First Sergeant retired. Morale plummeted, Article 15's were up, and re-enlistments down, but the colonel and the Sergeant Major were happy, because things were back to normal.

"The idea was to instill prisoners with a total feeling of helplessness from the moment they arrived; with a feeling of being totally at the mercy of an all-powerful system," explained our guide, staring absently at my face, but not seeing it. "New arrivals were searched and given uniforms, which were purposely always either too small or too large not only to increase their discomfort, their distress, and their disquiet, but also to make them feel stupid. To dehumanize them, prisoners were never called by name, but were only addressed by their cell number."

I don't know who was copying whom, but I remembered that same feeling from the Induction Station when I joined the Army. We didn't even have numbers. It was always: "Hey, you, troop!" Captain Goodwin knew everybody's name.

"No one ever escaped from Hohenschönhausen while it was under Stasi control, and everyone who didn't leave feet-first, eventually signed a confession," said our guide as he rounded off his tour. "You're all lucky that it's under new management."

Where was that joke when I needed it? I tipped him €20. It was a sop to my conscience. It wouldn't even pay for one visit to a psychiatrist, and I'll bet he still needed a few.

I had taken the M-5 tram up from Alexanderplatz, but decided to hoof it back to civilization to give my overloaded imagination a chance to cool off. It doesn't take a lot of fantasy to work up a good fright in a place like that.

The way back to town was through a perfectly normal neighborhood; not like those ugly and depressing Soviet-era residential areas full of prefab concrete apartment buildings. It wasn't long, however, before I realized that this was not the best idea in the world. The incongruity of a Stasi prison a block away, and a place where normal people lived normal lives just kicked my imagination up into high gear. I could hear the muffled ghostly screams coming over the wall and through the barbed wire.

I decided that it was time for something a little more cheerful, and stopped an old man to ask him how to get back to Landsberger Allee, where the lights glowed just a little brighter than here. I knew that there was an IKEA on Landsberger Allee out this way, and thought that a dose of retail therapy would improve my mood, not to mention the comfort food in the cafeteria, which is pretty tasty.

The layers of East Berlin street names are invisible to people like me who are only just discovering the East, but ask an *Ossie* how to get somewhere in East Berlin, and you're smack dab in the middle of East Berlin's identity crisis.

"Excuse me. Could you tell me how to get to Landsberger Allee?"

"Let's see. ... isn't that what you *Wessies* call Leninallee now. Down here. Turn right at the corner, and it's the first cross street after three T-intersections."

"Thanks," I said.

Not only are the *Ossies* disoriented by the name changes, they are not particularly thrilled at these constant reminders that their side "lost" the Cold War. The IKEA on Landsberger Allee née Leninallee would have had Lenin spinning in his grave if the street had still been named for him. And he's just one of many. Clara-Zetkin-Straße is now Dorotheenstraße. Isenburger Weg used to be called Ernst-Thälmann-Straße. And trying to figure out how to get to Torstraße can occasionally be speeded up, if you say "the old Wilhelm-Pieck-Straße."

On my side of the sector border, however, the name *Clayallee* still identifies the street that runs in front of the old Berlin Brigade Headquarters, named after the man who ran the Airlift. Then again, it's not all sweetness and light for us in the West. The City steadfastly refuses to name a street for President Reagan, despite his "Tear Down this Wall" speech.

The old names are instructive for those of a philosophical inclination, because they reveal the false certainties of political mindsets that didn't live up to expectations. Berlin streets should list all their past and present names not only to help the natives get around, but also to remind the politicians that things aren't as permanent as they may seem.

Clayallee would need a sign that said before 1949 it was Kronprinzenallee, named for Kaiser William II's first son. Theodor Heuss Platz, where the British PX and movie theater were, would need to say that it was once called Adolf Hitler Platz. On the other hand, I never ran into a real person who thought of it in those terms while I was in Berlin in the Army. I only discovered this interesting fact on this trip in the Berlin U-Bahn Museum on a map of the U-Bahn stations from 1936. This is probably for the same reason that I never met a German who fought against the Americans during World War II. They all claimed to have been on the Eastern Front, fighting the Russians.

Jewish Street, Spandau (2013)
The historical name of this street dating to the 14th century.
In 1938, the National Socialists renamed it Kinkelstraße.
Gottfried Kinkel, a German poet 1815-1882.
The old name returned in 2002.

A Book Debut

The sound of my name with an Irish lilt drifted across the room. That was my cue—as if I needed one—to go bask in Mary-Kate's lovely contoured grace. It's strange how the barely audible sound of your name can recall your consciousness from the arms of Morpheus, or the headlong rush of a train of thought, when it's carried by a particular voice. Women are the breath of life.

"Frau Asch called to say she has something for you," said Mary-Kate.

That was always good news, so I turned the smile I had aimed at the messenger up a notch or two.

"It never does any good to try and call back," she continued. "She's impossible to find in the stacks, Michaleen."

"I'll go over right after breakfast," I said, wondering if I could ever get her to accompany me.

"You wouldn't care to have breakfast with me?" said a voice that sounded like mine, before I was conscious of telling my mouth to go into action.

"You know I can't get away."

"Can't blame a fellow for trying."

"I could, but it clearly won't do any good."

It was uncanny. Impossible as she was to find in the stacks, Frau Asch always came in before I could get the chair pulled out from under the table to sit down. I was slowly coming to the conclusion that either Gunner Asch called the cell phone that she wasn't supposed to have to announce me when I picked up my badge; or she had ESP.

"Good morning, Doktor Troyan," she said in a librarian's whisper, even though she, I, and the besuited Professor Luschke were the only ones in the room at the time.

She put a tan-buff folder on the table, and whispered: "One of my people is bringing out a book on Thursday. It's based on her Stasi file, which we catalogue by the pound and not by the page. You might find it interesting."

"Thank you, Frau Asch," I said, recognizing her conspiratorial confidence for what it was. Was I ever glad that I had brought all those roses for her son to give to Fräulein Freitag. "That's most interesting."

"You're very welcome, Doktor Troyan," she replied, looking over her shoulder in Luschke's direction, before walking out of the room with that purposeful tread of hers that never seemed to make any noise.

I opened the folder. All it contained was a flyer from the Literary Colloquium Berlin for:

The Debut of

the Autobiography of Frau Doktor Hedwig von Wissmann-Schaftler

Title: *The Ant Who Frightened an Elephant*

Trade Paper: 316 pages

Publisher: Verlag Books on Demand

Language: German

The Literary Colloquium was right down the street from the Academy. I'd heard the eats were good. I pulled out my iTouch and entered "Literary Soirée" for Thursday.

I closed the folder and headed for the exit. On the way, I thanked Professor Luschke profusely for the excellent efficiency of his staff. I hoped that my comment would make it into Frau Asch's performance appraisal, or better yet promotion recommendation. I'd worked in the salt mines of bureaucracy long enough to know the coin of the realm, and how to mint it.

The Literary Colloquium was full on Thursday. It was definitely a bookish crowd, but that didn't make the line for the buffet any shorter or less pushy. I should have eaten before coming. Most of the people in line obviously hadn't. The food lived up to its reputation, which explained the line, but not the bad manners of the people in it.

I picked a quiet corner from which to survey the room with a professional eye. I spotted Frau Asch with a full plate of hors d'oeuvres, talking to a non-literary type next to a large potted palm. I started in her direction to say "Thanks" again, but she gave me a clear wave off, and maneuvered her companion's back toward me. His age looked right for her significant other. His build said 'street cop,' or 'case officer in a low-rent district.'

I quickly picked out the embassy and Station reps, who were at opposite ends of the room. Where else?

An older gentleman came in and started the same professional sweep of the room that I was running. It had to be a retired Stasi case officer, because there was an almost imperceptible hesitation when he got to the Station officer over by the fireplace. Another when he swept the place where Frau Asch and her companion were chatting. The embassy officer didn't evoke a thing. When he got to me, he returned my stare. I mimed a tip of my hat. He did the same. He headed for the buffet. I headed for the bar. This had the makings of a fun evening.

"Our speaker tonight needs no introduction," said the glitzy hostess, who probably taught Literature with a capital 'L' over at the Free University. "A heavyweight research scientist, and a tireless fighter against the intellectual repression of East German totalitarianism, her Stasi file weighs over twenty-five pounds."

The lady behind her waiting to take the podium was anything but heavy. Five seven, gray, blue, a hundred and twenty-five pounds soaking wet.

"With the arrogance of 20/20 hindsight, everyone can say that the Third Reich and the GDR were evil regimes that had to be resisted at every possible opportunity. This conclusion becomes less clear, however, when regimes like these define the reality of your day-to-day existence. Who amongst those prepared to cast stones at the people who collaborated with the Stasi and Gestapo could have mustered the courage not to cooperate, if they were in the same situation? Our speaker did, wielding the sword of humor like the Good Soldier Schwejk."

Schwejk's passive-aggressive idiocy drove the Austrians nuts. I suddenly had a vision of Bretschneider in a Stasi uniform, followed by the image of General Fink von Finkenstein behind Mielke's desk. The thought of Schwejk in a skirt made me chuckle, which brought a disapproving glare from the woman on my right.

"This evening we are introducing her autobiography, a book so controversial that no traditional publisher had the courage to publish it. Never one to remain inside the box that others tried to build around her, she resorted to the private publication of her story. Without further ado, ladies and gentlemen, I give you Frau Doktor von Wissmann-Schaftler."

There was a polite round of applause, inhibited by the fact that it's tricky to applaud with a plate in one hand, and a glass in the other. They should have held the buffet until after her talk. I wondered if the "privately published" thing was an indication of *Ostalgia*-fatigue in the publishing industry. I'd been seeing indications of that elsewhere. The Wall had been down for over twenty years, and some people were beginning to think that the GDR and the Stasi were old news.

Frau von Wissmann-Schaftler was clearly not one of them, nor was she one of those women who felt the need to conform to the current dictates of fashion. Sensible shoes, sensible dress, sensible hair. No jewelry, no make-up, a man's watch. The woman who introduced her was the exact opposite. When it came to personality, however, the Frau Doktor was the hands-down winner. I don't think they rejected her manuscript because it was dull.

"I couldn't put up with the lies of the nanny state," began Doktor von Wissmann-Schaftler. "The only reason that they put up with me was that I was very good at what I was doing, and had an international name in the field. If I had been another nobody, I'd have been packed off to *Bautzen in a nanosecond."

I wouldn't have wanted to be her Stasi case officer. She would have been *hard* to control. Not to be able to touch her because of her international reputation must have driven them bananas, which would have been really distressing, given how tough it was to get bananas in the GDR.

"The Stasi could make things *not* happen," she continued. "Your kids would not get into college. That apartment for which you had spent three years on a waiting list was no longer available. The new car that you had paid for in full at the start of a six-year waiting list for delivery was suddenly delayed, or postponed. The paperwork for the visa you needed for an international conference was mislaid until it was too late. And there was nothing you could do. There was no legal recourse, because nothing had been done. There was nothing you could prove. There were no documents. Everything was done by telephone, and it was never a direct order, just a 'word to the wise' and otherwise respectable people did what was expected of them."

This was very familiar ground. It would have made a good quickie review for the final in the course the Stasi taught with the textbook called *Methods of Reconciling the Interests of Society with the Interests of the Individual*. This tactic was not exclusive to the Sov's or the Stasi. It could also be found in any large bureaucracy, like the one where I used to work, or the Army. They could make things not happen, too.

When I was in the Army in Berlin, promotion was a big thing, because it meant more money, more freedom, and less BS. We put a lot of effort into gaming the system to make promotions come along as frequently as possible. The best analytic minds to ever crack a *call-sign rota turned their attention to the results of the promotion board. They studied the time-in-grade curve for Berlin and compared it to other Field Stations. They calculated each candidate's *STRAC number, which is the depth of the spit-shine on a candidate's shoes measured in inches, minus the length of his hair, times the sharpness of the creases in his trousers expressed as the cosine of the angle they form when standing at attention.

It came as no surprise that the higher your STRAC number, the better your chances of getting promoted, but some people with lower STRAC scores were getting promoted ahead of people who appeared to be playing the game right. After another round of analysis with a broader set of variables, the analysts came to the conclusion that the people who were not getting promoted despite getting all the other things right were the ones who sported moustaches. Even though they were permitted by regulation, moustaches were frowned upon by the local powers-that-be. They might not be able to tell you to shave it off, but they didn't have to promote you, if you had one.

"Freedom is the recognition of necessity," said Lefty, and went straight to the latrine to shave off his moustache. He got promoted on the next cycle. He also started growing his moustache back the day after he sewed on his new stripes.

When I next synced up with the Frau Doktor's speech, she was saying: "I persisted despite the Stasi's bests efforts to apply these repressive measures against me, because I wanted freedom so much that nothing was going to stop me. By that I mean the freedom to think what I want, to say what I think, to go where I want, and to live my life the way that seems best to me, rather than the way that some allegedly competent Party big shots want me to live it."

That was the way I felt about career-minded headquartercrats, or should that be headquarter-rats? The closer to the flag pole, the lower the IQ, and the fewer the principles.

I had once briefed a Senator—who my paranoia warns me should remain nameless—on a problem we were having with the Soviets. I told him exactly what the Sov's would do if we did 'A,' 'B,' or 'C.' 'A' was my recommended action, because it had the best outcome for us.

The Senator said: "Well, son, if'n I was a Rooshun, I wouldn't do that."

"I understand Senator, but you don't think like a Russian. That's what you pay me to do."

He dismissed me out of hand, and had his staffer show me the door. The Senator did 'C.' The Russians did exactly what I said they would do, and the whole thing was a gigantic fiasco.

"If the quality of the transcripts from the bugs in my apartment are any indication, the Party big wigs were not sufficiently well informed about me to make any kind of sensible decision concerning what I should be doing with my life. The transcripts were done by illiterates. One of them said that we were discussing the Russian writer 'Pulkakov,' when it was really Bulgakov we were talking about. Another spelled Kafka with a double 'FF,' and a third reported that we were talking about the writer "Höderlein" again."

That made me think of a colonel at the Field Station when I was there who was making an unannounced inspection of Tberg on a Mid, and took all the books that the operators on duty had brought to get them through the mind-numbing idleness of the graveyard shift.

"I haven't read a book in twelve years," he said as he collected the 'contraband.' "And it hasn't hurt me one bit."

A week later on Days, I was outside hammering in the guy-wire stakes for a new antenna mast when he walked by and went ballistic because I didn't have my hat on.

"The Army uniform has included head gear ever since Custer got his ass kicked at the Alamo," he said, "and I don't think that there's going to be an exception to policy just for you. Now get your hat on, troop!"

After her talk, there was an opportunity to buy signed copies of her book. I dutifully stood in line to get mine. I couldn't see the guy who had been talking to Frau Asch anywhere, but the three other pro's I'd recognized were in line ahead of me. Frau von Wissmann-Schaftler didn't say a word to any of them when she signed their books. When it was my turn, however, she looked up and said: "Rumor has it you're a retired CIA officer working on a book about how the Stasi controlled dissidents."

"I cannot deny that that rumor is a persistent one, Frau Doktor," I said, suspecting Frau Asch as the root of this particular grapevine. "Perhaps you could inscribe the book 'For Mike'."

I watched as she wrote "For Mike Wormold, Our Man in Berlin." The lady doing the introduction was right. The good Doktor had a sense of humor like Schwejk. Her book looked to be a fun read.

The line for getting books signed grew shorter, the crowd waned, and the amount of food on the buffet table was down to slim pickings. Word had it that our speaker would leave as soon as the signing was done. I stepped over to the bar when there were seven people left in line to buy a signed copy of her book. I got two beers, and got back in line.

"The word on the street is that you like a good Berliner Weiße," I said, extending the glass in my left hand towards her.

"You are well informed," she replied.

"And I also know that you were discussing Hölderlin, not "Höderlein." 'What has always made the state a hell on earth is that man has tried to make it heaven'."

"Particularly well informed," she said.

"Perhaps you would have been more impressed by our people."

"Perhaps so. Were you running an operation against me?"

"No, your publication record was impressive and we got everything we wanted from that," I replied.

"You're not interested in my philosophy?" she asked.

"Not on a professional level," I said, "but on a personal one, I wondered about your comments on the nature of freedom. What about all the German philosophers who said that freedom is a state of mind? 'Such cords can no one twine, with which my thoughts to confine.'"

"Freidank!" she said with surprise. "You *have* been reading much too much German philosophy. Thinking what I wanted wasn't enough. I wanted to act on it. I wanted what you've had all your life."

"And I wanted what you had: the courage to tell the truth. But you're right. I've read too much German philosophy, like: 'Freedom is the recognition of necessity'?"

"Engels. I'd never have taken you for a Communist."

"I'm not. Reading Marx and Engels was a part of my job. It was supposed to help us understand 'the enemy' better, but it just seemed to make us more like 'the enemy'."

"I read Marx and Engels because I wanted to understand what was going on in the GDR, but I never recognized the necessity of doing what the Party said. They were wrong most of the time."

"So were the people I worked for, but I chose Engels' definition of freedom nevertheless," I admitted with regret.

"I couldn't live with that choice. For me there was no spiritual survival without freedom," she said.

"You had the courage to say so, and to leave your prison. I had to wait until my sentence was up and I could retire."

"So now you're on a busman's holiday, writing a book about the Stasi?"

"Something like that," I said.

"I wrote mine for catharsis."

"Let's hope it works for both of us," I said, raising my glass for a toast.

"Your good mental health!" she replied.

Goulash Communism

Ilse remained unforgiving, and still wouldn't talk to me. This meant that all my expeditions in search of the Berlin of my youth turned out to be dismal trips down a memory lane that was awash in a knee-deep flood of memories from the times that Ilse and I had done this or that wherever it was I happened to be. I've always prided myself on being a master of the doable, so, I thought, if I can't solve the main problem of my return to Berlin—Ilse, I'll tackle something with a higher doability quotient.

Mark Twain had once said that a vacation was doing something different. „Alright," said my profoundly depressed psyche, „let's take a vacation from the 'old Berlin' and go to the new." That certainly sounded like good advice. I couldn't have bad memories of being somewhere with Ilse, if I went somewhere we'd never been.

The legendary Café MOCKBA on Karl Marx Allee was a must-see on my list of touristy sights in the East that had been off-limits for me in the nineteen-seventies. It had become the center of the party-hardy scene in the nineteen-nineties after the fall of the Wall, but it had recently been bought for a multi-million-Euro price, and was being converted into a conference center by a deep-pocketed entrepreneur. "This building is just as important a part of Berlin for me as Checkpoint Charlie," said the proud new owner who hadn't haggled over the price. Must be nice to have that kind of money.

The statue of a *sputnik* frozen in skyward flight at the corner of the building had been the promise of the bright shining future to come in the heady days of the mid-nineteen-sixties. It hadn't quite come true. Maybe it would in this Capitalist reincarnation. The restoration was progressing nicely and the papers said that the grand opening would be in February for the Berlinale. Too bad I'd miss it, but I already knew that I wouldn't get tickets even if I were still in Berlin. The papers said it would be for about 2,400 select guests, spelled with a '$.' That's the polite way of saying for the rich, spelled with a capital 'R.' In other words, for people who didn't have to ask how much the tickets cost. That's what left me out. I'd have to make do with this five-cent walk-around.

Café Moscow, Karl Marx Allee

The mosaic by Bert Heller looked like new, but the title he'd given to it had an anachronistic ring: "Scenes from the lives of the Peoples of the Soviet Union." Germany had reunified, but the peoples of the former Soviet Union had gone their separate ways. Maybe the distorted perspective that made the doves in the mural fly as high as the *sputnik*, or made the moose bigger than the Bratsk dam wasn't distorted at all, but just a reflection of the mentality of a system that elevated claiming that it was bigger and better to the level of an art form. Compared to the Russians, folks from Texas were more understated than British Lilliputians.

It was like the joke that was making the rounds in dissident circles during the Cold War. What's the difference between a writer and a politician? A politician is someone who can take a fiction and present it as reality, while a writer is someone who can take reality and present it as fiction.

When I briefed this joke in Washington to a bunch of politicians, nobody laughed, or even broke a smile. But when I told the joke at receptions along the lecture circuit after I retired, it always got a good response, especially if the person I was talking to happened to be a writer.

I was sure that there was some humor in my present predicament, but I couldn't see it just yet. The best laid plans of mice and men ..., as they say. I'd come here hoping to shake off the ghosts of Ilse-past, and had run into a herd of ghosts of Cold-War-past.

Alas, poor Cold War, I knew it well. It was a war of infinite jest and most excellent fancy, fought more often in the shadows of the mind than to the death, yet the lives of millions hung in the balance. It is a war without monuments, but not without casualties. 136 people were confirmed killed while trying to cross the Berlin Wall into West Berlin. Major Arthur D. Nicholson, the last casualty of the Cold War, was a classmate. That makes it very personal.

In all the years that I—and others like me—fought the Secret Cold War, it was under the banner of "Peace is our most important product." That was our motto, because the alternative was unthinkable. We accomplished our mission. The Iron Curtain came down without the Cold War turning hot. But when it did, we all suddenly found ourselves out of a job and unemployable, which was what, in a very roundabout way had brought me to the American Academy in Berlin. One of the walking wounded of the Cold War had returned to the scene of the crime.

Thoroughly depressed by this train of thought, I decided to skip the wide expanses of Karl Marx Allee. That was just more of the same "bigger and better" perspective of the Heller mosaic. Jacobystraße seemed to offer a more palatable dose of the good old days in the Workers' Paradise as a way back to Alexanderplatz. I could grab a quick lunch in the train station before I went to the Archives. Working there had to be less depressing than this.

„Ostalgia everywhere you look," I thought as I approached the *Haus der Lehrer* on my way to Alex. There is a huge Socialist-Realist frieze that runs all the way around the building at the fourth-floor level. There was a tour group off to my left admiring this marvel of the GDR aesthetic.

"This is one of the largest murals in Europe, extending over 130 yards in total," said the shapely young guide who couldn't have been more than a twinkle in her father's eye when the Wall fell. "It was done by the prominent East German artist Walter Womacka in 1964. While a number of his works have been destroyed 'post-Wall,' this one has survived, and there is now a society dedicated to preserving his art."

For her, Socialist Realist art was just one of those meaningless facts that the tour company had stuffed into her head when she took this job, as something to do while she waited to be discovered by the Babelsberg Film Studios. Unlike the pert, young guide, I had some personal experience with the reality represented by this Socialist frieze. For me, it wasn't just a disembodied representation of a failed regime.

Not only was Womacka's monumental frieze still around, so was he. And he was just as vocal as ever in defending the GDR, and as outspoken in his vilification of Capitalism and the West. Kindred spirits, he and I. We both missed the clarity of the Cold War.

From the frieze, the *NVA soldier with an AK-47 looked down at me as if he was getting ready to ask for my papers and hustle me off to the nearest Vopo station. Despite the sunny fall day, I felt an uncomfortable chill. I suppressed the urge to look over my shoulder to see if I was being tailed. This was post-Wall Berlin, after all, and I was retired.

The pretty young guide lifted her umbrella, and led her charges off in the direction of the marvels of Karl Marx Allee, the flagship boulevard where the May-Day parades were held in East Berlin. I sprinted across the street to Alexanderplatz, dodging traffic that would not have been there if the Wall were still up.

I hung a left towards the train station, through Alex, which took me by the infamous World Clock. It was one of the key elements of the great East German redesign of the square in 1969. It had been on magazine covers, postcards, TV. It was, and still is a great meeting point for everyone from locals to tourists. If you get lost, anyone can point you to it. And it's hard to miss since it is 33 feet high and weighs 16 tons. It features a revolving cylinder with the world's 24 time zones bearing the names of major cities in each zone.

It's ideal for a meet with an asset, because it's crowded all the time. You tell the asset that any time you name will be the time in Washington, not the time in Berlin. Anybody who overhears the time you set for the meet will be too early, because Washington time trails Berlin time by six hours. The clock very conveniently shows you Washington time, or any other time you want anywhere in the world. I'll bet it drove the Stasi crazy. I heard it was a godsend for the folks actively working Berlin.

At the train station, I dived into the first place to eat that wasn't a western fast-food franchise. I was hoping for a good currywurst, but the currywurst place I saw was a franchise too. It had a little machine that you dropped the wurst into to be cut up into little uniformly sized blocks, before it was covered in ketchup and curry. That was too industrial for my tastes.

The smell of the goulash said that I had other choices. It was coming from a place that was definitely not prepackaged and standardized. It had a bar with worn stools, and four wobbly tables with chairs. The tables were all full, so the bar it was.

The stool on my right was being kept warm by a gentleman of about my vintage with goulash stains on his tie. He was nursing a beer.

"Mahlzeit, Genosse," he said, as I sat down.

His use of the salutation "Genosse"—"Comrade" should have set off alarm bells, but I had my paranoia set to 'pick-pockets and panhandlers,' and he didn't fit the profile for either. My mouth was, therefore, on autopilot, so I just parroted what he had said, "Mahlzeit, Genosse." That got a surprised look out of him, but he didn't say anything more as he pondered what he'd just heard.

The waiter—cook—bottle washer—and probably owner came over to take my order.

"Goulash and a beer," I said absentmindedly.

"With, or without?" asked the waiter—cook—owner—bottle washer.

I had no idea what he was talking about, and didn't feel like asking, so I just said, "Without."

"Coming right up," said the guy behind the counter.

"You too?" asked the *Comrade* on my right.

"Me too what?" I countered, not quite sure why I was having this conversation.

"Can't afford the bread to go with the goulash, Genosse," he replied.

This time the word "Genosse" registered, and my paranoia switched into case-officer mode. I took in my interlocutor more carefully. The sleeves of his jacket seemed a bit threadbare, and the expression on his face more than a bit shopworn, but the eyes were as sharp as razors.

"We're getting by, Genosse," I replied, cultivating my American accent. "It's not like the nineteen-thirties, when you needed a wheelbarrow full of money to buy a loaf of bread."

"An American," he said, letting me know that the stealth message of my accent had gotten through. "In the old days," he said, switching to English, "I'd have tried to recruit you, but there's no point in that now."

"You wouldn't have gotten far," I replied. "Because I'd have been trying to recruit you. Let me freshen up your beer."

"Only if I can buy you bread for your goulash. We can't have it said that I've succumbed to the capitalist blandishments of the class enemy's *special services."

"No, we can't let that happen," I said. "And I'll have to do a contact report as well. Your English is very good. *HVA?"

"How perceptive. And you strike me as someone from the Station."

"Retired."

"What a coincidence. So am I," replied the Comrade, irony dripping from his every word. "Go back and tell the Station that this is the clumsiest of their 'so called' approaches yet, and I'm getting sick and tired of them coming around asking me to correlate the covernames of my sources with their true identities. You look like you actually have been a case officer, unlike the 'wet behind the ears' trainees they've been sending lately. You of all people should understand that my honor and my dignity as an intelligence professional prevent me from betraying my loyalty to a source. Those people trusted me with their lives, and that trust doesn't just evaporate because the country I was working for doesn't exist anymore. The trust was personal, not national."

He was right. I knew exactly what he was talking about. But he was wrong. This wasn't an approach. It really was a coincidence, but neither he nor I believed in coincidence with our paranoia set to case-officer mode.

"Your health," I said, raising my beer glass to clink against his.

He picked up his glass and touched it lightly to mine. "Enjoy your bread," said the Comrade. He drained his beer at one go, stood up and left without another word.

„A true gentleman, in the British sense of the word," I said to myself. „You don't meet people like that every day. If I'd only had the balls to say what he just said when they pressured me about Ilse."

The goulash was as good as it smelled. And the bread—one of those heavy German brown breads sliced by hand—was the perfect accompaniment to it.

See and Be Seen

The reception that night at the Academy was one of those "see and be seen" artistic things, where you are introduced to the literati. The *Mary Ellen von der Heyden Prize for Fiction* Fellow, Dorothea Dalrymple had read a chapter from her novel, *Good-bye Homeland*.

"Therefore," she concluded, "as John Galsworthy puts it in his *A Modern Comedy*: 'One had to leave one's country to become conscious of it.'"

There was a polite but unenthusiastic round of applause. That meant it was time to grab a drink and a bit of finger food, before the obligatory mingle with the guests. The guests had come to see the tame Americans, and we were supposed to be absorbing the intellectual atmosphere of Berlin from the distinguished personages who had graced us with their presence.

I was making the rounds with a champagne glass full of ginger ale, an old trick from when I was on the diplomatic reception circuit. If you can keep your head while all others about you are losing theirs, you are clearly not drinking the alcohol that flows like water at diplomatic functions. The pretense of imbibing is best served up with a slight slur to your speech, and a fuzzy focus in your eyes, achieved by looking at the point of the nose of the person you are trying to fool, rather than at their eyes.

"Let me introduce you to a famous East German playwright who was exiled from the GDR in 1966," said the party mixer-upper with one of those wallpaper smiles that never wilted. I had always been envious of people like that, until I realized that they never seemed to rise above being a facilitator at receptions. Their only promotion path seemed to be to marry someone who needed a live-in hostess.

Before I could protest, she had me face to face with Herr André H. Büchner. His suit was a study in classic GDR low fashion. He was clearly dressing the part that people expected him to play.

"Herr Büchner fell afoul of Ulbricht," she gushed, "for a line in a play called *Footprints of Stone*. It opened and closed on the same night in the East, but ran for two years to great acclaim in the West."

Wife: "Why didn't you sign the petition, you coward?"

Communist Mayor: "I wasn't ready to give up. I thought that I could still change things. If I had signed it, it would have been the beginning of the end of the GDR."

It was the end of the GDR for Büchner. Shortly after his play closed, he had been sent on a cultural tour to a theater festival in Munich, and they didn't let him back in.

"They are doing a revival of one of his plays at the Schaubühne on the Kudamm this week," said the mixer-upper with creamy elegance, leaving us in a cloud of expensive perfume as she went to find more people to herd.

"I'll get you tickets," he said, his eyes focused on the end of my nose.

"Yes, I'd like that very mush, Herr Büchner," I replied, focusing on the end of his nose.

"Come now, Doktor Troyan," he said, refocusing on my eyes. "There is no need to overplay your part. The theater is my profession."

"That obvious?" I asked.

"Only to a theater professional who has not been drinking. Under normal circumstances, it would be quite convincing. It was, however, the quality of the makeup used to mitigate your scar that convinced me your drunkenness was an act. It's very expertly done."

"Thank you," I replied, rather pleased with a compliment on my makeup technique from a theater professional. We had had some good instructors showing us how to use our disguise kits. I'd have to tell Louise the next time I ran into her. She would be delighted to hear that I'd earned a theatrical's approval.

Now that we had both admitted that we were frauds, we could get down to the exchange of serious ideas.

"What do you think of *Good-bye Homeland*?" I asked to get the ball rolling.

"A pseudo-émigré, who thinks that now that she's been outside America for the first time, she understands the loss of one's homeland, and can write about it."

"You and I know better, don't we, Genosse?"

"Hm, an American who says 'Genosse'?" he pondered. "Let me guess: Army Intelligence, or the CIA?"

"Army Intelligence," I replied, being thrifty with the truth. "Here in Berlin, actually."

"Then you, Genosse, like I, have indeed lost your homeland," he said. "Everything the Americans had built up here is gone. The Amerika Haus has been turned into a venue for quirky exhibitions like "German-Turkish Week." The Benjamin Franklin Clinic in Steglitz is so poorly maintained that the doctors must be afraid that the ceiling is about to come down around their ears. The American Shopping Center at Truman Plaza is being turned into luxury apartments. You must feel like I do when I visit the East and think about the old days."

Amerika Haus
Private Property: No Trespassing

"It's not just the places that have disappeared," I responded. "I miss the clarity of the Cold War. You knew who the bad guys were, and you could look yourself in the mirror full of moral righteousness."

"You sound like William Hood in *Mole*," he responded. "'The only justification a soldier or a spy can have,' said Hood, 'is the moral worth of the cause he represents.' But we've come a long way since the halcyon days of the Cold War. Today, everything has degenerated into an unsatisfying relativistic righteousness," pontificated Büchner, pressing the tips of his fingers together. "The moral high-ground you thought to command has turned into the shifting sand of political correctness that seeks to offend no one, but leaves everyone offended by its insincerity."

"Would you have a character say that on stage, Genosse?" I asked

"If I did, it would be the beginning of the end of my life in Germany."

"Another one-way ticket to a theater festival?"

"Something even worse. They would quit inviting me to cultural events like this, where I can at least hint at the truth to those with ears to listen."

"Like a member of the former class enemy, late of the special services?"

"No, I prefer to think of you as a compatriot in No-man's land whose country has also left him."

"Two fellow-travelers on the road to the Undiscovered Country," I replied. "Your very good health, Genosse," I said, lifting my glass.

"Shakespeare and Trotsky in the same line," he said with a touch of surprise. "You mind if I use it in a play?"

"Be my guest," I replied.

"You know, the process of saying good-bye changes your whole viewpoint. At first, when I was prevented from returning to the GDR, I was outraged, irate, and furious. The GDR had left me. I had not left it. But now that there is no GDR to go back to, I look back on it with a feeling of unreserved pity. There were a lot of people—and I was one of them—who believed we could create a system that would eradicate the *angst* of survival inherent in the Capitalist system. The fear of being unemployed, homeless and unable to feed one's children, for example."

"A worthy goal, but what went wrong with the GDR?" I asked.

114

"I think it was that we forgot the mental legacy of the Germans," he replied. "There were people, who from either a sense of their own importance, or a fear of the power of the State, abandoned their ideals, and became careerists, but this is not entirely a German trait, you'll agree?"

"Of course," I said, remembering a few of the last things that happened at Headquarters before I was retired.

"The fatal flaw of the system was that German careerists always do what their leaders want, exactly the way the leaders want it done. For hundreds of years the Germans have preferred to let things fail, rather than to tell their leaders that they are wrong. That led to Hitler and the occupation; and to the SED and Reunification, none of which were very pleasant."

"You should put that in a play," I suggested, recalling that when the careerists had taken over at Headquarters, they introduced a zero-defect culture that rewarded cautious mediocrity, and penalized risk taking. It became more important not to embarrass the organization than it was to achieve anything. This new culture gave birth to the proverb: *"Big operation — big risk; small operation — small risk;* no operation — no risk." In other words, if your plan doesn't work, your ass is in a sling before you get to make the necessary adjustment that will get it to work, and you get an irredeemable black mark in your file."

"No producer would touch it. Forgetting is very popular these days."

"Forgetting is dangerous," I countered. "You know what they say about a people who don't know their history."

"I know. I'd very much like to do something about forgetting, but I can't afford to produce it myself. That's one of the failings of Capitalism."

"Then pick a medium you can afford," I suggested. "That's the way Capitalism works. How about a T-shirt? They're cheap to produce, but get a lot of visibility." Doability had always been my strong suite.

"In California, perhaps," he said, "but in Berlin it's too cold for them, except in the summer."

"Which means that T-shirt season in Berlin won't compete with the theater season," I parried.

We exchanged a few more meaningless pleasantries before a different mixer-upper in a low-cut evening dress swished by to herd me along to the next mingle.

My next partner for this game of musical conversations had no idea who I was, which was good, because she would have been embarrassed if she'd remembered me from the Archives.

"Frau Schreiber," said the mingle herder, "I'd like you to meet Doctor Troyan."

She extended her hand, palm down. I took the cue, and played gentleman, like they'd taught me, making a slight bow to kiss her hand.

"Frau Schreiber is …," began the mingleress, but I cut her off in mid-spiel.

"The incomparable Romaine Schreiber needs no introduction," I waxed complimentary. I didn't need a meaningless introduction. I'd read up on Romaine Schreiber right after I'd taken that peek at her reconstructed file. "I've read all your novels," I lied.

"I didn't know that they had all been translated into English," she parried.

"They haven't," I said, switching to German without a moment's hesitation. "The ones that were translated were well done, but great literature should only be read in the original."

The guest herder looked surprised. They obviously hadn't briefed her on me. I was sure that her next stop would be for a quick look at my CV.

"Then you're either a professor of German literature, or a CIA agent," said Schreiber. "And since I don't recall any of the new group of Fellows being German professors, you must be CIA," she lunged.

"That's a general misapprehension," I said, but instead of making this cryptic remark any clearer, I executed a riposte, and bored her witless with the details of my book.

"Did you know that before the fall of the Berlin Wall, there were 189,000 active Stasi informants in East Germany, roughly 1.13 percent of the population?" A scowl flashed across her face. I knew that she knew one of them personally, but she didn't know that I knew, so the scowl was quickly replaced by her 'pretending not to be bored' mask. I pretended not to notice.

"Since the Stasi files were opened for public inspection, about 2.8 million people have submitted requests to see theirs." She smirked at the thought of being a statistic.

"Why in 2012 alone, 80,611 requests were filed." The soporific power of statistics began to take hold, and her 'pretending not to be bored' mask slipped just a bit.

"And just this last Saturday, 487 people requested their Stasi files," I continued.

"Fascinating," she said, looking desperately around for the mingle-herder. Her glass was empty. I signaled to a waiter with a drinks tray.

She looked relieved when the waiter showed up, so I changed tactics and told her how lovely her dress was.

"Your shoes and your handbag set it off perfectly," I said, using script 57a from the tradecraft course, the one for approaching a beautiful woman at a formal reception.

Her smile looked genuine, even if my comment was not. 'Ask about her work' was the next item in the script. Now it was my turn to be bored.

"I think it hardly overstates my case," she replied, warming to her topic, "to say that everything in the observable post-war universe definitely has its origins in Berlin. If we go back to the crack of the post-war dawn that the Germans call the "Year Zero," we have the four allies facing each other across a conference table. We hit the "Next" button on our post-war DVD, and we come to the East-West confrontation that resulted in the Berlin Airlift in 1948. From there, we fast-forward thirteen years to the epicenter of the Cold War, the construction of the Berlin Wall. From that point on, we are stuck in a slow-motion dance of political posturing across a floor as sticky as flypaper. We can still see the shoes of some of the dancers that were trapped by the flypaper: Kennedy's highly polished, stylish 'Ich bin ein Berliner' oxford, and Reagan's comfortable 'Tear down this Wall' loafer."

I could see why her prose was so highly valued in literary circles. I found myself nodding in time with the rhythm of her voice, as if I were listening attentively.

I'm not talkative the way women are, unless, of course, I've rehearsed it. When I was a kid, my mom would worry about me, because I'd go for days without saying anything. The peace and quiet of not saying anything is too useful for thinking to be wasted on an exchange of sounds and breath, signifying nothing.

I heard my name somewhere in the stream of sound that was her voice. It brought me back from the refuge of my own thoughts. I hadn't been listening, and she'd asked me something that required an answer. I caught her look and smiled innocently, focusing on her nose.

"I hesitate to express an opinion on that," I said with drunken sluggishness, parroting the response they taught us in school for exactly this situation.

"Why?" she barked. "Because she's a Fellow at the Academy, and you don't want to disparage a fellow American?"

That told me that she had finally gotten around to the question I was sure she was going to ask when this non-conversation started.

"Well, if you insist," I said disingenuously, feeding her Büchner's answer to the question. "Her story only has the banality of reality. It lacks pathos and a sense of mourning. How would you cure that if you were her editor?"

"So you were listening!" she exclaimed. "I thought you were miles away."

I had in fact been many mental miles away, but that's not the kind of thing that you admit to a woman, if you can avoid it.

She never did tell me how she would have fixed *Good-bye Homeland*. The guest herder with the wallpaper smile and dazzling black strapless cocktail dress that was somehow defying gravity showed up about five minutes early to move me along to the next stop in the evening's roster of people I had to meet.

When I saw that she was leading me over to Professor Johnson, I excused myself to go to the bathroom, and played hooky from the rest of the reception. I didn't know if Ilse had finally told him why she hit me. Either way, it would have been an uncomfortable conversation for the both of us. This was one of those "discretion is the better part of valor" moments that some people term cowardice.

The next day, when I tried to get tickets to Büchner's show for the following week, I found out that it had closed early due to disappointing box-office results. I guess he was right. Forgetting is in style. It probably wouldn't have helped if I had taken him up on his offer of tickets. Closed is closed, even if the author did give you the tickets.

I did, however, manage to pick up one of Schreiber's novels from a remainder table. There was always hope that I would read it before I left, but not much.

The Facts of Life

The subject line of the eMail said: "Fan Mail from a Flounder." An eMail with that subject line could only come from one person: my daughter Samantha. She's as big a *Rocky and Bullwinkle* fan as I am. Her sabbatical tour of the European art museums wasn't due in Berlin for three weeks, so I was surprised, but pleased to hear from this flounder.

"Here's an unbirthday present for you. I just got through listening to an interview with the legendary East German conductor Phillip Harmonecker, the one who had a falling out with Ulbricht in the mid-nineteen-sixties. Heard some things that sound like they belong in your book. You can <u>download the podcast</u> here."

I like unbirthday presents. They balance out the yearly present curve nicely. This one was doubly appreciated, because it gave me an excuse to do something other than the next item on my to-do list, which was an indexing pass on the chapter I had finished last night.

A couple of mouse clicks, and the wonders of modern technology brought Herr Phillip Harmonecker to my doorstep. I had a sense of déjà vu as the podcast started. It was almost like being back at work, doing an audio op.

"A number of people from the arts," said Harmonecker, "were '*invited*' to come be briefed on the big picture of German Socialism, and to be enlightened on the role that artists played in advancing the cause. Ulbricht gave this boisterous speech from on high, berating us for not doing enough to advance the cause of Socialist Realism. A week later, having had a chance to re-evaluate our role in society, we were '*invited*' back to begin a dialogue with the Party about what we could do to improve the situation. Everyone had to say something. When it got to be my turn, I opened my big mouth and said: 'After the way you spoke to us the last time we were here, I feel that no dialogue is possible until you apologize'."

I laughed out loud. Here was a man whose sunny innocence brightened the dark, dank, dangerously sharp-edged world in which he lived. It's a wonder that it hadn't cut him to shreds.

"This was followed by three years," said Harmonecker, "during which I was unofficially unemployed. I did not have an orchestra of my own, and I was not allowed to accept guest conducting invitations in the West."

The same thing happened to the leader of one of the Surreptitious Entry teams out of Headquarters. They sent his team on a poorly prepared rush job that almost got them all killed. He demanded that both the Chief of Station and Division Chief who pushed the job through get reprimands and apologize to his team. He was 'promoted' to a job with no duties.

"How did you manage to keep it to just three years?" asked the presenter.

"I simply got tired of all the play-acting," said Harmonecker, "and decided to use my international reputation while I still had one. When the *Musikverein* invited me to Vienna to do the New Year's Concert, I accepted. When I got their confirmation of my acceptance in the mail, I called the Minister of Culture, and announced that I was going to Vienna to do the concert. 'If,' I said, 'I don't get a visa to go, I will tell the world that it is your fault.' I had my exit visa before noon the next day, delivered by special courier."

The Surreptitious Entry team leader tried blackmail too. He threatened to tell the targets they'd been had. Headquarters offered him 500 grand and early retirement, but all he wanted was his job back and an apology. Too bad he hadn't had to take the course for case officers on Marxism-Leninism. If he had, he'd have known Engels' dictum about freedom being the recognition of necessity. He didn't take their offer, and they fitted him up with a five-year sentence in a Federal slammer for extortion. It was either that, or 40 to life for espionage: take your pick. As neat as any of the Stasi ops I'd read about.

"Weren't you worried," asked the program host, "that they wouldn't let you back in like they did with Büchner?"

"It was a calculated risk," said Harmonecker, "but a small one. I had come to the point where I decided that playing music was more important than where I played it, and I was willing to take that chance. Music is, after all, not quite as political as the stage."

„Or as dealing with Headquarters," I thought. In the course of my career, I'd been too successful by taking too many chances, which made me too many political enemies. When the opportunity presented itself, my enemies were only too happy to 'promote' me to a do-nothing job back at Headquarters. Before I could even clutter up my desk sufficiently to make it usable, I was given to understand that the advantages of the great *RIF following the end of the Cold War were especially suited to my situation. I had been to the course where they taught Engels, and the lesson of the Surreptitious Entry guy hadn't been lost on me either. I retired.

"When the Wall fell," said Harmonecker, "they thought that manna from Heaven would rain down on Earth. I've never seen such happy faces as I saw on that day."

I remember seeing those same faces on TV the day the Wall fell. I was TDY in Vienna from Prague to meet with someone we couldn't send behind the Iron Curtain. I'd turned on the TV before breakfast to get a quick overview of the news, and had to pick my jaw up off the floor when I saw the pictures. I couldn't believe it. Afterward, when I was still giving briefings on the situation in the "former East," I'd ask for a show of hands of those in the audience who—before the Berlin Wall actually fell—believed that it would fall during his or her lifetime. I never saw a hand go up.

"They were happy because they had hope," said Harmonecker. "but on our side of the border, the hope implied by the process of Reunification was unfulfilled, resulting in more pain than gain. I know several people who committed suicide because they had lost all the things that gave stability to their lives."

That was the way I felt when I retired. I had the hope of endless new opportunities opening before me, but I quickly discovered that I was unemployable. My paranoia said that Headquarters had put the word out on the street that I was untouchable. It was nothing you could prove, but the same tactic was on page 187 of *Methods of Reconciling the Interests of Society with the Interests of the Individual.*

Graffiti on a Wall at Charlottenburg S-Bahnhof (2013)

"The strangest thing about the Revolution," said Harmonecker, "was that it started and ended on Monday. On Tuesday everybody was back at work, as usual. After a while, however, you could see a change in the eyes of the young people. The sparkle that was there when they stood up to the regime to chant the Wall down was gone less than a year after Reunification."

That's about how long it took in my case, too. I used to be an optimist: the kind of guy who'd say "half-empty, but the waiter is headed this way." My first Chief of Station was a pessimist. He could make a sunny summer day seem overcast just by walking into a room. He enjoyed being a pessimist, and he let everybody know it.

"It's a win-win situation," he explained. "If things turn out better than I expected, I am happily surprised. If they turn out bad, I'm still happy, because I was right all along. They can't be worse than I expected, because I always expect the worst."

"But without the hope of optimism," I replied: "You don't have any incentive to do something. If things are going to Hell in a hand basket anyway, why bother to do anything?"

"Absolutely right," he said. "If the op is going to go bust anyway, why take the risk? You think that Headquarters will back us up if it goes south? You've got a lot to learn. That's not pessimism, that's a fact of life."

"But if all you ever do is sit behind your desk bemoaning the lack of intelligent life at the other end of the circuit to Headquarters, and feeling superior, nothing will change for the better. If you don't believe that you can make a difference, we might as well pack up and go home."

"You want to feel optimistic? Everyone has the right to be stupid, kid. Just don't overdo it, or do it at somebody else's Station. There's too much paperwork if you get PNG-ed or killed."

I'd finally come round to his way of thinking.

"The third generation of East Germans not only lost their historical identity," said Harmonecker. "They lost their future as well. This generation feels superfluous, and some of them have given up trying to find a job, because they have discovered that they can live perfectly well on government benefits, with an odd job or two to earn a little extra on the side."

That's the thing about beating your head against a brick wall: it feels so good when you stop, that where you stop isn't as important as it seemed when you started. So, I reinvented myself, and set a new course that steered around the rocks off the cape of useless spite into waters that Headquarters seems not to care about. It doesn't pay well, but with my retirement it keeps body and soul together.

"Is there anything you miss about the GDR?" asked the presenter.

"What I miss is the kind of support that the musical arts got from the government," said Harmonecker. "Every year, for example, every orchestra in the GDR had to perform a world premiere of a work by a young composer that had been commissioned by the State."

What I miss is the work, and the people, and the sense that I was doing good by defending American lives and interests. They took away the job I loved. I just wanted to be a good case officer, but their idea of good and mine didn't coincide, so they took my job away from me.

"For most West Germans, continued Harmonecker, "the word *Ostalgia* has a negative connotation. To them it suggests a feeling of nostalgia for a failed political system that split a country in two, and imprisoned half its people. To my East German friends *Ostalgia* is the memory of their childhoods. It is a part of their roots, and defines who they are, even for those who had a bad experience with the Stasi, because the pervasive atmosphere of repression and constant feeling that we were being watched engendered a sense of community and camaraderie. We had to stick together to keep them from sticking it to us. Life in reunified Berlin doesn't have that."

"I know exactly what you mean, Phil," I said out loud to the disembodied voice in my iTouch. "We had the same 'circle the wagons' sense of community at both the East-Bloc embassies I was assigned to. I still call a lot of those people my friends, while I can't even name most of the folks I served with in Berlin, Vienna or Munich."

"No one has forgotten," said Harmonecker, "that people were shot and killed for trying to leave the country, or that the Stasi had spies everywhere, even in my entourage, or that there were political prisoners."

I wonder what the word is for a longing for the way things used to work at the Agency? "OSStalgia"? I remembered how it was, but the longer we worked against our Cold War enemies, the more we became like them. The whole process eventually got co-opted by political expediency, and diverted into covert action away from intelligence collection.

Political prisoners? We had 'em too. Guys and gals like me and the team leader from Surreptitious Entry, sitting around in do-nothing jobs that kept us where they could keep an eye on us, but where we were out of the way.

"A dictatorship was not part of the original premise of Communism. It all began with the idea that each individual is of equal worth. It is the way that it was implemented that was the problem," said Harmonecker.

I couldn't have said it better myself.

"There is a line in *The Third Man* that—for me—with a slight paraphrase seems to encapsulate the counterpoint between Capitalism and Communism," said Harmonecker.

124

"In West Germany, for 40 years under the Capitalists, they had Guest Workers, the Red Army Faction, poverty, and crime, but they produced the economic miracle, social mobility, and the BMW. In East Germany under the SED they had what the Communists called democracy, peace, and social equality—but what did that produce? Economic ruin, social stagnation, and the Trabant."

Foto: Deutsche Fotothek via Wikimedia Commons

While we were the people who brought you *AZORIAN, *MHCHAOS, and *MKULTRA, we also were the people who pulled off *TKLUSTRUM. Even a BMW nine series can't top that.

"The Wall will be with us for a very long time," said Harmonecker, "in the memories of the lives we lived yet cannot disavow, no matter how hard we try. Even after all this time, I still have to fight the fear of being controlled and watched. If you were on their list, your life could be very unpleasant."

I was on Headquarters' list. I knew exactly what he was talking about. I wondered briefly if the eMail from Sam with the link to his podcast had gone into my dossier. Why was I wondering? I knew it had been filed. I used to do paranoia much better. I was on Headquarters' list.

All in all, a great unbirthday present. Sam knew my tastes to a 'T,' and always got me great gifts.

Berlin's New Main Train Station

Day Train to Berlin

Sam was coming in on the train from her Rijksmuseum stop in Amsterdam. I told her I'd meet her at the train station. She didn't speak German, and might need someone to run interference for her.

Her train was due in at 13:13. In my day, only the Brit duty train crossed the 115 miles of East Germany to Berlin during daylight hours. The American Duty Train to Frankfurt was scheduled at night, because the Soviets had asked us to run the trains during the hours of darkness, and like the good guys we are, we had complied. The Brits just told them to stick it in their ear. The Sov's were worried that we'd be taking pictures of military operations and facilities from the train. We had better sources than that.

Still, the Duty Train was done up right: all sleeping cars with berths. You departed Berlin at 20:31 and arrived in Frankfurt at 06:53. That's ten and a half hours to cover 300 miles. It wasn't that the train was pulled by snails, but that the Sov's stopped it for everything imaginable and unimaginable. The train could only be pulled by a West German locomotive from the Lichterfelde train station near Andrews to the sector border. It stopped there to switch to an East German locomotive and engineer, and to let the Sov's check the documents for everybody on the train.

"This man's documents are not in order," said the Soviet major in charge of processing the Duty Train. "His identity card says 'Michael A Troyan,' but his Flag Orders say 'Michael A. Troyan.' You will have to correct that before I can allow the train to proceed."

They changed locomotives again at Marienborn for the rest of the trip to Frankfurt. To annoy us, the train stopped at sidings all the way across East Germany for other, 'higher priority' East German trains to pass. It didn't bother me. Once I got to sleep, I didn't wake up till Frankfurt.

There was this one guy I knew who had made a daylight crossing of East Germany on the American Duty Train. Dangerous Dan had been on the train the time it got stopped by a blizzard just across the border into East Germany. They were stuck in frozen diplomatic limbo for ten hours.

"The Russians guarding the train looked cold as Eskimo hell," said Dan. "I wish I'd had my camera, but I never take it on the train, because it's normally too dark to take pictures."

Dangerous Dan was one of the couriers who escorted the shipment of classified materials out to Frankfurt on the Duty Train twice a week. He came by the name honestly. As a courier he was authorized to pack a loaded .45 automatic on his hip. That was the Army's way of making sure that the classified information in Dan's care on the train stayed classified.

"I shoot first and ask questions later," said Dan, to those who got too close to the secrets under his care. "That is, if you're still alive to answer questions."

Some folks thought he'd actually shoot. Others not. The consensus of opinion was expressed in his nickname. I wasn't prepared to put Dan to the test just to find out. He was as nutty as the rest of us.

The Monday-night train out to Frankfurt, the Tuesday-night train back; out again on Wednesday night, and back on Thursday. Other than that his time was his own. That was his official payback for living on the train four days a week.

His unofficial payback earned him a few hundred dollars a month extra. He did a fairly brisk trade in Russian flags, and uniform insignia, like belt buckles and hats. The flags were from the flag shop here in Berlin. They cost three dollars apiece.

"Dirty 'em up a little, so they look used," he would say, "then sell them to the GI's in Frankfurt for twenty-five dollars. That's three dollars for the flag, two dollars for the delivery, and twenty dollars for the story about how I stole it off the flag pole at Spandau Prison, the month that the Sov's had guard duty there."

His other sideline was a barter-based import-export arrangement with the Russian enlisted men who cordoned off the Duty Train, ostensibly to keep one of us from sneaking off, but in reality to keep the East Germans from sneaking on. Those furry Russian winter hats were popular, and went like hot cakes for $30 a pop. His supplier wanted western-made watches. They were five bucks in the PX.

"It's always the same guy with hats to trade," he said, one Saturday night at *The Scum*, after a few beers. "I couldn't figure out how he got so many, so I asked him. Turns out he's as big a wheeler-dealer as I am."

"I'm the first one in the mess hall going, and the first one out coming," said Dangerous Dan mimicking a Russian accent

"The going price for uniform buttons, insignias, badges, belts and buckles," said Dangerous Dan, "is *Playboys*. I'm waging my own personal psywar op[*] against the Sov's by translating all the cartoons in the *Playboys* into Russian. Mark my words, this dose of Capitalist decadence will lead to the fall of the USSR in fifteen years time."

Dan wasn't off by much. It was sixteen years, and the analysts at Headquarters were surprised when it happened. If he'd worked for us, he could have gotten a citation and a cash award, but he didn't. Word had it that he went back home to work with his father selling cars.

Dangerous Dan also liked to brag that he removed all the centerfolds from the *Playboys* he swapped with the Russians. I wouldn't trust anybody who would do that as far as I could throw him, and neither would the Russians. That kind of trick would have worked only once, yet he did a land-office business. You paid your money—up front—and your purchase was delivered in a week, like clockwork. So, taking out the centerfolds probably was a fairy tale told for the entertainment of those who would listen. *The Scum*—the usual venue for the telling of such tales—was, after all, a place where lies are seldom heard, but where falsehoods are the coin of the realm. Either that, or the Russians were getting something else besides *Playboys*, like secrets.

He had the opportunity to get them and to hand 'em over. The 'absence of information' axiom applied in his case. He hadn't been included in MUSIK reporting thus far, so it could be him. Then again, if he was just fishing us about the centerfolds, his sideline could have been enough to

---

[*] Psychological warfare operation

account for all the money he seemed to have. But who knew how much money he really had. "Not I," said the little red hen.

A straight cash-and-carry recruitment was more than common enough for me to put him on my list, even without the 'absence of information' axiom. The more competition for Ilse that I could think up for the title of MUSIK, the better.

The American Duty Train station in Lichterfelde had been torn down, and Bahnhof Zoo had lost its title of West Berlin's main station to the new, improved Hauptbahnhof, which could have swallowed both Lichterfelde and Bahnhof Zoo whole, and had some room left over for dessert. So much for the Berliners' sense of history. Everything's bigger and better and *new* in the new Berlin.

I showed up at the train station early to give me some time to find the right track for Sam's train. I needed it. Did I say the station was big? Sam's train pulled in with atypically German inefficiency an hour and a half late, but her car number stopped right on the spot it was supposed to be. That's no way to run a railroad. That kind of thing was unthinkable in my day.

She was wearing sensible traveling clothes like I'd taught her. Comfy brown slacks that don't show off stains, or her legs; a cozy matching sweater that didn't show off her bust; and what we called 'tennis shoes' in my day, but that now go by a myriad of jazzed up names intended to justify the price on the box. It's a lot easier to negotiate European cobblestone streets and train stations in those than in heels.

"How's my favorite flounder?"

"Getting along swimmingly," she replied. "Your scar doesn't look as bad as I'd imagined it would be."

"Things like this always sound worse in the telling than they are in person," I said, not wanting to disillusion her by pointing out that applying makeup was one of my spooky skills.

"Lunch?" I asked.

"No, I ate on the train."

Food on the train was another thing that was just like the Brit Duty Train. Not only did it cross 'East Germany' during the hours of daylight, there was a dining car. The Sov's had told the Allies to cut out the dining cars on the Duty Trains. The Americans did as they were told. The Brits put on a second car. The food was great, too.

130

Even though she packed light, I didn't feel like lugging Sam's luggage around on public transportation, so we took a taxi to the Academy.

"Mom asked if I'd be so kind as to *not* give you her regards."

"Tell her 'Hi!' for me," I replied. Someone had to be the first to turn their back on the siren call of revenge, and to hold out an olive branch, otherwise everybody would end up dashed on the rocks off the cape of useless spite. I wondered why it always had to be me, but I already knew the answer. If I waited for someone else to stand up and take the lead, nothing would happen.

"How's your book going?" asked Sam.

"Better than I'd expected. It turns out that I do have a Stasi file, and that someone was reporting on me when I was here at the Field Station."

"Someone?"

"I don't know who it was yet. All I have is from partial reconstructions of a few Stasi files that talk about the source using a covername. It's almost like being back at work again," I said.

"You didn't really want to quit, did you?" asked Sam.

"You noticed that? I didn't think it was that obvious," I answered.

"Your spy antennae must be broken. An elephant with a flashing neon sign in a small room would have been more inconspicuous."

"No, it wasn't exactly my idea. They made me an offer I couldn't refuse," I replied.

"They can take the spook out of the game, but they can't take the game out of the spook," said Sam.

"Yeah, that's me all over: one of the lost tribe of Cold-War case officers. With peace breaking out all over Europe in the wake of the Cold War, all those who had been gainfully employed as spies suddenly found themselves out of work, not because there was nothing left for us to do, but because the people holding the purse strings believed the Russians when they said they were our 'friends.' Nobody remembers the good things we did, because nobody was allowed to know in the first place. Hm, I'd better get down off my soapbox. What do you want to see in Berlin?"

"My favorite spook, Nefertiti, *The Man with the Golden Helmet, and the East German aesthetic for a start," she said, bringing a smile to my face.

"Your favorite spook and *The Man with the Golden Helmet* aren't quite what they seemed when they were 'undercover'," I responded.

"That doesn't make either of them any less interesting," she said.

"Nefertiti moved since I was here last, but I've got her new address. The first time I saw her, she captured my soul. We can drop by to visit any day, but she's open late on Thursday, Friday, and Saturday," I said.

"And the East German aesthetic?" she asked.

"That's a more nebulous request, but I've got a few leads we can follow, like Heller, Womacka, and Frankenstein," I answered.

"What's that? A ghoul's gallery?"

"They're world famous in East Germany," I countered.

"Which no longer exists," she parried.

"Oh, it's very much alive in some quarters," I rejoined.

"This isn't going to turn into a political dissertation about the relationship between aesthetics and politics in the Communist State?" asked Sam, who had heard me up on my political soapbox more than once or twice.

"What do you expect, when you ask an old Cold Warrior? Everything is political in the Socialist State; not to mention in the Fascist State, the Capitalist State, large three-letter bureaucracies, and in the modern trend to political correctness."

"You always were an equal opportunity cynic," she said with a laugh.

The taxi pulled up to the Academy gate just in the nick of time.

We dumped her luggage in my apartment, and went down to meet Mary-Kate, who would undoubtedly debrief her about me, while she got her officially registered. I discreetly made myself scarce so that I wouldn't inhibit the interrogation.

Checkpoint Charlie

Checkpoint Charlie was the face that the media put on the epicenter of East-West tensions during the Cold War. Now, it looked more like a cheap vaudeville act. If it hadn't been so sad, it would have been laughable.

I'd only been there when it was a going concern a couple of times, and neither of those had been what you'd call 'white knuckle' tense. There was that time we went across the sector border on the Special Services tour that was in my Stasi file. It was like going to the zoo to watch the lions. You knew lions were dangerous, but you knew you were safe on the other side of the glass.

Then, there was the time my mother came to visit. She asked especially to see it. We walked up to the Wall. We visited the *Haus am Checkpoint Charlie*. We took pictures. That was hardly the stuff of sweaty palms. I had more adrenaline pumping watching James Bond drive through in *Octopussy*. It obviously had more oomph when tanks with live ammo were facing off there in 1961, but I was still in school then.

Today's visit fell into the same category as the visit with my mother. It was a suggestion that I couldn't refuse. What do you say when your mother says: "Let's go see Checkpoint Charlie!"? The same thing you say when your daughter repeats the request: "Sure. The sun's out. Let's go."

I'd been following Checkpoint Charlie in the papers since I got back. The story read like some comic operetta sponsored by a company that makes soap. The dramatic tension was supplied by the political fight about where to put the museum that will curate the period of the Cold War and Divided Berlin. The comic relief was in the name of the show. It was called "Snackpoint Charlie." It was a good pun for the greasy-spoon food court that had sprung up there after the Wall fell, but it seemed to ignore the fact that this could have been the place where World War III started.

The tone of the discussion in the papers raised the question of whether the Berliners just thought of the memory of the Wall as a tourist magnet, or if they had actually retained any of the lessons that could be learned from what went on here. I was leaning towards Büchner's assessment: "Forgetting is very popular these days."

There was, however, no question about who won the Cold War. Hungry tourists could grab a bite to eat at the McDonald's right across from the replica of the "Checkpoint Charlie" guard shack, or at the Starbucks just a bit further on.

"You have to take a picture of me in front of Checkpoint Charlie," said Sam, striking a pose between the two flag-waving actors, doing a bad job of pretending to be American MPs. Their uniforms were a mix-and-match combination of a Class-A jacket with fatigue pants. Any First Sergeant who saw that would have gone nuts.

"That's a Euro apiece," said the one on the left, with an accent that marked him as a real American.

"Here you go," said Sam.

"Thanks," said the American, whose wrinkled, patchwork uniform wouldn't have passed an ASA inspection, let alone a real army one.

"Спасибо," said the guy on the right whose five-o'clock shadow put the finishing touch on a uniform that was a size too big.

Now that was a slant on *Détente* that you never saw during the real Cold War. The Russians stayed on their side of the border, and wore their own uniforms. These days, there were over 300,000 of them living the good life in Berlin, that is, if you could call working as an actor at Checkpoint Charlie for a Euro a pose the good life.

I stepped back and framed the shot, but no matter how I tried, I couldn't get Sam, the two fake GI's, and the guard shack in frame without the Golden Arches playing peek-a-boo in the background. I gave up, and snapped the shot that was there with the obligatory 'Say Cheese,' thinking that something to eat might not be a bad idea right about now.

There was already a line of people forming behind me to have their pictures taken in this 'classic' Berlin still life with tourist. Maybe this was the good life for that Russian. Looking at the line, I figured he was making 30, maybe 40 Euro an hour, easy.

"You takee our pikcha?" asked the young Chinese couple behind me. This was another thing that would have been impossible at the real Checkpoint Charlie.

"Of course," I said, taking the proffered camera. They smiled. The fake GI's smiled. The Golden Arches smiled. I pressed the button, then swung my camera up for a second shot before they could un-pose. My photographer's fee. They'd never believe this back home, if I didn't have photographic proof. Too bad that there was nothing in the image that said the guy on the right was a Russian. That was going to be a hard sell without a tape recording.

"It's not quite what I expected," said Sam, when we regrouped.

"No, the barbed wire, concrete barriers, and swarms of East German border guards are long gone," I said. "These days, the Berliners call it 'Schreckpoint Charlie'."

"What's that mean? That's way out of my depth in German."

"'Fright-point Charlie,' but it rhymes with 'Checkpoint' in German."

"I want to do an establishing shot," I said, backing up so that I could get the famous 'You are entering the American Sector' sign in the frame with the guard shack.

"The sign's a replica, you know," I said, "and not a good one. There's a typo in the Russian. You'd think with a Russian on the staff, pretending to be an American, he might notice and get them to fix it."

"There are two in the French," said Sam.

„That's my girl," I thought. She could afford to speak French. French went a long way in the art world. I'm sure it was a big help in dealing with the Louvre. Where I worked, all those poor souls who saw themselves on the way to the City of Light to use their French were unpleasantly surprised. Paris was out, and Francophone Africa in for French, so I studiously avoided giving any hint that I could speak or read it.

"I could use a chocolate milkshake," said Sam, looking in the direction I was pointing the camera."

"Sure," I said. I always did. It was tradition.

As we started across the street, I saw a gaggle of kids coming down the sidewalk, skipping arm in arm, singing: "Mr. Gorbachev, tear down this wall" to the tune of that old German 'favorite,' "Happy Birthday to You." I also saw a team of dippers working the crowd that had stopped to listen to the kids.

"Wait a minute," I said, as I pretended to re-tie my shoe. I fiddled with it till five, no make that six of Berlin's plain-clothes finest detached themselves from the crowd, and attached handcuffs to the team of pickpockets. There was a brief scuffle as one of the dips foolishly tried to hit his cop and leg it. They very solicitously picked him up off the ground.

"You didn't have to do that," She said. "You could have just told me why you didn't want to cross the street at precisely that moment. I'm a big girl now."

"I keep forgetting," I said. "You'll always be a little girl to me."

"I'm not. So give," she said.

"It was a bunch of pick-pockets working the crowd the kids created."

"You're not going to tell the police?" she asked.

"You see any cops around?" I parried.

She looked right and left, in a slow scan like I'd taught her. "No."

"They're part of the crowd. Did you see the guy fall down? The guy holding him up is a cop. Very efficient, the Berlin cops."

I suddenly had an irresistible urge to go someplace with friendly people, people whose faces projected something other than that inane smile that all strong-arm artists seem to wear, like it's a part of their uniform. You tend to need bandages the minute that smile vanishes. Just ask that pickpocket, if you don't believe me.

"Let's go get that milkshake," I said.

"I guess having a spook for a father can come in handy now and again," replied Sam.

I'd never thought about it like that. I guess she had a point. The wall-to-wall paranoia that goes with being a spook can keep you out of normal trouble too.

We took the long way around the guard shack to McDonald's to give the crowd more time to disperse, and the cops a chance to stuff the guy with a broken leg into an unmarked car. We got in line behind a mother with a precocious little boy who wanted a kid's meal with fruit and milk.

"Mommy, who was Charlie, and why is this place named for him"

You only get questions like that from kids with smart parents, so I was expecting something intelligently didactic, but the petite 5'2" blond, blue in the stylish green dress that made her look like Tinker Bell had the quality that Einstein said was greater than intelligence. She had imagination.

"There were three brothers: Alpha, Bravo, and Charlie. Alpha lived in Helmstedt. Bravo lived in Dreilinden, and Charlie lived here on Friedrichstraße …"

She stopped because their food was ready. Too bad, 'cause I'd have liked to have heard how her story ended. Her suggestion that Charlie was a real person triggered an old memory. "40-klix Charlie" was the toast of the town when I was in the Army here.

"Two chocolate milkshakes," said Sam.

"You want fries with that?" asked the girl behind the counter, with an exhausted glance at her watch.

'40-klix' Charlie's claim to fame was that he had beaten a speeding ticket from the MPs. This wasn't just any speeding ticket. It was one that could only have been written in Berlin. Charlie was driving down a street in one of the American areas, where the speed limit was marked in Miles Per Hour. The sign said: "25 MPH." Charlie saw the MP in his mirror, and checked the speedometer of his beat-up American-made Ford that he'd bought twelfth hand from someone rotating out of Berlin. It said: "25 MPH." The MP was driving a locally procured Opel, with a speedometer calibrated in kilometers. It said: "40 Klix per Hour."

Unlike the people at the Field Station, the MP was not someone who could have worked in rocket science. He saw 40. The speed limit was 25. He did the math. '40 minus 25' equals Charlie doing 15 over the speed limit. He switched on his siren and his bubble-gum machine.

"Going a little fast, aren't you, buddy," said the MP.

"I was only doing 25," replied Charlie.

"My speedometer says '40'," said the MP. "If you want to make something out of this, we can just continue it with my captain, back at the MP company."

Charlie actually did go to work in rocket science, as I recall, and wisely chose not to make something out of it.

The adjudication of the ticket was done at the Field Station, where there were people who could subtract 25MPH from 40KPH and get it to equal zero. Unfortunately, none of them was deciding what to do about Charlie's ticket. The military equation that kept this from happening factored in the MP's eighteen-year career, and the variable that a black mark like this on his record would keep him from being promoted to SP-5. It didn't matter that Charlie was up for promotion to SP-5 as well. He was only on his first enlistment. The MP was a career soldier. The Army—in the person of the First Sergeant—wanted to take care of its own, no matter how wrong the MP was.

"Just pay the fine and shut up," said the Sergeant Major, when Charlie tried to get some sympathy from the head shed. "You're getting out at the end of your enlistment, but the MP is retiring in two years. The difference in his pension will be a big deal for him."

Charlie appealed to the *JAG, where the case was given to a short-time captain who applied the judgment of Solomon. He tore up Charlie's ticket, annulled his fine, and arranged over drinks at the O-club for the MP to be transferred to the Duty Train, where he wouldn't need to know the difference between miles and kilometers. The fewer cases like this that he had to deal with, the better.

"It's an open and shut case," said the JAG captain. "You should get out at the end of your enlistment, just like I'm going to. You don't belong in army green any more than I do."

The MP got promoted, but Charlie didn't. Someone conveniently replaced the ticket that had "officially" been taken out of his packet for the promotion board.

A revenge pitch might have worked. Money, I think, would be what would get the door open, "to make up for the financial loss he suffered by not getting promoted." I put him on the list of MUSIK possibles. Charlie knew all the things that MUSIK had reported so far.

"Remember me?" asked Sam, prodding me with a tray holding two milkshakes and an order of french fries.

"In a word, could I ever forget?"

"That's four words."

"I'm a big tipper."

Wittgenstein and the Duck-Rabbit

"It says in this guidebook that currywurst is characteristic of Berlin fast food," pronounced Sam, waving around a weighty-looking paperback tome. "I can't say I've been to Berlin and admit that I did not have a currywurst."

"Probably not a defensible position to take," I replied, wondering why she believed the guidebook and not me. I must have said the same thing a hundred times since she'd been here.

"The guidebook says that *Curry 36* on Mehringdamm is the wizard of curry. Let's go there."

I figured that any place in a guidebook was probably a tourist trap, but I also knew that this was not a discussion, so I didn't make a counter suggestion. Besides, this place was close to the Stasi hotel that had been in the papers last week. We could do Tempelhof and the Airlift Monument at the same time. They were just across the street from one another. Very conveniently located for a Stasi hotel. The closer to the target the better.

"I've already got it mapped out," said Sam. "It's just down the street from the Mehringdamm U-Bahn station."

"I'd better get my hat," I said, and we were off to see the wizard of curry.

It *was* very touristy, but there was a long line, which is always a good sign. You could see a lot of Berliners, from blue-collar workers and taxi drivers, to suits with lawyers and accountants in them. The ties were the giveaway to who was who.

"*Doppelte Curry, 'ohne,' mit Pommes,*"[*] I said when it was my turn.

"Next," said the lady behind the counter, who was a bit too big in the bust for her stained apron.

"What he said," said Sam in English.

"Sure thing, honey," said the lady behind the counter with a smile that said she had put us together the wrong way.

"Single curry for my daughter," I added.

"Got it. That'll be €6.40," said the lady behind the counter, shifting her face back into neutral. "Next."

The price was right, the service was fast and the currywurst more than eatable. The french fries, however, were soggy. A quick scan of the other tables didn't find any french fries. I should have done the scan before I ordered.

"While we're here," I said, "I'd like to walk down to the Airlift Memorial."

"Is that close by?" she asked, oblivious to the blob of curry ketchup that just missed her linen skirt on its way to the sidewalk.

"Just down the street," I replied, "and right across the street is Hotel Luftbrücke."

"What's that?" she asked, stepping in the curry ketchup spill.

"It's a hotel that was run by the Stasi."

"The Stasi ran hotels?" asked Sam.

"Sure. They had a contract with the Americans at Tempelhof Air Base to provide rooms to aircrews who were turning around planes overnight. A cheap but effective op, run by some apparently unsavory characters. Glad it wasn't mine, though. The case officer complained that he spent more time providing marriage counseling to the couple that ran the hotel than he did running the op."

"Not some place you stayed in your misspent youth?" wondered Sam.

"No. It's just a part of my self-guided spy tour of Berlin," I answered, throwing my empty paper plate and plastic fork in the trash.

---

[*] Double curry, no (casing), with french fries.

"Wipe that blotch of ketchup off your jacket before we go," she said, chucking her half-empty plate after mine. She ate like a bird, and was always throwing food away whenever I took her out to eat.

About a block and a half away, Sam made an abrupt stop that would have driven our surveillance nuts, if we'd had any, but I'd been checking, and we were black.

"Stencil graffiti is clearly the dominant art form around here," said Sam, pulling out her camera. "This stylized portrait of Wittgenstein, flanked by two duck-rabbits, is a very good example," she continued. "It'll go great in that lecture on 'street' art I'm planning for when I get back."

I'd forgotten all about Wit, but when Sam pointed out the portrait, it all came back to me. "Wit" was short for Wittgenstein. He was a philosophy major, who had done his thesis on Wittgenstein. He was always throwing in Wittgenstein quotes to help make his point in an argument.

A linguist from BRANDFLAKE—I think his name was Jerry—got tired of Wit showboating with all these quotes, so one evening at the Swing meal, he made a big deal of writing a couple of them down, and announced to one an all:

"He's making this shit up. I'm going to hit the library tomorrow, and prove it."

141

Wit wasn't making it up.

"Whereof one cannot speak, thereof one must be silent," said Wit when Jerry threw in the towel. "That's from *Tractatus Logico-Philosophicus*," if you want to look it up.

"Never stay up on the barren heights of cleverness, but come down into the green valleys of silliness," said Jerry.

"Touché," said Wit. "*Culture and Value*. 'For a philosopher there is more grass down in the valleys of silliness than up on the barren heights of cleverness,' also *Culture and Value*. Let me buy you a beer."

After that they were good buddies. I even heard that Jerry was the best man at Wit's wedding.

Like Wittgenstein's duck-rabbit, it's all about how you look at something. Going back over my misspent youth at the Field Station from a case-officer's perspective, I was amazed at how the Army seemed to bend over backwards to make it easy for the Stasi and KGB to approach people. I'd have had a field day doing recruitments.

It was the army-green valleys of silliness that would have given me the hook I needed to recruit Wit. There was a huge Warsaw Pact Exercise going on, and we had so much magnetic-recording tape turning that we almost ran out. They had to fly in a special shipment for us all the way from the States. The scanners and scribes couldn't keep up, and there were stacks of tapes on the floor, on top of the positions, and on the analysts' desks. Break had been cancelled, people were working extra shifts, and they had set up the spare recorders from the maintenance shop so that more scanners could work on tapes.

Wit had been working full out since the WAREX started.

Somewhere around 80 hours after he came on duty he said: "Sleeping on a stack of tapes is as dangerous as stopping to rest when you are walking in the snow. You doze off and die in your sleep. I need a break, so let me drive down to the flats for the shipment of tapes."

He parked the truck next to the *ARFCOS room, so he could be in and out quick. "Quick" and 100 boxes of 40 seven-inch tapes each are only synonymous when you have a forklift. With no forklift and no dolly, they form an oxymoron equal to a minimum of 25 trips between the ARFCOS room and the truck if you are alone, like Wit was.

The motto of ASA is *Semper Vigilis*, but with four boxes of tape stacked high in your arms, it's not easy to be vigilant about what's in front of you, because the boxes get in the way. The result of this invitation to disaster was that Wit bumped into the object of our eternal loathing, Lieutenant Dumb Bar, whose presence qualified as a calamity even in the best of times, and these were far from the best of times.

I don't often take a positive dislike to someone at first sight, but in his case I made an exception. He couldn't pour water out of a boot with instructions on the heel. I doubted there was anything he could do to make me change my mind, ever. I was right. It only got worse. And Wit was less tolerant than I when it came to stupidity.

"You're just one of those *swaydo intellectual languagists*, whose rooms are full of books in German, and other egghead crap," said Dunbar, with imperial anger.

Wit had trouble suppressing a smile at the lieutenant's mispronunciation of "pseudo intellectual linguists," but he knew that failure to do so would certainly make matters worse. The lieutenant was unknowingly wont to make himself the laughing-stock of the Field Station by trying to use the big words that he heard the men under his alleged command use, but he most often only succeeded in distorting them in bizarre and amusing ways. If he wasn't such a prick, we could have felt sorry for him, but he was, and we didn't. If he wasn't the source of the expression "more fun than a barrel full of second lieutenants," it was the brother he didn't have.

The NCOs and junior officers who were the most successful at "leading" their gaggles of wise-guy, egg-headed escapees from a Mensa convention, prudently either got the big words right, or skipped them altogether.

"You're a disgrace to the uniform," said Dunbar. "Your uniform looks like you slept in it. Your shoes aren't shined. You haven't shaved for at least three days, and your hair is over regulation length. You've got thirty minutes to correct these *deafitionsies* [SIC] and report back to me."

"Sir, yes, Sir!" said Wit sensibly, because the lieutenant's flushed face and barely controlled scowl gave him to understand that any attempt at discussion would be ill received.

Wit's loyalty to the mission and to the guys who were waiting for him to get back with the tapes was more important than any lieutenant. He bundled everything into the truck, and took off for the Hill, without giving another thought to a clean uniform, shined shoes, a shave and a haircut.

The WAREX ended three days later, and Wit had spent the whole time on the Hill doing tapes like everybody else. His uniform looked even more slept-in, because it was. His beard and hair were three days longer than when Lieutenant Dumb Bar told him to get cleaned up within 30 minutes.

When Wit didn't show up in the allotted time, Dumb Bar went ballistic. He filed an Article 15 against Wit for disobedience of a direct order, and for being AWOL, because it didn't dawn on him to look for Wit in ops.

Wit, of course, had good, justifiable reasons for being in the state he was in and ignoring the lieutenant's order, but it would take a mind at least as brilliant as a mushroom's to guess what they were, so there wasn't much hope that Lieutenant Dumb Bar would get the point.

When they announced the decision to bust him one grade, Wit said, "Of course you realize that any chance you had of convincing me to re-enlist just evaporated." It was a great throwaway line, because there was never any possibility of Wit re-enlisting. It did, however, make Dumb Bar frown, which was its intended purpose.

With my case-officer hat on, I would have plied Wit with money. Getting busted one grade doesn't do anything for your financial situation. And I would have sung the siren call for revenge. I could have hooked him. I was good. Another name to add to my list.

"Why haven't you asked me what a 'duck-rabbit' is?" said Sam, with that tone in her voice that her mother used to use when she suspected me of some chicanery. "You're going to pretend that you know, aren't you?"

"Pretend? No," I said calmly, so as to keep from escalating this 'discussion' to the level that her mother would have taken it. "The block that your old man has been around more than a couple of times was not just full of sleazy Stasi hotels, bribery, and dead drops."

Putting on a cheap theatrical German accent to suggest that there were no hard feelings, I said: "A 'duck-rabbit' is a perceptually ambiguous figure originally introduced by the American Gestalt psychologist Joseph Jastrow around 1900 in his book *Fact and Fable in Psychology* to prove his point that perception is not just a reaction to a stimulus, but also the result of mental activity. Someone looking at a 'duck-rabbit' may see either a duck or a rabbit, but upon prompting, may be able to make it shift back and forth between the two repeatedly. This chameleon figure is more commonly associated with Ludwig Wittgenstein and his influential *Philosophical Investigations*."

"You wanna come guest lecture to my class when I get to this lesson?"

"No problem," I said. "My honorarium is a piece of chocolate cake."

"I think that can be arranged," she said. "But drop the German accent. It was terrible."

"It was supposed to be a cue that I was not out for your academic scalp."

"Let's get back to that sleazy Stasi hotel, and the spooky father I know and love," she said.

"Keep it down! You'll blow my cover," I joked.

We set off back down Mehringdamm, and I launched into a spy story she'd heard a dozen times before. She pretended to listen for about 200 meters, but suddenly stopped again. I automatically took the opportunity to check for surveillance. We were still black.

"What's this say?" she asked, pointing to a stencil on a gray wall.

"It's the third time I've seen it."

"Gay Museum," I replied. "Berlin's been around the block a few times too."

I added Benedict to my list. These days, nobody cared, but in the old days, I could have gotten to him with a blackmail pitch. The more competition for Ilse in the MUSIK sweepstakes, the better.

Plaque at Kaiser-Friedrich-Straße 57

This is where the Snack Bar was located, at which on 4 September 1949,

Herta Heuwer (30 June 1913 in Königsberg — 3 July 1999 in Berlin)

invented the spicy Chillup®-Sauce for Currywurst that in the meantime has become famous worldwide. Her idea is tradition and an everlasting pleasure.

Bar Gagarin

"Let's go to the Sunday Brunch over at Bar Gagarin in Prenzlauer Berg," said Sam. "Several people recommended it."

When it was a part of the GDR, Prenzlauer Berg was a workers' district, but now it is *the* place go to in the new reunified Berlin for a dose of old East Berlin *Ostalgia*. Since I had never been there with or without Ilse, I was hoping for a ghost-free morning. I would be OK, as long as Sam didn't talk about her mother. We all have our own personal ghosts, but I seem to have more than most, which is why I seem to keep running into them everywhere.

"I checked the website," she said. "We take the U-2 U-Bahn line to Senefelderplatz. It's an easy walk from there, only 453 meters."

Modern technology is great. I remember doing the same kind of planning to fill a dead drop with TOP SECRET black and white overhead photos and a wooden ruler. Now you just call up a color satellite shot on your computer, and a program calculates the walking distance between two clicks on the screen. For Sam, this wasn't progress. It was just the way things were.

The last stop before Senefelderplatz was Rosa Luxemburg Platz.

"Rosa Luxemburg Platz?" asked Sam as we pulled into the bright yellow station, and the big name-sign caught her eye. "Is this where they have a garden of Luxembourg roses?"

"I don't even want to think about what they didn't teach you in that expensive college you went to," I replied. "A number of streets in the 'East' still bear the names of prominent Communists like Käthe Niederkircher, Karl Liebknecht and his partner in Socialist martyrdom, Rosa Luxemburg."

"A rose garden was a very logical conclusion," she retorted. "I'll have you know that the rose is the national flower of Luxembourg."

"No, I didn't know that." What else could I say? I didn't know.

"There are at least 234 Soupert & Notting registered rose cultivations," she added, taking intellectual coup. I knew better than to ask who Soupert & Notting were. It was a very good college. Political history, however, was not her major. Art was. She took after my mother.

It was a pleasant walk from the U-Bahn station to Bar Gagarin, along a street of five-floor walk ups. That was as high as they thought they could reasonably ask people to climb when they built them, somewhere around the turn of the last century. Five floors carrying a load of groceries in each arm is a long haul. I'd made it myself more than once. These days, they have to put in an elevator for the third floor, but they don't generally build them that low.

The décor of our brunch spot was retro nineteen-sixties GDR kitsch, anchored by a mural of the bar's namesake, his arms open wide to embrace the vastness of a stylized solar system revolving around a dirty-yellow sphere emblazoned with the name "Bar Gagarin." What attracted everyone's attention, well, Sam's at least, was the red star that had replaced the dot over the letter 'i,' "which is a not-so-subtle graphic comment drawn from the clichéd pallet of Soviet iconography," observed Sam. Like I said, she's an art major.

"You should go see the doors to the bathrooms," she said when she got back. The door to the Ladies' has a sketch that is a modern version of the Venus of Willendorf. I'd know her anywhere. She was in my *Art History 101* textbook. And inside, there's every toiletry you could think of."

I dutifully got up and went to look at the door to the Ladies'. That was the lady from Willendorf alright. I wasn't an art history major, but during that tour in Vienna, I'd been to the Natural History Museum where she lives more than a couple of times. It was a great spot for making a brush pass. Miss Willendorf was not my taste in ladies, but probably all the rage in pin-ups 24,000 years ago, give or take a few.

Unapologetic linguist that I am, what I noticed was that the signs on the doors were in three languages: German, English and Russian. The

Ladies' said "Frau, Woman, Хозяйка", and the Men's said "Man, Mann, Мистер." The Russian was clearly in honor of Gagarin, but it had been done by someone whose knowledge of Russian was limited to the alphabet and a cheap dictionary. Translated, the Russian read "Lady of the House," and "Mister." At first, I though this was strange in a part of Germany where Russian was an obligatory part of the school curriculum, but then I realized that hadn't been the case for over twenty years. None of the wait staff looked old enough to have gone to school under the old system.

Come to think of it, the German on the door was a little strange, too. Normally the Germans mark these doors with the letters 'D' and 'H,' which stand for "Damen," and "Herren." When I was in the army in Berlin, we used to play tricks on the newks, telling them that 'Damen' stood for "The Men," and "Herren" was "Hers plural." More than a few of those poor naive souls actually went in the wrong toilet to screams of laughter from us old-timers on the outside, and screams of outrage from the ladies on the inside. After that, they weren't so trusting any more, which, in general, was a good thing.

I decided not to go into the "Frau, Woman, Хозяйка" to see what the toiletries were like. In the "Man, Mann, Мистер," however, they had everything from razors, to aftershave, to toothbrushes. I hadn't eaten yet, so I didn't need a toothbrush, and it was too early for my five-o'clock shadow to be noticeable, so I left.

Before I got back to the table, Sam's voice climbed out of the incomprehensible swirl of voices mixed with the clatter of dishes to attract my attention. I could understand her as clearly as if she were standing next to me, and not across the room at the buffet. She had played a bit of summer stock, and knew how to project for the cheap seats in the back of the house. It was her way of alerting me that she might need a back-up.

"You clumsy oaf!" she said, with the staccato, precise enunciation that she reserved for lower life forms, which occasionally included me. Her mother talks like that too, especially when talking to me.

I turned toward the buffet just in time to see the plate of eggs and bacon that Professor Johnson had plastered on the front of her embroidered Belgian blouse slide down her plain cotton skirt to land on the floor and bounce like any good plastic dish should.

I quickly scanned the room, looking for Ilse. I didn't see her in the dining room, but she could have been at a table outside, or in the 'Ladies'. A waiter and I seemed to be the only ones in the place who took any notice of what was going on. He picked up a broom and dustpan, and sauntered over to the spill as if this kind of thing happened all the time.

I couldn't hear what Professor Johnson was saying, but he looked extremely apologetic. He extended a hand with a napkin in it to help her wipe off the front of her blouse, but he was brought up short by Sam's staccato delivery of "What do you think you're doing?" If he had touched her, she wouldn't have said anything, and he would have been of the floor, sporting a black eye. She packed a punch and a half. I taught her that. It didn't look like she needed any back-up on this one.

Sam's part over, this vignette continued as a silent movie with Professor Johnson reaching into his shirt pocket to pull out a business card. She raised her hand to take the card, and he bowed low to kiss her hand. I'd have to remember that trick. She didn't slug him.

Professor Johnson picked up an empty plate and handed it to her, signaling that she should precede him making the rounds of the buffet. He got himself a plate and followed her through the line. I could not see any signs of interaction. She kept her back to him, and he wisely kept his distance. At the end of the buffet table, she headed back for our table, and he walked over to a table set for one on the other side of the room. At least that meant that Ilse wasn't here, about to pounce on me when I wasn't looking.

"Did you see that clumsy oaf?" Sam said as she came back to the table. "He just turned right around without any warning, and walked into me."

I uttered a noncommittal sound. I knew that she didn't want me to interrupt her monologue. She takes after her mother that way.

"I'll never be able to get this blouse clean, and my skirt is ruined."

"Just tell him to buy you new ones," I said. "He's loaded. He has a chauffer-driven Mercedes."

"You can tell that just by looking at this bum across the room. He has faded jeans with a hole in the knee, and a shirt with frayed cuffs. I knew you were a good spy, but this borders on the paranormal."

"But he has an embossed business card with a gilt edge," I said to throw her off the track.

"How could you possibly know that?" she asked. "I haven't shown you his card," she added, putting on that bemused, insincere suggestion of a smile that she reserved for me when she knew I wasn't telling her everything 'for operational reasons.' I didn't need the look to tell me what she was thinking. The minute she calls me 'a spy,' I know that she's got her spook-detection radar set on high.

"Actually, I know him. He's the head of the Stasi Archives where I'm doing my research, and I've ridden in his Mercedes," I said, neglecting to mention that it was on the way to the hospital.

She pulled out Johnson's business card and read it:

HERR PROFESSOR DR.
WERNER M. JOHNSON

Bundesbeauftragte für die Stasi-Unterlagen
Federal Commissioner for the Stasi Archives

Her face switched to an amused, delighted smile that would fade the minute she noticed me paying attention to it. I got up and went to the buffet to get my own food so that I would miss the transition. I liked that smile.

'Werner' was Ilse's father's name. I wondered what the 'M' stood for.

I was trying to decide if I wanted to make a trip to the dessert bar, when I noticed Professor Johnson get up from his table and head our way. Sam hadn't seen him, and I pretended I didn't.

"Doctor Troyan," he said when he got into hailing range. "I hate to disturb you and your, er, 'niece'," he hesitated.

"My daughter Samantha, Professor Johnson," I interjected quickly, trying to keep him from putting his foot any further into his mouth.

His stern professorial mask slipped just for a second, revealing the hint of a smile. Sam noticed too. I'd taught her a few other tricks, besides how to punch a guy out.

"Professor Johnson," she said coldly.

"Werner, please," he corrected. He'd never said that to me. "May I call you Samantha?"

"Doctor Troyan will do," she said icily to pay him back for that 'niece' crack.

"My daughter's Ph.D. is in Art History," I explained.

"I'd never have guessed," he replied, recovering nicely. "You look much too young to have a Ph.D."

"My blouse and skirt are ruined," she countered with a glare, but I could tell she was pleased with the compliment.

"Please allow me to replace them," he parried. "I know an exclusive boutique with that kind of Belgian embroidery, not far from where I work. They are closed today, but I could pick you up tomorrow for lunch and we could go there afterward."

"Why don't I come in to your office tomorrow with my father?" she offered. The "Belgian lace" remark had scored a blitz smile.

"Certainly. If you come in at about 11:00, I can give you a tour of the Archives, and we can have lunch at, say, 12:00?"

"Someplace without wearable food," she quipped. Her eyes sparkled ever so slightly, belying her frown.

"I know just the place. Berlin's finest cuisine, served on a paper plate, and you only wear it, if you're a sloppy eater."

"A currywurst place?"

"A true Berlin delicacy," he said. "It's as typical for Berlin as baked beans are for Boston, pizza for Chicago, or Beignets for New Orleans. Culturally, it's very proletarian. It's the snack of choice for countless police inspectors in German whodunits. When German politicians want to look like the average German on the street, they do a photo-op at a currywurst stand."

"It's a date," she smiled. It was a real smile. I was going to have to keep an eye on this guy.

Good Morning, Frau Doktor

We arrived at the Archives stylishly late, around elevenish, rather than case-officer punctual at 11:00. Gunner Asch had obviously not only been well briefed, but was alert. I saw him pick up the telephone to report our arrival when we were still 50 feet out.

"Good morning, Frau Doktor," he said, ignoring me. "We've been expecting you. Fräulein Freitag will be right out to collect you."

Sam gave me a quizzical look, so I translated, but when I got to the part about 'Fräulein Freitag,' I said "Doctor Johnson's secretary."

I opened my briefcase and took out the rose that had become a part of the routine of going to the Archives. The exchange of rose for badge came off just seconds before Elisabeth Freitag bounced out of the building, heading our way.

"That's Werner's secretary?" said Sam.

"Yes, but she has her sights set on someone else. Watch."

Elisabeth opened the door and began gushing a warm welcome in German. I cut her off mid-word. "My daughter doesn't speak German."

Elisabeth didn't miss a beat, and started over in English.

"We've been expecting you, Doktor Troyan. Professor Johnson said to bring you to his office the *minute* you arrived."

Turning to Gunner Asch, she said: "Why doesn't Frau Doktor Troyan have a badge yet, Herbert?"

"You have to sign for her," he replied, handing her the clipboard with the sign-in sheet and a rose where the pen would normally go.

While Sam was taking in this vignette with feigned disinterest, I leaned over and whispered in her ear: "Don't tell her where the rose came from. You'll blow my op."

I was rewarded with a sardonic look I'd seen often enough before to know that my 'secret' was safe, but that there would be an interrogation later to pay for it.

Sam and Elisabeth disappeared in the direction of the upper reaches of the Archives' bureaucracy, and I withdrew discreetly to the hushed confines of the Archives' reading room. Frau Asch was already waiting for me at my usual table. Her pleated skirt was a good color match for the blue-buff folder in her hand. It was good, because the color of the folder said that it contained a reconstruct. The blue skirt didn't really do anything for her. Her color was red.

"Your daughter looks very lovely, Herr Doktor," she said, as she placed the folder on the table in front of me.

I wasn't even going to try to figure out how she knew that. It was more than clear that the Stasi Archives had information distribution honed to a fine art. I focused on the reconstruct instead.

MUSIK reports that on the recent visit of Air Force General (4-star) Lloyd to the Teufelsberg facility, specialist William Hoffmann stole the general's rank insignia from his uniform. Case officer comment: this is hardly sufficient for a blackmail approach, especially since …

These things always broke off just when they were getting interesting, but as with any TRASHINT project, you took what you could get when you could get it.

Everybody at the working level knew, and some of the people at the "call me Sir" level suspected that Slick Willie was the one who made off with the general's stars. What was missing from MUSIK's report was the fact that the general had been a good sport about their disappearance.

"Don't worry about it, colonel," said the general according to the version I heard on the Swing that night. "Happens all the time. My aid has a supply of spares in his briefcase."

That had been a part of the story of the general's stars that I told to Ilse, and if she had been MUSIK, that would have been in the *Report of Meeting* too. I started to cross Ilse off my list, but stopped as the idea flitted across my brain that the missing part of the 'case officer comment' could have been "the general was a good sport about it." I wanted something a lot more substantial to cross Ilse off my list.

"I remember the incident, and I remember Hoffmann," I said to Frau Asch, "but it does not tell me who MUSIK is. It does say that it cannot be Slick Willie, because the report is about him."

"Slick Willie?" asked Frau Asch.

"Yes, that was Hoffmann's nickname. Last I heard, he was teaching law at one of the Ivies."

"Thank you, Herr Doktor," she said, as she made a note on the reconstruct. "I'll check the nickname."

She found me about ten minutes later in the snack bar, washing down a *Berliner with a diet coke.

"There is a card for 'Slick Willie,' Herr Doktor," she said without preamble. "It lists him as one of the founders of the subversive, anti-army organization 'WGAF.' The source given is a file number, but it is in one of the number series that was confirmed destroyed."

This shower of words caught me mid-bite. As I shifted from concentrating on my Berliner to concentrating on her words, a glob of jelly plopped onto the table.

"I haven't heard, or thought about 'WGAF' since I left Berlin," I said, when I quit chewing and swallowed. "It was an abbreviation for "Who Gives a Fuck?". You mostly saw it scrawled across notices about shoe shines, haircuts, and instructions to clean up the office that were left in the Pass-on Book. I also recall having seen it a time or two in the latrine. It was certainly 'subversive,' and obviously 'anti-army,' but I'd never thought of it as an *organization*," I said to Frau Asch, as I wiped up the glob of jelly. "Somebody's paranoia must have been in overdrive to call 'WGAF' an 'organization.' Can I get you a cup of coffee? A Berliner?"

"Yes, thank you, Herr Doktor," she said, pulling up a chair.

That was a surprise.

"Cream? Sugar?" I asked.

"Two creams, one sugar," she replied.

I got up to get her a coffee and doughnut, which gave me a chance to think about what was going on. The "Herr Doktor" in her reply made it clear that this had nothing to do with my boyish charm. I'd been finessed by experts, and while this was not the smoothest approach I'd ever been subjected to, it was not shabby. Frau Asch's father had taught her very well indeed.

"I'm sure, Herr Doktor," she said, when I returned, "that you realize I've been more than forthcoming with information for your project."

"Yes."

"And as my father always says, 'for every tit, there is a tat'."

"Yes."

"Elisabeth and I want to know how your daughter met Professor Johnson."

"And where he's taking her for lunch today?" I replied in agreement, now that I understood the motive, and recognized the opportunity this gave me to access other information, both on MUSIK, and on Sam.

"How insightful of you, Herr Doktor," said Frau Asch.

I told her all about Bar Gagarin, and promised a follow-up report about lunch the next time I came in.

"Where did he take you?" I asked Sam when she sailed in with a pyramid of packages. We were well past the accusations of GESTAPO interrogations that teenage daughters level at their fathers when they get asked this question. I'd convinced her that I really was interested, and not just out to ruin her life.

"To a place called Konnopke's," she replied. "It's just two U-Bahn stops further than Bar Gagarin. It's some kind of East-Berlin chic that's been there since the nineteen-thirties. Apparently it survived Hitler, the bombing, the occupation, and the Communists."

I was going to ask if the currywurst was any good, but I couldn't get a word in edgewise.

"It's under the tracks for the U-Bahn," she continued. "Isn't that an oxymoron? Elevated tracks for the U-Bahn. You said the 'U' in U-Bahn meant 'underground'."

"Yes, that's right, but this is Berlin," I said. "Everything about Berlin is unique."

"So I suppose that Berlin pigs have been known to fly?" retorted Sam.

"And oafs have been known to be quite charming," I parried.

She put on her polite, cultured, Ph.D. mask. For normal people polite masks are relatively effective, but in my case, they have holes in them, where the eyes look out. When you know what to look for they make the rest of the mask as useless as a cell phone with a dead battery. The eyes behind the mask told me I'd struck a nerve.

"How were the eats?" I said, changing the subject in the hope of turning off the mask.

"Simply scrumptious," she replied, the mask shifting into a real face again. "You should go there. You're always going on about currywurst in Berlin. This was much better than the one you had me try."

Being able to deliver a riposte about currywurst gave her face a chance to save itself.

"I'll have to do that," I replied, much relieved to have avoided a confrontation by ignoring the fact that *she* was the one who took *me* to *Curry 36*. "What else did you do?"

"He took me to this perfumery called 'Frau something or other.' It's somewhere in the wilds of East Berlin. I'd never be able to find it again," said Sam.

It wasn't hard to believe she'd never find it again. She had a terrible sense of direction.

"A rather nebulous description," I said. "Got anything more substantial?"

"Here. Smell this," she said, holding out her left arm, wrist up. "This was Marlene Dietrich's favorite scent."

I took her hand, and the mesmeric smell of violets caressed my nose. I lamented the fact that *A Foreign Affair* hadn't been done in smell-o-vision. Marlene, Berlin, and a little espionage were irresistibility cubed. That smell would have taken it to the fourth power. All those years on the job, and nothing like that ever happened to me, but even a case officer can dream, can't he?

"You picked the right one for me. You know how big a Dietrich fan I am. What about Professor Johnson?"

"Werner? He liked it so much that he bought me a whole flacon," she said, opening up the small package that was at the top of her pyramid of boxes.

The label said "Reines Veilchen — Made in Berlin by Frau Tonis Parfum." The packaging said "exclusively expensive." I didn't say anything.

"Then we went to this really great boutique," she said, opening the next box in her stack of purchases, and pulling out a stylish blouse with lace trim that was clearly worth three of the one that had been ruined by an application of bacon and eggs.

I started to say "He's obviously got the budget to match your good taste," but a little warning voice put the brakes on my tongue. Instead, I said, "Very pretty," as she held it up for me to admire.

"And the skirt," she said, opening the bottom box in her stack, "is simply gorgeous."

"Quite an ensemble," I said, recalling a similar smile on Ilse's face during a much lower-budget shopping spree with me.

"He's really quite charming, once you get to know him," she said. "And his mother is very elegant. She helped pick it out."

"His mother was there?" I asked, trying to keep the surprise off my face, but not sure if I succeeded.

"Ilse? Yes, she's very nice," said Sam. "She speaks American English."

"How did he introduce you?" I said, trying to sound like this was not an interrogation.

"He said that I was the daughter of one of his researchers," she replied.

"No, I mean what name did he use for you when he introduced you?"

"He called me 'Samantha.' Is this some kind of spooky social dynamics analysis?" asked Sam.

"You could call it that. He didn't use your last name?" I persisted.

"No, and what's the significance of that?" she asked with lessening patience.

"He's smarter than the average bear," I said.

"How so?"

"See this scar on my cheek?" I asked, pointing to be sure she could find it under all the makeup.

"What does it have to do with Werner?" she demanded, her self-control slipping another notch.

"His mother put it there," I replied. "She won't tell him why, and I'm not going to explain it to him or to you until she talks to me."

"She won't talk to you?" said Sam, raising her voice to an unusual level for talking to me. I usually rated studied restraint, no matter how big an idiot she thought me to be. I had once explained to her that "it's the power and logic of your words, not the volume of your voice that has the most chance of convincing me you're right and I'm wrong." She'd taken this to heart, after actually having convinced me she was right a time or three or four.

"No."

"What kind of horrible things did you do to her?" asked Sam.

"And what makes you think they were 'horrible' things?" I responded, knowing that I wouldn't like the answer.

"Mother won't talk to you, and she told me about all the horrible things you did to her," answered Sam.

"But you still talk to me," I said, wondering how much longer that would be going on.

"You never did any 'horrible' things to me," she said. "You were always fun to be with. It was as if you planned everything we did together to be fun."

"Most of it I did. You've made more dead drops and more asset meets than some of the junior officers at the Station here in Berlin. Those were all carefully planned."

"And I just thought we were having fun," pouted Sam.

"That was a part of the plan. An old case officer I used to work with once told me that if your mother had been one of my cases instead of my wife, we'd have gotten along much better. I know how to deal with a case. I always get into trouble with real people."

"So, all I am is a case to be run," said Sam, her face growing more clouded.

"No, you're much more than that. I learned my lesson with your mother. I treated her like a real person, but I treat you like a case, because the case-officer me is a much nicer person than the real me."

"I don't know whether to be flattered or insulted," said Sam.

"You should be flattered," I replied. "I don't do this for just anybody. Only for the people I love. It's a high-energy effort."

"And why didn't you do this for mother?"

"Because I didn't learn this cosmic truth until it was too late for us."

Marlene Dietrich Square
Berlin, Tiergarten

Marlene Dietrich 1901-1992
A world-famous star of screen and song from Berlin
In recognition of her commitment to freedom and democracy
For Berlin and Germany

Fun, Travel, and Adventure

This morning, for a change of pace, when I got off at Magdalenenstraße U-Bahn Station, I turned right and headed for the distant exit. I thought it was about time to see the other half of Frankenstein's pictorial history of the German Workers' Movement in the Twentieth Century.

The whole station is decorated in an unearthly green. Even though the Berliners call the station "Frankenstein's Crypt," the *Frankenstein* they are talking about is not the character in Mary Shelley's novel, but rather Wolfgang Frankenstein, the German artist who moved East in 1953, while other sensible people were moving West. Mielke was a big fan of Frankenstein's, and had one of his oil paintings hanging in his conference room. The painting had been a gift on the occasion of the tenth anniversary of the construction of the Wall.

"Those aren't mosaics. They're just cheap brushwork on bathroom tiles," said my favorite art critic slash daughter the first time she saw them, and she hadn't been back to Magdalenenstraße with me since.

I couldn't blame her. Frankenstein's work was not what I'd call great art, but he had his *Ostalgic* supporters these days, just like Womacka, and he wasn't going anywhere anytime soon. Sam, on the other hand was going places, but she no longer needed to take the U-Bahn to Magdalenenstraße to get there. A chauffeured Mercedes came by the Academy for her.

"Good thing they're on the opposite side of the tracks from the traveling public," I said on our first day through, "or they'd be covered in graffiti."

Sam nodded appreciatively, but I knew she wasn't listening. She was taking pictures for the lecture she was planning to give when she got back off sabbatical.

"Berlin is too cool for its own good," I continued on the off chance that she really was listening. "Graffiti artists love Berlin, and Berlin loves them back. Much of the western side of the Wall was blanketed with graffiti, and graffiti-covered segments of the Wall can still be found here and there around town. The Allied Museum has a couple of nice ones."

"Um-hum," she said between shots.

"The city's skyline," I went on, encouraged by this indication that I was getting through, "may be defined by the architectural power of buildings like the TV tower on Alex, the ruin of the Kaiser Wilhelm Church, and the Brandenburg Gate, but its streetscape is largely molded by graffiti. Kreuzberg seems to have been the cradle of Berlin graffiti in the early nineteen-eighties. It was surrounded on three sides by the Berlin Wall, which offered miles and miles of blank wall to color, no numbers to follow, and little police scrutiny."

"There's police scrutiny here?"

"Yes, there is," I said, pointing to the cameras around the station. "That's why the east side of the wall remained a pristine and orderly gray. That, and the fact that getting close enough to paint the Wall's east side meant entering the death strip, a bit higher price than most graffiti artists are willing to pay for the sake of their art."

"I guess that is a lot to ask just for art's sake."

"All that changed when the Wall fell in 1989. Vast new vistas of blank Wall face opened up virtually overnight. As young people flooded East Berlin, taking the center of youth culture from West to East, the drab, pockmarked walls of East-Berlin neighborhoods like Mitte, Friedrichshain, and Prenzlauer Berg were soon festooned with colorful spray-paint squiggles. There were slogans ranging from '1984 is now,' and 'Are you really free?' to 'The wild, wild East,' and 'Capitalism is the name of the crisis.' Some of it was art."

"Good art," said Sam. "Good enough art to get written up in *The New York Times*, if that is any measure of success. There was this long article about Berlin's graffiti."

"Some of it, however, was a waste of space and paint, typified by a poster I'd seen plastered over several graffiti-smeared walls:

```
I would have preferred a blank wall rather than
        this great piece of shit."
```

"You'll have to show me one of those," she said.

"Next time we're in Kreuzberg."

Turning right instead of left only added five minutes to my walk to the Archives, but it was enough that Frau Asch was waiting at my usual table when I came in. I'd given up trying to figure out how she did it, but she could come to work on my team any time, that was if I ever had a team again.

"Your name is not on this fragment, Herr Doktor," she said, "but you are the only identifiable person correlated to MUSIK. Tit for tat."

She placed a reconstruct of the lower quarter of a "Meeting Report" form on the table in front of me. It had been put together from about 40 pieces.

```
Photo Analysis requested case officer to inquire if
MUSIK could elucidate on the significance of the
letters 'FTA' that are clearly visible in night-
time imaging of the central antenna tower at Object
115. MUSIK replied without hesitation that 'FTA' is
an abbreviation for an anti-army slogan that
contains a profanity. MUSIK said that to MUSIK's
certain knowledge the 'FTA' had been applied to the
skin of the antenna enclosure by John …
```

Wouldn't you know it? Just when it was getting interesting, the report was continued on the next page, and there wasn't a next page.

"Was there a photo in the same bag with this fragment?"

Like a magician pulling a rabbit out of a hat, Frau Asch produced half a photo, pieced together from about 25 pieces, and put it on the table.

"The annotation on the back says that this is 'Object 115'," she added.

"No doubt about what that is," I replied. "Teufelsberg at night."

The photo was a close-up of the top tier of the central tower, just below the radome with the 30-foot dish. Scrubbed into the dust on the inside of the enclosure skin was a huge FTA. It would have only been visible at night, when the lights inside the enclosure were on. They were spaced around the edge of the enclosure at regular intervals pointing out to keep the big dishes from casting a shadow that would tell the Russians and *East Herms which way the antennas were pointing.

"I can't remember his last name," I said, "but I do remember John."

"If you do remember, Doktor Troyan ...," she said, and disappeared together with the reconstruct and the photo on those silent feet of hers.

There had been plenty of claimants to the title of author of the huge FTA on the antenna enclosure skin, but none of them seemed credible.

"You're just trying to fish us into buying you beer," said Slick Willie, when Dangerous Dan tried to lay claim to the title.

"It was worth a shot," said Dan. "You got any idea who really did it?"

Even if I could have identified the mysterious FTA artist, it wouldn't have given me the leverage I needed to recruit him. They might have busted him a grade for it, but he wouldn't have had to pay for another beer for the rest of his tour. I knew plenty of people who would have been willing to make that trade-off.

The name that I most associated with FTA was John. If John wasn't the one who had carved out the FTA in the dust on the enclosure skin, he'd have been the first in line to buy a beer for the guy who did. John was always extremely flush with cash. That would raise his profile for any good case officer, but I suspected that he made his money openly, rather than surreptitiously. He was a wheeler-dealer from Idaho of all places. He'd found a shop in town that made cloisonné pins cheap. He ordered a gross of FTA pins.

They sold like hotcakes on Swings and Mids. He couldn't sell them on Days. There were too many *day-weenies around who didn't appreciate the joke. Maybe he wasn't earning as much as he'd have gotten from selling secrets to the Stasi or the KGB, but he was as rich as Croesus compared to normal *SP-4's. He charged six dollars apiece for the pins, and I'd be surprised if he was paying more than four marks—about a buck—for them.

The story of Lieutenant Dunbar confronting John in the Pit about the FTA pins he was selling spread through the Field Station like wildfire.

"Soldier," said the lieutenant, "selling those 'Fuck The Army' pins is nothing short of seditious. I'm going to bring you up before the colonel for a court martial."

"Beggin' your pardon, Sir. I don't understand, Sir," said John, cool as a cucumber.

"The pins with 'FTA' on them, soldier," said the lieutenant, raising his voice to match the climbing level of his blood pressure.

"Oh those pins, Sir," said John, his face aglow with blissful innocence. "I'm afraid there's been some misunderstanding, Sir. 'FTA' means 'Flying To America.' It's a short-timer's pin for those about to rotate back to the States."

"You can't possibly expect me to believe that, Smith," screamed the lieutenant.

"Why not, Sir?" continued John calmly. "I've never heard the lieutenant's expansion of 'FTA' before. I couldn't even bring myself to say the first word in the lieutenant's expansion out loud. My mother would never approve."

Lieutenant Dunbar opened his mouth to say something, but no words came out. He executed a by-the-book about-face, and marched out of the Pit.

"The guys in the Pit were busting a gut, trying to keep from laughing out loud," said Harry, who was relating the story to a bunch of us at the Swing meal on the day this confrontation took place. His listeners, on the other hand—including me—let loose an appreciatively vocal roar of laughter. John used more swear words than most of us put together, when he wasn't talking to lieutenants, or his mother, that is. He could get four curse words in a seven-word sentence.

I crossed John off my list. Anybody who could fart off Dunbar that calmly would have no trouble farting off a simple blackmail approach.

FTA was a state of mind. You could see reflections of FTA every-where you looked. It was the reaction to our "alleged" leaders who thought that polished shoes, razor-sharp creases in your fatigues, and short hair, or my personal favorite, Character Guidance by the Chaplain at 10 in the morning after a Mid, were more important than the mission.

The impulse to exhibit some FTA behavior could usually be traced to being told to drop the operational task you were working on, and clean the position, the latrine, or the all-time, site-wide favorite, collect and clean all the headsets.

"Yes, that's right. All of them at once," said Lieutenant Dunbar, when questioned about his order by the Pit Boss. "And I want to see my face in them!"

The only logical interpretation for being given an order like that was that the person who gave the order didn't care that the intelligence you should have been collecting would puddle up on the floor and evaporate. That seemed *criminal* to us. A clean position didn't make it any more efficient, but shutting it down to clean it certainly did make it less efficient.

As soon as the person who gave the order was out of earshot, the person who received the order generally intoned the FTA motto: "Screw the mission, and clean the position!" I must have heard it, or said it myself, a couple of thousand times while I was in Berlin.

On the other hand, cash is a motive I can trust, and anybody as entrepreneurial, read greedy, as John might have been up for a few dishonest dollars. I was about to put him back on my list, when I realized that anybody MUSIK was reporting on couldn't have been MUSIK.

Ostalgia

Sam's plans for the day called for a visit to Boxhagener Platz. It's home to a weekly flea market on Sunday, and that was today. She had heard that 'Boxi' was a good place to go for cheap GDR kitsch to take home for presents. I hoped that she wouldn't ask me to help her pick out something for her mother.

Her sightseeing list was beginning to give me the impression that Berlin's center of social gravity had moved East lock, stock, and barrel, but that was just me. Sam didn't have any sense of East or West. To her, it was all Berlin. I'd have to take her to look at the Wall, if I could find some. Potsdamerplatz and Checkpoint Charlie had a few wall segments sprinkled about and a double row of paving blocks to show where the Wall used to be, but I wanted something a bit more imposing. Maybe the Berlin Wall Memorial over on Bernauer Straße, near Nordbahnhof?

The overflowing market was packed with great people-watching opportunities. There were bohemian students shopping for vintage sunglasses, and respectable mothers looking for unusual crockery. A young couple—obviously tourists—was looking through a bowl full of "genuine" pieces of the Wall. An old couple—obviously locals—was shopping for chairs at a stand that had enough chairs to equip a small theater; no two of them alike.

Sam stopped to rummage around in a tin box full of "worthless" GDR coins that had prices much higher now than their face value ever had been.

"I've got some of those at home," I said. "A souvenir of Prague."

"Of Prague?" she said. "But these are East German."

"Yes, of Prague." I replied, trying not to sound too patronizing. "I was in Prague when the East Germans figured out that if they could get into a West German Embassy, they would be let out to the West. The West German Embassy was just up the street from ours. I got called in to report on what was going on, and had to park on the street, because, at the time, I didn't rate a parking space on the compound. A veritable deluge of East Germans soon overflowed the German Embassy grounds and poured out into the street. By the time I got my report written, the street was so flooded I couldn't get out the door, let alone move my car. I stayed inside, and slept on the floor.

The next morning, after the busses had taken all the East Germans away to a new life in the West, I went out to the car. It hadn't been damaged at all, and there was a note on it that said, 'Thanks for letting us sleep on your car. We won't need these anymore, but maybe you can use them.' On top of the note was a pile of East German coins."

She bought five of the overpriced coins anyway. "These are for people at work," she explained. "I'll tell them your story, and say they came from you, not the flea market, when I hand them out."

"Not a bad idea," I said. "Coins with a story are better than without, even if the story and the coins don't come from the same place."

She smiled a woman's smile, one of those enigmatic expressions that only women can pull off.

About three stalls further down, Sam stopped to point at a faded print in a battered wooden frame. "Shouldn't I know the man in the picture?" she asked.

"Yes, you should," I chided. "That's Mikhail Sergeyevich Gorbachev, the man who let the Wall fall."

"Give me a break," she said. "It's a mug shot, not art."

"You're right. It's not art," I said. "It's a cheap print run off by the thousands."

"Exactly my point."

"It's ironic," I smiled. "Way back when, he was the man of the hour. Now he's a cheap historical artifact that my daughter the artist doesn't recognize."

"I refuse to let you insult my intelligence like that," she quipped. "Let's ask the guy running the stall."

"Excuse me," she said, waving to the twenties-something guy in dirty jeans and a torn sweatshirt on the other side of the table from us. "Who's that in this portrait here on the ground?"

"Some commie big wig," he said. "Egon Krenz?"

"You get my point?," said Sam.

"Yes, I get it, but that doesn't mean I have to like it."

"The frame's good," said the torn sweatshirt. "A steal at ten Euro."

"No, thanks," said Sam, as we moved on. "We were looking for Gorbachev."

"Sorry," said the sweatshirt. "Good luck finding him."

About four stands further along, I saw an old gray plastic, rotary-dial phone, and went over to pick it up. The bottom was stamped "VEB Fernmeldewerk Nordhausen." That was hardly a surprise. If you had seen one East German-made phone, you'd seen one from Nordhausen. The model number stamped under that, however, made my mouth fall open.

"Close your mouth please, Michael, we are not a codfish," said Sam. I'd always said that to her when she got that open-mouthed surprised look as a kid, and now I was being hoist on my own cliché.

"Fifty Euro," said the girl in faded designer jeans whose tight sweater proclaimed "Wir sind das Volk,"* the slogan with which the East Germans shouted down the Wall in 1989. She was clearly an up-and-coming young capitalist who was going to sell most of the items on her stand today.

"Why so much?" asked Sam who had inherited my paranoia.

"Because it belonged to the great East German novelist Romaine Schreiber," replied the girl.

"And you have a provenance?" countered Sam, putting on her art curator's hat.

---

* We are the People.

"Better than that," said the girl. "I have my grandmother right here. Just a second, she's signing a book." Turning around, she called, *"Omi!"

"And I'm just supposed to take your word for it that she is this novelist whatshername?" said Sam, shifting her professional skepticism into overdrive.

"No, you can take my word for it," I said, cutting her off in mid-frown.

"Frau Schreiber," I said, bowing to kiss her hand.

"Herr Doktor Troyan," she gushed. "The gentleman who has read all my novels. What a surprise."

Now it was Sam's turn to be a codfish.

"Your granddaughter was just telling us that this used to be your telephone," I said.

"Yes. We were cleaning out the attic, and I decided to get rid of it. *Ostalgia* may be popular with the young people, but I would just as soon forget," said Frau Schreiber.

"Yes," I replied. "Some things are better forgotten."

We exchanged a few more pleasantries, but we didn't buy the phone. Sam did, however, buy a copy of one of her novels in English, signed, of course. She would probably read her copy before I read mine.

After we got about five stalls away, Sam asked, "Are you going to tell me what's amazing enough about that piece of junk to turn you into a codfish? Or is this one of those spooky things that I don't have a need to know for?"

"Private phones were few and far between in the GDR. Offices would have a phone, but you wouldn't have a phone at home, unless you were somebody with a capital 'S,' as in SED or Stasi. Normal people didn't have phones at home, unless the Stasi wanted to keep tabs on them," I explained.

"In other words, they gave her a phone so they could tap it?"

"It's a little more Machiavellian than that," I continued. "That was an 'alpha' AB45-00100. The standard 'alpha' series model was the N45-00100. The designation 'AB' instead of 'N' in the model number indicates that this was an *Abhörtelefon*—a bugged phone. The microphone remains connected to the subscriber line even when the handset is on-hook. That way the Stasi could 'bug' any room that had a model 'AB' phone in it without having to enter the room and install something. All they had to do was plug in a tape recorder at the central switch."

"You mean that they were bugging her house?" exclaimed Sam.

"Yes. Without a doubt," I replied calmly.

"We should go back and tell her," said Sam, pulling on my arm.

"I think not," I replied, holding my ground. "She said she wanted to forget, and it's easier to forget something you never knew."

We were heading into clothing territory now. There was a school of shoppers swimming in a sea of leather jackets. A gaggle of young ladies— and I use the term loosely—was picking through an assortment of designer clothes that probably fell off the back of a truck last week.

A naked mannequin was peeking out from between two racks of dresses on hangers. That was evidently to attract the male escorts of the women shoppers so they would bring their wives, daughters, girlfriends, and "nieces" over to look at the merchandise. It was obviously a successful sales technique; I was headed that way.

A dress on the end of a rack had caught Sam's eye. It was a classic cotton, flowered print, in rather good shape for a flea-market dress. She held it up in front of her by the hanger, and looked in the mirror that was hung on the end of a rack with a skirt hanger clipped onto its green plastic frame. The lady who ran the stall obviously understood what her female customers wanted.

"What do you think?" asked Sam, turning around so I could get the full effect.

"You're asking the wrong person," I said, with a forced smile. It looked exactly like a dress that I had bought for Ilse. So much for our ghost-free visit to a flea market that didn't exist when I knew Ilse. It had been gorgeous on Ilse. "Your father's not the one to ask if you look alluring."

"You can ask me," said Werner Johnson's voice from somewhere behind me.

"Well, do I?" she asked.

"Look alluring?" he said. "Yes, very much so. You should buy it."

From the look on Sam's face, I could tell that I would be having lunch on my own. I was going to have to talk with Ilse about them.

Lefty

They politely invited me to accompany them to lunch. "I know this place that does a really great quiche," said Werner. Two's company, but three's a crowd, especially when one of them is the girl's father.

"I like a good quiche as much as the next guy," I said, hoping that it sounded sincere, "but when I'm in Berlin, I'm a slave to a craving for currywurst and potato salad. I spotted a currywurst stand on the way in, and have my mouth set on it."

I turned around and headed back into the junk section of the market, while Sam and Werner went out through the clothes section in search of trendier climes.

Walking back down the row between the stalls gave me a different perspective on things, and I saw a bunch of good junk that I'd missed the first time through. There was a nice tea service with the MITROPA logo that identified it as being from an East German railroad dining car. Back then, the logo was what kept it from being stolen. Now, it was what pushed the price up. A bit further along, I found a DVD of *Unser Sandmännchen, Our Sandman*. It was the GDR's answer to the West German TV kids' program *Das Sandmännchen, The Sandman*. I bought myself a copy. They did great kids' programs all over the eastern side of the Iron Curtain. In Czechland, Sam gave me an excuse to watch *Večerníček* to treat my inner kid.

The next thing that caught my eye was an old, beat-up seed spreader. This, however, wasn't a case of *Ostalgia*. Seeing the seed spreader reminded me of Lefty, and put him on my list of suspects for the title of MUSIK. He could have known all that information the Stasi had in my file. He was a Russian scribe in TREADMILL. His room was just down the hall from mine. I bumped into him all the time on the Hill, in the mess hall, and at the PX.

He wasn't called "Lefty" because he was left-handed, but because he was always quoting Marx and Lenin; first in Russian, then in German, and finally in English for those who spoke neither. I would have been after him with my case-officer hat on, but not for his political leanings. Headquarters was always pushing for politicals, but his behavior didn't have the ring of sincerity that I would have been looking for to make a straight politically motivated recruitment. The quotes were a teaser. There was nothing else in what he said and did to back them up. Headquarters could have screamed and jumped up and down all they wanted, but I wouldn't have made a political approach.

Statue of Marx and Engels
Marx-Engels-Forum, Berlin

No, my hook for Lefty would have been his FTA lawn, but I couldn't decide if a straight blackmail pitch or a chance for revenge would have worked better.

The FTA lawn was a feat of legend at the Field Station. It all started on a Wednesday. Lefty had just come down off a Mid, and the First Shirt grabbed him to do some gardening because Lefty foolishly decided to skip breakfast, and go straight to his room, so he could change and get downtown to his girlfriend faster. Skipping breakfast, however, took him past the Orderly Room at exactly the wrong moment: the moment in which the First Shirt decided that he needed a warm body to work on the lawn in preparation for the IG inspection the next day. If Lefty had gone to chow with the rest of us, the First Shirt would have known he had worked a Mid, and would have left him alone, but since Lefty was "wandering" through the company area in uniform when he should have been at chow, he was fair game as far as the First Shirt was concerned.

"Szczymanski," said the First Shirt, "just the man I was looking for."

That kind of greeting didn't bode well for this encounter, but Lefty was tired. "You were, sergeant?" he said naively. "Not about my promotion, sergeant, is it?"

"The IG is coming," said the First Shirt, ignoring Lefty's question. "I need someone to do some gardening. Get a lawn mower, and trim up the company lawn out front."

"I just came off a Mid, sergeant," replied Lefty.

"The Trick bus ain't down yet," replied the First Shirt. "I suppose my aunt Tilly drove you down."

Lefty didn't have a lot of options open to him. Punchin' out the First Shirt was not really a good idea. Beatin' feet was out; the First Shirt knew his name. Talkin' back was the same as volunteering for some even shittier detail, so Lefty wisely said, "Where do I get one?"

"From Supply," said the First Shirt.

In a unit that was full of Mensa candidates, good ideas are a dime a dozen. By the time Lefty got to the bottom of the stairs on the way to the supply room, he had an idea that bordered on genius.

"First Sergeant sent me," said Lefty to the Supply Sergeant, who didn't even know what Mensa is. "I need a lawn mower, a bag of grass seed, a bag of fertilizer, and a grass seed spreader."

The First Sergeant's word—even if it's not really his—is everyone's command, and five minutes later Lefty was on his way to the company lawn with his supplies. If Lefty had just done what the First Shirt had told him to do, life would have continued in its daily rut, and Lefty would have been one of those names I couldn't connect with a face. But he didn't, and life turned off the beaten path of uniform military order and discipline into the uncharted realm of chaotic individualism.

First off, Lefty mowed the company lawn. It wasn't that big, and he was done in under fifteen minutes. Then he mixed the fertilizer two to one with the grass seed in the seed spreader, and carefully walked off a six-foot-high FTA in the center of the company lawn, pushing the seed spreader in front of him.

The IG came and went. He was pleased. The grass was cut. The rocks that marked the edge of the lawn were a freshly painted white. The floor that led to the Orderly Room was so highly polished that you could see your reflection in it. The company's paperwork was in order. The dinner that the colonel had hosted for him had been superb. And he'd found a cuckoo clock to take home to his wife in Virginia.

Two weeks later, when the IG visit was but a faintly unpleasant memory, the First Sergeant noticed that the grass in the middle of the company lawn was greener and taller than the rest of the lawn. He just thought that the last grass-cutting detail had sloughed off the middle of the lawn, and ordered it cut again. That didn't help, but he didn't think any more about it, until he was doing a walk through inspection of the third floor with the Company Commander.

The First Sergeant heard a helicopter flying low overhead, and looked out the window to see if he could catch a glimpse of it. From the noise it was making, it was close by, but he couldn't see it. He figured it must be directly over the building. The noise was going to wake up the troops who had come down off the Mid, and there would be a lot of grumbling. He'd catch the brunt of it.

The rotor wash from the chopper had picked up a copy of the *Stars and Stripes* from somewhere, and it was fluttering around in front of the window. He would have to get someone out to pick it up, before the colonel noticed.

Much to his relief—and to the relief of the Trick that had come off Mids that morning—the helicopter soon flew off, taking its noise with it. The wind from the chopper died down, and the swirling sheets of the newspaper slowly settled down onto the company lawn. As he followed their leisurely descent to the grass below, the First Sergeant's gaze fell upon the six-foot-high verdant green letters FTA that were clearly perceptible from the height of the third floor, but invisible from his ground-floor office.

The First Sergeant had climbed to his august position by reason of the fact that he understood how things worked in the army. He did the math for helicopter overhead and FTA on the ground, which equals the general in charge of Berlin Brigade calling the colonel in charge of the Field Station in less than twenty minutes to complain about a seditious message in the grass in front of his company Orderly Room.

"Captain," said the First Sergeant to the Company Commander. "I think we should postpone the inspection to a later date, so that I can prevent a crisis that will hit here in about twenty minutes."

The Company Commander had no idea what he was talking about, but he had learned to trust the First Sergeant's sense of impending military disaster.

"Of course, First Sergeant," he said. "I'll be at ..."

"I hear that Harnack House is doing a particularly good lunch special today," said the First Shirt, who had absolutely no idea what the Officers' Club was serving for lunch that day.

"I think I'll go try that out," said the Company Commander.

Five minutes later, two guys who had been innocently walking past the Orderly Room on their way to the mess hall were turning over the company lawn with a tiller.

"Be sure to start in the middle," said the First Sergeant. When he said that, the two victims of being in the wrong place at the wrong time didn't need to ask why they were going to be late for lunch. The secret of the FTA lawn was out.

Those of us at the working level had known about the FTA lawn for over three weeks. The guys who lived in the third-floor rooms overlooking the FTA lawn earned themselves a bit of spending money, charging a quarter a head for a look out their windows; fifty cents if you wanted to take pictures.

Intelligence on the identity of the person responsible for the FTA lawn had taken a little bit longer to develop. Lefty hadn't bought his own beer in over two weeks.

"This one's on me, Lefty," said Fast Eddie, putting a bottle of Beck's on the table.

"No, it ain't. It's my turn to buy him a beer," said Charlie, setting down a Berliner Weiße.

"Thanks, guys," said Lefty, picking up the Beck's in his right hand and the Weiße in his left.

The SECRET of Lefty's authorship, however, was strictly limited to those deemed to have a true need to know, that is to say, all the enlisted men. For some strange reason, the officers and NCOs were not on the access list for this category of intelligence, and were never briefed on it.

By the time the general's irate call reached the colonel, there wasn't a blade of grass left to be seen. By the time the colonel and the Sergeant Major marched over to the Orderly Room to read the riot act and restore order, the only thing they could do was watch the paint drying on the signs at each edge of the company lawn that said:

Freshly Seeded
Keep Off!

"Must have been a trick of the light, sir," said the First Sergeant. "I can assure you, sir, that no such thing could ever happen in my company."

"Come on, Pat," said the Sergeant Major, when the colonel had left. "You can tell me."

"Tell you what, John?" replied the First Shirt with a straight face, though I can't imagine how he did it. He knew he was being double-teamed.

"Why you reseeded your lawn."

"Been on my to-do list for weeks," said the First Shirt. "Today was the first chance I've had to get around to it."

When the First Sergeant tried to find out who was responsible for the FTA lawn, he was met with a silence that would make a Mafia *omerta* look like a radio talk show.

I'd have done a blackmail approach. Even though the First Sergeant had "proved" to the colonel and Sergeant Major that there never was an FTA lawn, Lefty wouldn't have wanted the First Sergeant to learn that he was the one who planted it. The First Sergeant could make your life miserable all by himself.

Lefty went on to become a Congressman from a liberal state that shall remain nameless. He would have been quite a feather in the cap of the case officer who recruited him. I could have done it.

"Look what we found," said Sam, as she bounded in after her lunch date with Werner, holding up a white T-shirt overprinted with a color cartoon in the best tradition of a nine-panel Sunday comic strip.

Her use of "we" signaled a new stage in their relationship. I smiled innocently, and hoped that she mistook my reaction to "we" as interest in her T-shirt.

"I'm going to use it in my art seminar when I get back, as a part of the section on the GDR aesthetic," she gushed. "And I bought six in various sizes to take home for friends."

"I can see the potential," I replied.

"Werner explained it all to me," she continued. "The title is 'Ostalgia.' That's a pun, based on the German word for 'east.' It means a longing for the attractive features of what in retrospect seems a simpler way of life than the freedom of choice and challenges of Capitalism. It blends them into a sort of kitsch of the 'good old days,' leaving out the Stasi and the fact that people got shot trying to escape the country."

"I'd consider that a major drawback to life in the East, but it's not my shirt."

"The tag line says: 'Remembering the good old days of the GDR. Not everything was good, but a lot was better'."

"I know some people who might say that," I said, trying to hold up my end of the conversation.

"The guy with the beard is Karl Marx," she said, pointing to the familiar face near the top of the shirt.

"I always thought Groucho was funnier than Karl," I said, and, recalling our pointed discussion about Gorbachev, I didn't mention that I had seen his face more than a few times before. I decided that a little détente would go a long way. She is my daughter, after all, which means that she'd already had full portions of my snide wit.

"You can consider him the German poster child for Communism."

That line would go over well with her students.

"There was more time for love, says the first frame. That's why there's a couple kissing and a lot of hearts."

The girl's face reminded me of Ilse.

"The second frame says: 'There was good daycare for the kids'," Sam continued, pointing to where I should be looking.

That's good instructional technique.

"Werner explained that childcare was free, and it was easier for women to combine work and children. The third frame, the one with the guy on the ladder picking apples, handing them to the guy with a bucket on the ground, says: 'We still had friends and neighbors'."

„Them against us encourages that sort of thing," I thought to myself, so as not to interrupt her spiel.

"The fourth frame, with the guy carrying the wooden crate who looks like he's sleepwalking, says 'there was work and training for everybody'."

"When you present that one in class, you should tell the old joke about work in the GDR to explain why the guy looks like he's sleepwalking. It went: 'They pretend to pay us, and we pretend to work'." She frowned at my joke, but I figured she'd use it anyway.

"The fifth frame says: 'coffee and beer were 50 *Pfennigs*'. Werner couldn't say exactly how much that is in today's money, but said it was real cheap."

"That's one way to put it," I replied. "There were a hundred *Pfennigs* in a Mark. There were eight east marks to the west mark, which, in my day, was just under four west marks to the dollar. That makes fifty east *Pfennigs* about six west *Pfennigs*, or about four dollar cents."

"Those were the good old days," she said. "You can't get a cup of coffee around here these days for less than a Euro fifty."

"I've seen it a tad cheaper here and there," I said, "but it's still a long way from fifty east *Pfennigs*."

"The next frame, with a happy family and a car, says 'we enjoyed our darling car for a long time."

"You might recognize the car as a Trabi," I replied. "One of those rattle-traps from the outrageously kitschy "Trabi Safari" that you went on."

"Oh, yes, now that you mention it."

"They had to enjoy it for a long time. The waiting time for a Trabant was six years, and you had to pay the full price in advance when you placed your order."

"That must have cut down on traffic congestion."

"Oh, yes. It did," I answered. "Public transportation, on the other hand, worked and was cheap."

"The seventh frame with the naked couple says, 'Nudist beaches were no problem.' Werner said that the West Germans are more uptight about nudist beaches; less so than the Americans, but more than the East Germans."

"I'll bet your class will get a kick out of that one."

"The boys will probably be asking me to recommend some beaches in East Germany for Spring Break."

"You'd better prefix this lecture with a little political history to cut off that question," I said. It was scary to think that all her students had been born *after* the Fall of the Berlin Wall.

"The eighth frame with an old gentleman sitting on a park bench with his arm around his wife says 'retirements were secure'."

"They were peanuts in dollar terms," I said, "but they went a lot further than Social Security."

"Werner says that there is a piece of street graffiti on Potsdamerplatz that will help underscore this point when I give my lecture. He's taking me there to get pictures tomorrow."

The five *Werner*'s in the ten minutes since the 'we,' said that I was *really* going to have to keep an eye on this guy.

"The last frame with the happy couple chilling out at home says 'rents were reasonable.' Werner told me that you might have had to live with your parents for a few years after you were married before your name made it to the top of the waiting list for an apartment, but once you got it, you could afford it."

"So, this is what folks miss about East Germany according to Werner?"

"Really according to the artist, who Werner says is some famous playwright: André H. Büchner," replied Sam. "You can see his signature down here at the bottom."

„Good for him," I thought to myself. He'd taken my advice.

"Yeah, I know him," I said to Sam.

"Is there anybody you don't know?"

"A few people," I replied.

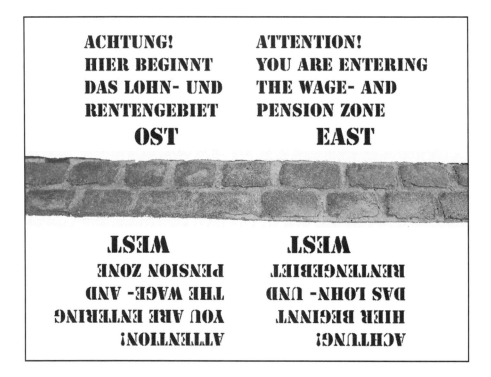

Potsdamerplatz (2013)
The double line of paving blocks marks the path of the Berlin Wall.

The Subscriber You Are Calling
Is Not Available

The growing attraction between Sam and Werner made it clear that a talk with Ilse was going to be necessary sooner rather than later. I had lost my excuse for not calling when the bandages came off, but had given in to the siren call of 'why do today what you can put off till tomorrow?' … especially when you know it's not going to be any fun.

I wrote out a couple of speeches to give, depending on how she reacted when she picked up the phone and realized it was me. I rehearsed in the mirror, polishing my delivery like an actor on opening night. I had the same butterflies I always did before an op.

„Curtain up," said a little voice in the inner recesses of my brain.

I dialed her number. The phone rang three times. I was speechless when she actually picked up.

"I don't know if you remember …" I started, but she cut me off.

"We Germans are good at forgetting. We conveniently forgot National Socialism and Hitler; forty years of Socialist Unity and Honecker; the Airlift and General Clay, but I haven't forgotten you. You bastard!"

I started the groveling apology that I had planned for just this kind of reaction, but the line was already dead.

It used to be that to express your anger with someone you were talking to over the phone, you could slam the handset down with a soul-satisfying bang. They made them to last in those days, and nothing would happen to the phone when you slammed it down. To get the same feeling of satisfaction these days, you need to throw your cell phone against the floor as hard as you can. This, however, not only terminates your call with extreme prejudice, but your cell phone as well. I suspected that was what Ilse had just done. I pressed "Redial".

"The subscriber you are calling is not available," said a disembodied female voice that was what passed for an operator in the digital age. The voice was as dead as Ilse's cell phone. There was no warmth or humanity behind it, and telling it my troubles wouldn't get me any sympathy or a date, so I pressed "End Call".

John Le Carré, the man who could find ambiguity everywhere, even where there wasn't any, would have been very happy with what was going on with me. My new life in Berlin had standing-room-only ambiguity. I know how to deal with ambiguity. Running a case is never black or white, but the system at Headquarters had degenerated into one that only can deal with clear-cut problems. Dealing with ambiguity requires autonomy, intelligence, and decisiveness, which Headquarters doesn't want you to have. When you confront a real-world problem full of the human variables, you've got to be able to fly by the seat of your pants. You have to be able to formulate a plan quickly, and then be able to step back to see if it's working, and make adjustments if it isn't.

It used to work the way Ian Fleming said, when he explained why an under-funded, under-staffed operation like MI-6 could beat the hyper-funded and hyper-equipped KGB. "The right man is better than the right machine." The more we studied the 'enemy,' the more we became like them, until Headquarters got to the point that it wanted things in the field run like a machine, just like the Sov's ran their ops.

Mediocre used not to be good enough, but it looks to be the standard now. The system used to work by rewarding prudent risk taking. Blowing an op would mean a lateral assignment to a *good housing post with a low profile, but that was not necessarily the end of your career. Getting promoted required some risk taking, and some adaptation; not just getting along and not rocking the boat.

The first DCI's didn't run the place for the benefit of the Headquarters staff. They believed that Headquarters was there to provide competent support to operations. As time went on, however, you saw more and more Headquarters officers rotated to a Station to get some field time, and then rotated out quickly before they were too inconvenienced by local conditions and the ambiguity of operations.

When these pseudo-field-officers got back to Headquarters, they thought they understood field operations better than real field officers, and usurped more and more control over field operations, until the field lost all its autonomy. Everything had to be approved in advance by Headquarters.

For this particular case, I didn't have to get Headquarters' approval, but I did need some professional help, because one of the first things you do when you make an ops plan is to identify the things you can and cannot do yourself. Never having been assigned to the Station in Berlin, I didn't know any of the local stringers. Going to the Station was equally out of the question.

The thought "local help" echoed in my cavernous skull, which was apparently empty of gray matter. Maybe it was a trick of my imagination, but one of the echoes seemed to say "goulash communism." I headed back to that greasy spoon on Alex, where you meet the occasional ex-spook.

Third time's the charm, as the saying goes. After having staked out the place on Tuesday and Wednesday, I made contact on Thursday.

"I need a professional for a personal job, Genosse," I said, knowing that I wouldn't have time to beat around the bush.

"Not another trial balloon for the Station?" he asked with a frown.

"No. This is personal. I need a pair of hands for an op I can't run myself," I said, sliding an envelope across the counter toward him.

He motioned to the waiter—cook—bottle washer—and probably owner, holding up two fingers. He looked in the envelope while two beers found their way to the counter in front of us. I paid for the beer, growing more cheerful. I was on my home court now. I knew he was short of funds, and that money would be the fastest way to 'yes.'

"Obviously a small job," he said, counting the money in the envelope.

"That's right. Something I can't do myself, because it would contaminate the DNA sample I need for a paternity test," I replied, looking him straight in the eyes, searching for a predictor for his reaction.

"Very personal indeed," he said, taking a sip of his beer.

"The targeting data and delivery instructions are in the envelope," I said, taking a sip of my beer.

"What do I have to sign?" he asked.

"Nothing. Like I said, it's a personal op."

"An equal payment on delivery?" he inquired.

"It's a pleasure doing business with a professional," I replied.

"The health of your children, Genosse," he said, with a wink, lifting his glass for a toast.

"And of yours, Genosse," I replied, clinking my glass against his.

We placed our two empty glasses on the bar, and I stood up.

"Next Thursday, I think," he said. "Fall-back is Monday."

"Good hunting," I said, as I headed for the S-Bahn that would take me back to the Academy. I knew he would follow me to confirm who I really was, so I didn't do anything to make it hard for him. He kept a discreet distance for a crowded train station, but didn't do anything to conceal that he was behind me. We both knew the drill for confidence-building measures.

We got off the S-Bahn at the Wannsee Station, and I headed straight for the Academy. I checked in with Mary-Kate, so that he would have someone to ask "Who was that gentleman you were just talking to?".

"These flowers were just delivered for Samantha. Can I give them to you?" she said, holding out a bouquet of roses.

I put the roses down on the counter, and pulled out the card.

It said: "I know they can't compare with your beauty, but they will have to do until something better comes along."

Werner had stolen my line!

"Why don't *you* keep them, and consider them a present from me?"

"You're wanting me to take roses that you shanghaied from another woman? That's asking an awful lot, Michael Troyan, and if you don't have an awful good reason, you'll be eatin' 'em."

Mistakes about a woman can never be corrected. I learned that the hard way, so I decided to tell her the truth.

"I have to put the brakes on this relationship for a week, while I try to get the answer to the question that Professor Johnson's mother won't respond to. The roses won't keep that long, so you might as well enjoy them. If I get the right answer, I'll replace the roses, and put the same card back on them. If not, eating a bunch of roses—thorns and all—will be a lot easier than what I'll have to tell Sam."

"A week is it? I'll just mark that down in me little book."

"Thanks. Could you just add 'Lunch with Michael' to that while you're writing?"

I had a prickly feeling of unease, as she paused, trying to make up her mind. Something sparkled in the depths of her eyes. Her right hand moved over her appointment book, and wrote: "Dinner with Michael."

"Dinner it is. And not a word to Sam," I said.

All I got in return was a wry smile.

I could sense that I had overstayed my welcome, so I made myself scarce, but not too scarce, because I wanted to watch what happened at her desk next.

I didn't have audio for this op, but I could imagine the way the conversation went:

My spook: "Who was that gentleman you were just talking to?"

Mary-Kate: "One of our Fellows. Doctor Troyan."

She pulled out a copy of the American Academy's house magazine, *The Berlin Journal*. Even from this distance, I could recognize the cover. It was the one with the article introducing the new batch of Fellows. There was a group photo, and an alphabetical list of short bios. That would give him enough information so that he could run some checks to confirm who I was. I'd have done the same thing. It's just good tradecraft.

Profuse *thank-you*'s, and a 'How do I get to the toilet?,' which is where he went next.

The delivery of the roses for Sam meant that things were moving faster than I had expected. I needed to talk to my contacts at the Archives to see if I could side-track things on that end as well. Back to the S-Bahn. This was not something I wanted to discuss on the phone.

Frau Asch, blue-buff folder in hand, emerged from the curtained door to the stacks before I made it to my usual table. Her red, pleated skirt was much more to my liking than the blue one that matched the color of the folder. It undulated with each silent step she took. She placed the folder in front of my briefcase without a word.

I flipped it open. There was a hand-penned note paper-clipped to the left side of the folder, and a reconstruct on the right. I read the note first.

Prof. J sent her a dozen roses this morning. He's never done that before.

I made a small annotation to the note:

Snack bar in 10.

I turned my attention to the reconstruct about MUSIK on the right side of the folder.

```
MUSIK reports that his prohibition on the use of
the elevator at object 115 continues to be
circumvented by the enlisted men. MUSIK reports
that when the posting of an NCO to control access
proved insufficient to keep the enlisted men from
using the elevator, he instituted a key-access
system. MUSIK reports that in less than 3 weeks
from the installation of the locking mechanism,
everyone at object 115 seemed to have a key. Case
officer comment: copy of the key was provided to
case officer …
```

„Gotcha!" said a little voice in my head. „Proof positive that it wasn't Ilse."

The mistake in the text of the reconstruct that told me it wasn't Ilse was very much out of character for the regular MUSIK case officer who could come up with six different synonyms for the verb 'reports.' The meet must have been set up on such short notice that the regular case officer couldn't make it, and they had to send somebody else to talk with MUSIK. Judging by the blunder in the report, it must have been an ops trainee. It couldn't have been a real case officer.

That was great news, but I had that feeling of uneasiness you get from half realizing you know something important, but not being able to bring it into focus. It would catch up with me eventually, but right now, there were other mysteries that I had to solve.

Ten minutes later, I was sitting in the snack bar with a diet coke, a cup of coffee and two Berliners in front of me. Frau Asch showed up on time, and sat down unobtrusively. I briefed her on their meeting at Boxi, and she smiled appreciatively.

The next part was where it got tricky. I needed Frau Asch and Elisabeth to help run interference for a week, but I couldn't let my co-conspirators know why. It's not like this was the first time that I'd had to be thrifty with the facts for the other people working with me on an op.

Everyone is economical with the truth, or lets themselves be misunderstood at some time or other. It just happens to me a little bit more often than it does to normal folks. Truth may be the hallmark of civil society, but lies are the glue that keep the veneer of civilization from peeling off.

"Could Elisabeth be a little less efficient for the next week as far as facilitating contact between Professor Johnson and my daughter? I have a small matter I need to resolve, before this can go any further. I should have it taken care of by the end of the week."

"You suspect Professor Johnson's father of being MUSIK?" she asked. "I saw the way you reacted to the last reconstruct I showed you. You think it has your answer?"

I love people who supply you with the answer they want you to give to their question. I could have kissed her, but she'd have slapped me, or poured her hot coffee in my lap, or both. I hoped my enthusiasm didn't show.

"Yes," I replied. "I just need to check it out. If he is, I don't want Samantha caught in the fall-out. If he's not, I'll join the cupid conspiracy."

A smile danced across her otherwise enigmatic face.

I donned a pleasant 'but you're too kind' smile, and hoped it looked convincing.

"Tally ho!" as the guys from MI-6 would say. "The game's afoot!"

Building #1 of the Stasi Headquarters Compound

MUSIK's Finale

On Friday morning, Frau Asch sat down unceremoniously at my table in the snack bar, disturbing my tête-à-tête with a Berliner and a diet coke.

"My father asked me about you last night, Doktor Troyan," said Frau Asch, clearly displeased that I had intruded into her family circle.

"That's interesting," I said with surprise.

"He emphatically told me to be sure to give you his regards. This is clearly some kind of spooky, case-officer thing. What are you two up to?"

"He's doing a little research for me," I replied. It was nice to know who I was working with.

"Not for your book he's not. He wouldn't give a CIA officer, retired or not, the time of day, if he thought it had to do with his old job."

"A very principled man, your father. I applaud him for it."

"So what are you two cooking up?" she demanded.

"I'm afraid I'm not at liberty to say," I replied with what I hoped was a deadpan look.

"That's what my father said. That's what he always said about work."

"You and my daughter should have lunch to swap stories about your spooky fathers. You probably have a lot in common," I suggested.

"You're not going to tell me, are you?" she said in frustration.

"You didn't really expect me to, did you?" I said.

She left in rather a bad mood. I hoped that she'd be professional enough not to let this influence our common op of side-tracking Sam and Werner for a week. Sam had always held up her end of being a case officer's daughter. If Frau Asch shared her father's principles, we were safe.

A week later on Thursday, when I showed up for the meet with Frau Asch's father at the greasy spoon on Alex, he was already there. He had a table in the corner. There were two bowls of goulash—with bread—and two beers. It hadn't been there long. The beers were cold and the goulash hot.

"How was the hunting, Genosse?" I asked.

"Successful," he said. "Here are the receipts from the lab for the samples," he continued, pushing a small envelope my way.

"Thank you," I replied, sliding over the envelope with the second half of his payment.

"You have a lovely, intelligent daughter," he remarked.

"I can return the compliment, Genosse. To the health and happiness of our daughters," I proclaimed, raising my beer. "You've a fine grandson as well," I added, raising my glass again.

"Whom you've been supplying with roses for his girlfriend," he countered.

"Your own info, or did your daughter tell you?" I inquired.

"My daughter," he said with a touch of pride.

"I suspected as much. She's very observant. You taught her well. How's the romance progressing?"

"Satisfactorily," he answered.

"I think they'd make a good couple."

"And I thought you became a florist just to develop a low-level source," he responded.

"That may be true, but it has nothing to do with my assessment of their suitability for one another," I added truthfully.

"A practical man," he said, as he finished his goulash.

We both stood up, and went our separate ways without another word. Like I said, it's a pleasure working with a professional.

Thursday night found me babbling on and on to the amused Mary-Kate, encouraged by her laughter. I have no idea why women laugh at me the way they do. I don't seem that funny to myself, but I'm not the audience I'm playing for. I guess I'll never figure it out, unless one of them happens to tell me while I'm listening, which is not always the case.

"*Sláinte,*[1] *mavourneen,*" I said, lifting my beer in the hope of changing the subject to the matter of a repeat dinner invitation.

"And just where would you have learned a word like that, Michaeleen?" she said switching to an Irish brogue as heavy as any I'd ever heard in Dublin. "It's a pretty word to turn a colleen's head, but your name's not Irish, is it?"

Mavourneen had just sort of slipped out. It was a souvenir of that long TDY I'd done in Dublin under alias. Officially I'd never been there, so I couldn't very well go telling her that I'd been there working the IRA problem with the Brits. For one, because I hadn't checked to see if she was IRA, and even if she wasn't, the best I could do would still be a lie.

"In Dublin's fair city, where the girls are all pretty," I said. If you've got to lie, try and keep it as close to the truth as you can. It's easier to remember that way. "On a packaged tour."

"Now that's not a word, Michaeleen, that a fair colleen of Dublin would be a wastin' on a tourist," she continued, hanging on to her brogue. "And there's nothing in your CV about you being there for as long as it would take to get to *mavourneen.*"

I knew that she'd been reading up on me, but that TDY wasn't in the CV that I'd filed with my application for the fellowship.

"I'll not have you lying to me, Michael," she said, backing up to my full name to underscore her displeasure. "If I catch you at it, I'll give you a matching scar for your other cheek. Me red hair's no lie."

That was a warning I'd learned to heed the hard way. Real red hair on an Irish woman's head was as sure a warning sign of an evil temper as ever you'll see. The lady who had taught me *mavourneen* had also taught me that. Hell hath no fury like an Irish redhead scorned. I'd spent a month "in hospital," as the Brits say, recovering. The wounds still acted up when it was

---

[1] *Sláinte* is used for drinking a toast in Ireland. It means "your health."

cold and damp, even though you could barely see the scars. The surgeon had been justifiably proud of his work.

I tried a disingenuous smile, like a little boy found with his hand in the cookie jar.

She stared at me overlong, with one of those non-smiling bemused expressions that women project to make men squirm. She was good at it, and she knew it. I had no idea what to expect next; no idea what associations *mavourneen* had triggered, and her face wasn't telling me anything. She'd clean up at a poker table with a face like that.

I had learned that in times like these it was best to keep your mouth shut, but I heard a voice that sounded like mine saying, "I don't think this is about some colleen I met in Dublin before I knew you, so you're going to have to tell me what is wrong."

The expression on her face changed to decision. I hoped that was good, but it wasn't.

"Michaeleen," she said, "I'm giving you the benefit of the doubt. I almost believe you, but not quite enough to bet my life on it. That means I'm not going to shoot you unless you do something stupid. Please put both your hands on the table palms down."

Well, at least I knew where I was at. She was a pro. I looked her straight in the eyes, and did exactly as I was told. There was no hint of hesitation in those eyes. She did have a gun and she would pull the trigger. Definitely IRA.

"I'm not armed," I said.

"Now, I can believe, Michaeleen," she said, "that an ex-CIA officer would be knowing he should say that when he's face to face with a colleen with a gun, but not that he would be knowing how to charm her with *mavourneen*."

"I worked with Five in Dublin, on loan from the CIA," I said calmly. When it came to a choice of blowing my cover, and getting blown away, there was no choice.

"And that's what the man from the Army would be saying, Michaeleen, if he'd come to settle an old score," she replied. "You'll not be surprised if I don't really believe that."

"No. Not at all," I replied. She sounded annoyed. That was good. Annoyed is generally safe. It doesn't get you shot like exasperation does.

At least now I knew what the problem was. She wasn't concerned about the other redhead. She thought I was an IRA hit man. That meant she was probably a relocated IRA informer. I knew how to deal with that problem a lot better than how to deal with jealousy of another woman. I don't know why. I'd had about the same amount of practice with both situations, but that's life for you. There are some things you can do, and some things you can't. Dealing with armed women was a snap. I'd had a course on it. Dealing with unarmed jealous women was, however, a mystery. There wasn't a course on that, and if there were, I'd probably flunk it anyway.

"This is a fine Mexican stand-off, Michaeleen. I've either got to trust you enough to walk away, or I've got to shoot you. Which is it?"

"Walk away. Set your emergency contact signal, and ask for a trace," I said. "Then have dinner with me on Friday night. We can go to the *Dicke Wirtin* again."

"The nerve of the man, asking for a date with a gun pointed at him," she said with the hint of a smile. "You're on, Michaeleen. But if you're not who you say you are, then it's your wake I'll be a holdin' on Friday night."

"I can recommend the currywurst," I said. I was on solid ground here. Just like in the old days when you made a recruitment. You could always tell when it clicked.

"If you twitch when I stand up, you're dead," she said.

"Hands where you can see 'em the whole time," I said. "I like your dress by the way. The color suits you. Wear it on Friday."

She stood up, and walked toward the restroom as if nothing out of the ordinary was going on. She didn't need to look back. She could see me in the mirror on the wall. I didn't move until she'd disappeared from view. I waited another five minutes before I got up and paid the bill. My carcass had been ventilated enough already.

Mary-Kate wasn't at the reception desk when I checked in Friday morning. I'd have been surprised if she had been. The guest herder with that gravity-defying cocktail dress whom I'd first met at that 'see and be seen' was holding down the fort. Her present elegant, but understated ensemble was more suitable for daytime wear, but it looked completely out of place behind a desk.

"Your mail, Doktor Troyan," she said, handing me a largish, official looking envelope.

I thanked her for the envelope, and told her how pretty she looked. She smiled that same wallpaper smile that never wilted.

"Mary-Kate?" I asked.

"Called in sick," she replied.

I retreated to a comfortable chair to examine my envelope. It was the one I had been expecting from the lab. Inside was a single sheet of paper, generated by a computer, untouched by human hands. That was really the only way to actually ensure secrecy.

The DNA samples to determine the paternity of the two possible children of subject A show a Combined Paternity Index (CPI) of 99.999% for the male child. This means that only 1 person out of 100,000 could have contributed this DNA pattern to the child, and paternity is considered established. The female child shows a CPI below the level required to establish paternity, and subject A is deemed not to be her father.

That confirmed my suspicion about why Ilse was not exactly happy to see me, but at the same time, it put an end to my concerns about playing cupid for Sam and Werner.

I was tempted to tell Sam, to score points against her mother in the constant battle between us for Sam's allegiance, but I also quickly recognized the potential for blowback, and decided not to risk it.

The wheels in my brain made another revolution, and presented me with a rather more beneficial use for this particular piece of intelligence. Ilse was protecting some equity by not telling Werner I was his father. She obviously hadn't told him, because otherwise he wouldn't have been asking me why she hit me with a Meissen plate full of currywurst at his reception.

I didn't need to know who or what she was protecting, just that she had something to protect. I figured a straight swap would work. I keep her secret, if she keeps mine. Mutual Assured Destruction was the cornerstone of the big Cold War. It could work for our small Cold War. I would have to tell Ilse that Sam is not really my daughter anyway, so Ilse won't say anything out of place when Werner gets more serious about Sam and finally tells Ilse her last name.

Everything will be copasetic as long as we both keep our mouths shut about the kids. It would be nice if I could also work out some kind of Cold-

War truce in what would be an in-lawship straight out of a smoke-filled wilderness of mirrors, where nothing is really what it seems. She'd only have to tolerate being in the same room with me on rare occasions, like the wedding, and say, a christening. I could sell it. I'd made tougher sales before. The scar would get my foot in the door, if I washed off the camouflage makeup and added a few gruesome red highlights.

I headed straight for my favorite Berlin florist. Trudi was in another of her never-ending series of flowered smocks. It had bird of paradise plants all over it. I ordered two dozen roses to be delivered to Sam, and gave Trudi Werner's card to go with it. She didn't even bat an eye. That's why I love dealing with professionals. They take everything in stride, while Headquarters would be forming a committee to study the problem.

"And a dozen roses for Mary-Kate at the Academy, and two dozen packed individually to go," I said.

I grabbed a card to go with Mary-Kate's roses, and wrote: "The Dicke Wirtin at 19:30. Wear the same green dress. Sam's roses being redelivered as you read this."

My two dozen to go were ready before I had the card written.

Gunner Asch looked a bit surprised when I walked in with two dozen roses and asked him to call Elisabeth to the guard shack, but he kept his professional demeanor and dialed the phone.

As soon as he hung up, I handed him a dozen roses, and said: "Give these to Fräulein Freitag, and ask her out to dinner at 18:30." That produced a rather large smile. "But wait until I'm gone to ask her."

Elisabeth was efficient as always, and bounced into view three minutes later. I shoved a dozen roses into her hands and said: "OPERATION CUPID is a go. Give these to Professor Johnson, and tell him to pick my daughter up at the Academy at 18:30 for dinner. She thinks I'm taking her, but I have other plans."

That produced a smile almost as big as Gunner Asch's. She turned around without saying a word, and headed back to her boss to boss him around like any good secretary should.

"Tell your mother that I'm going to the snack bar, if she's got a minute," I said as I left the guard shack.

I ran into Frau Asch just in front of the paternoster—one of those vertical escalators that were popular in Germany, before the nanny state shut them down to protect the unsuspecting public from these 'dangerous' contraptions.

There had been one in the IG Farben Building in Frankfurt. I remember dragging six courier pouches on to that one to get them to the ARFCOS office upstairs. You had to do it all in one go, because you couldn't be separated from your pouches. I don't know how I got them all in there and off again without getting separated from a bag, an arm or a leg, or my head, but I did. I wondered absentmindedly how Lieutenant Dumb Bar could have locked up a paternoster—if we'd had one at Tberg—to make all the enlisted men use the stairs. It would be like trying to put a gate on an escalator so that only those with a key could use it: impossible.

The half a suspicion I had that I knew something important was suddenly reconnected with its missing half.

"I wonder if you could look up the name *Dunbar*?" I asked Frau Asch without a preamble. "No first name, but he would be a lieutenant in the U.S. Army."

She looked skeptical, but wrote the name down.

"Now let me buy you a cup of coffee and a doughnut. OPERATION CUPID is a go."

"Yes, I know. Elisabeth told me."

I don't know how they did it.

Three quarters of an hour later, Frau Asch came into the reading room, and floated silently over to my table.

"I found a card for Lieutenant John Q. Dunbar, Field Station Berlin. That's all that's on the card, except a note to refer all inquiries to Major Kaufmann."

"Bingo!" I said. "Kaufmann was the case officer of record on the first "Report of Meeting" reconstruct for MUSIK, the one that you found with my name misspelled."

"That's not enough to implicate Dunbar in the MUSIK case."

"Not by itself, but it dots the 'i' for the clue in the 'elevator key' reconstruct you showed me. Dunbar was the one who had the lock installed on the elevator. 'To help keep the enlisted men in shape,' he said. We hated him for that, and other things too."

With 20/20 hindsight I see how I could have made the recruitment. A disgruntled martinet, whose authority is ignored by the people allegedly under his command. I'd just offer him the recognition and respect he wasn't getting in the U.S. Army. He wouldn't take money. We'd offer him a commission in our army, and eventually promote him to colonel, maybe even general, if he delivered enough. Pomp and circumstance all the way, with him in full parade uniform at each promotion ceremony. A medal every now and again, presented by a general would grease the way to bigger and better things. Yeah, I could have finessed it.

I contacted the Station in the normal way, by ███████████████. They confirmed my ID with Headquarters, who just happened to have my file out, because of Mary-Kate's trace, and I was invited in for lunch in the bubble.

The Chief of Station and I played 'Do you know?,' while the young case officer who was the day's duty gopher went to get take-out. The CoS and I knew a few people in common, but had never run into one another before, which is not surprising, because Berlin is a liaison Station now, and the CoS was clearly well suited—as in Savile Row—for his job. I doubted that he'd ever made a dead drop.

I was surprised when the duty gopher got back, because he brought döner kebab.

"I get it at this place just down the street," he said "It's real typical Berlin fast food. My German tutor says that it was invented here in the nineteen-seventies by a 'guest worker' from Turkey."

"Now that you mention it, I had noticed a lot of döner kebab stands around town," I replied.

I wondered if he would come back to Berlin forty years from now, looking for a good döner, and run into his 'Ilse.' It could happen. He didn't have a wedding ring on. Maybe she was his 'German tutor.' Ilse had taught me practically all the German I know.

I had to give him his due. The döner kebab was really tasty. I can recommend it, if you're ever in town.

"Knowledge is a tricky thing," I said, when we got down to business. "It might not stand up in a court of law, but I know that ..."

You know the whole story, so I won't bore you by repeating it here.

The CoS wrote up my tale, and sent it in to Headquarters.

The response from Headquarters was terse:

```
THANK NARULA (P) FOR HIS REPORT, WHICH HAS BEEN
PASSED ON TO THE APPROPRIATE ORGANIZATION. GLAD TO
SEE HE IS MAKING GOOD USE OF HIS RETIREMENT.
```

About three months later, I got a promotion *and* a cash award. There was no explanation in the cover letter, just a "Thank you for your excellent work," which suggests that my identification of Dunbar was right. What else had I done for them lately? The promotion and cash award show that somebody cared—a lot. Dumb Bar must have been very high up, and still active.

In the salt mines of bureaucracy, promotions and cash awards are the coin of the realm, which, though they make life more comfortable, are not the only side of the coin. The other side is, as one of my old Chiefs of Station once explained, "not the money or the piece of paper that you can't hang on a wall, because it's classified. It's the fact that someone was impressed enough with what you did to go to the trouble of completing the mountain of paperwork required to get it for you."

I wonder who did it. If I ever find out, I'll buy 'em a drink, ... or two, for as much as I got. For that kind of money, Dumb Bar must have been someone on the Director's staff. I'll have to ask around.

More importantly, the trace for Mary-Kate confirmed who I am, so she didn't shoot me, which would not have been any fun at all, as I can tell you from personal experience. Mary-Kate is good company, understands living your cover, not to mention the fact that she and Sam get along exceptionally well, which is going to be important, if things with Mary-Kate keep progressing the way I hope.

You know what they say:

A son is a son, till he takes a wife,
But a daughter's a daughter for all of her life.

I couldn't mess up what I had with Sam, not even for somebody as good as Mary-Kate.

The Academy fellowship to Berlin turned out better than I expected after the rocky start it got.

Manhole Cover
with a 'round-the-town' view of Berlin's main sights

Starting at 12 o'clock: the Kaiser Wilhelm Memorial Church,
the Olympic Stadium, the German Federal Chancellery,
the Victory Column (Siegessäule), the Brandenburg Gate,
the TV Tower on Alexanderplatz, and the new Reichstag.

Design by Marcus Botsch (2006)

Bookcode

A bookcode is code that encodes a word in clear text with the location of that word in a book. To function properly, it is essential that both correspondents not only have the same book, but the same edition of the book.

The attempt to use a bookcode in *The Good Soldier Schwejk* by Jaroslav Hašek, is undone when the novel *Sins of the Fathers* by Ludwig Ganghofer is designated as the code key. The novel is in two volumes, but *Schwejk*, assuming that the novel is to be read, only brings the first volume, because the two together are too heavy, and there won't be enough time to read both while they are on exercise in the field.

The locations of words in the book serving as the code key are given in seven-digit groups. The first three digits indicate the page, the next two digits the line of text on that page, and the last two the number of the word in that line. For increased security, the first position of each element of the group can be padded to make it less obvious that the group is from a bookcode. For a book with less than 300 pages, the page element of the group could represent page 189 as 389, 589, and 789. (See the chart below)

First Digit	Page Number		
	1st value	2nd value	3rd value
0	0	True	True
1	1	True	True
2	0	True	True
3	1	True	True
4	0	True	True
5	1	True	True
6	0	True	True
7	1	True	True
8	0	True	True
9	Spell - 0	True	True

If the book does not contain the word in the clear text, then a page element beginning with the digit 9 points to a word in the first 99 pages that begins with the appropriate letter.

Books commonly have 30 or fewer lines per page, so that the line element of the group can be padded as well, using the same technique. Line 12 could be represented as 52 or 92.

Line Number			Word Number		
1st Digit	1st value	2nd value	1st Digit	1st value	2nd value
0	0	True	0	0	True
1	1	True	1	1	True
2	2	True	2	2	True
3	3	True	3	0	True
4	0	True	4	1	True
5	1	True	5	2	True
6	2	True	6	0	True
7	3	True	7	1	True
8	0	True	8	2	True
9	1	True	9	0	True

The word number element can be similarly padded, based on the assumption that there are seldom more than 29 words per line. Word number 22 could be represented as 22, 52, and 82.

One of the security features of the bookcode is that the code book can be hidden in plain sight, thereby eliminating the compromising presence of an easily identifiable coding key. The choice of book, however, must be appropriate to the user's library. This is what led to the compromise of the key book in *Our Man in Havana*. Charles Lamb's *Tales from Shakespeare* did not fit in Wormold's library, and was thus easily identified for what it was.

The Author on U-Bahn Video Surveillance Monitor
Fehrbelliner Platz

About the Author

T.H.E. Hill served with the U.S. Army Security Agency at Field Station Berlin in the mid-nineteen-seventies, after a tour at Herzo Base in the late nineteen-sixties. He is a three-time graduate of the Defense Language Institute (DLIWC) in Monterey, California, the alumni of which are called "Monterey Marys". The Army taught him to speak Russian, Polish, and Czech; three tours in Germany taught him to speak German, and his wife taught him to speak Dutch. He has been a writer his entire adult life, but now retired from Federal Service, he writes what he wants, instead of the things that others tasked him to write while he was still working.

Also by this author:

The 9539th T.C.U. does to the secret Cold War what the 4077th M.A.S.H. did to the Korean War.

Voices Under Berlin: The Tale of a Monterey Mary is the tale of one of the early skirmishes of the Secret Cold War told with a pace and a black humor reminiscent of that used by Joseph Heller (*Catch-22*) and Richard Hooker (*M*A*S*H**). It is set against the backdrop of the CIA cross-sector tunnel operation to tap three Russian telecommunications cables in Berlin in the mid-nineteen-fifties.

It is the story of the American soldiers who worked the tunnel, and how they fought for a sense of purpose against boredom and the enemy both within and without. One of them is the target of a Russian "honey-trap," but which one? Kevin, the Russian transcriber, Blackie, the blackmarketeer, or Lt. Sheerluck, the martinet?

The other end of the tunnel is the story of the Russians whose telephone calls the Americans are intercepting. Their end of the tale is told in the unnarrated transcripts of their calls. They are the voices under Berlin.

• Dr. Wesley Britton, author of *Spy Television, Beyond Bond: Spies in Fiction and Film,* and *Onscreen and Undercover: The Ultimate Book of Movie Espionage*, calls *Voices Under Berlin* "a spy novel that breaks all the molds."

• Po Wong writing at *bookideas.com* says "Kevin is a hero in the mold of McMurphy, the rebellious asylum inmate who is the protagonist in Ken Kesey's *One Flew over the Cuckoo's Nest*. Kevin manages to do his job despite the blind obedience to stringent regulations that frequently overrides common sense and intelligence in large military operations, and despite the widespread ineptness around him. ... *Voices under Berlin* is a coherent, funny, and often sardonic look at real espionage work. The detail is so realistic that you may find yourself wondering, as I did, whether this is a novel or the memoirs of an actual intelligence agent. Of course, if you're looking for James Bond, you won't find him here. What you will find is a fascinating account of what it must have been like to be toiling away at an important but often dreary job underneath the streets of Berlin during the Cold War years.

• *Midwest Book Review* says one of the things that sets this novel apart is "the author's combining a genuine gift for humor with a deft literary astuteness in telling a story that fully engages the reader quite literally from first page to last."

For more information about this novel, please visit:

www.VoicesUnderBerlin.com

206

Want to learn more about Berlin in the early 1950s?

Then read *Berlin in Early Cold War Army Booklets.*

This is a reprint of a series of six army booklets on Berlin, covering the period from 1946 to 1958, two years after the Russians shut down the CIA cross-sector tunnel that served as the background for the novel *Voices Under Berlin.*

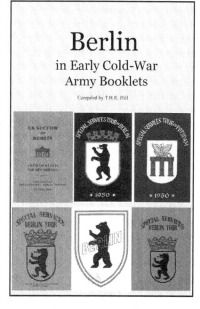

When read in parallel, the booklets create a sense of living history, because, while they cover the same topics of interest about Berlin, their coverage of these topics changes as time goes by. The value added to the booklets by reprinting them in a single volume is that the single-volume reprint makes it possible to compare the texts and see the changes.

As the series progresses, the role of Hitler and the Nazis moves further and further into the background, as does the amount of war damage noted. At the same time, the relationship between the USSR and the USA can be seen to rearrange itself. The reprint is indexed and the changes in the text from one edition to the next of the individual booklets are highlighted for ease of comparison. To help better define the historical context of the booklets, the reprint is provided with a Berlin Chronology.

The decision to reproduce these booklets was based on a number of considerations, number one of which was preservation. A number of the copies in the author's collection are distressed, and this project will put a stop to their deterioration. In addition, not a single one of these booklets is to be found in a search of WorldCat, the on-line catalogue of a consortium of libraries, headed by the Library of Congress. Reprinting will make them available for research libraries to add to their collections.

To learn more about *Berlin in Early Cold War Army Booklets*, we invite you to visit:

www.VoicesUnderBerlin.com/1950.html

The Day Before the Berlin Wall: Could We Have Stopped It?

An Alternate History of Cold War Espionage

The plot is based on a "legend" that was still being told by U.S. Army soldiers in Berlin in the mid-nineteen-seventies. According to the legend, American Forces knew in advance of the plan to build the wall, and also knew that East German troops had orders to halt construction if the Americans were to take aggressive action to stop them.

In Hill's version of the tale, a young American sergeant is the one who gets this piece of intelligence, but he is in East Berlin and has to get back to West Berlin to report it. The Stasi (the East German secret police) have killed his postmistress, and framed him for her murder. Now it is not only the Stasi, and the Vopo's (the East German "People's" Police), but also the West-Berlin municipal *Polizei* and the U.S. Army MP's who are after him. It is the day before construction is scheduled to start, and time is running out, so the sergeant is running as fast as he can to prevent the wall from being built, and to keep himself out of jail.

The key question of the novel is "even if he is lucky enough to make it back across the border, will anybody in the West believe what he has to say and take action on it before it is too late?" History says that he either didn't make it, they didn't believe him, or they ignored his information. Join T.H.E. Hill in this alternate history of Cold War espionage to find out what might have happened.

To learn more, please visit: www.VoicesUnderBerlin.com/DayBefore.html

Made in the USA
Lexington, KY
10 August 2013